Chapter One

"THERE ARE AT LEAST THREE DEAD BODIES IN THERE."

Tess Harrow stood in front of the log cabin, mentally calculating where each of the corpses would be found. The basement would have one of them. She could see damp seeping up from the underground barracks, the stonework crumbling from neglect. It would be a crime *not* to store a body there. The lean-to off to one side of the cabin, which was living up to its name and looked one strong breeze away from toppling over, was ideal for another. The chimney was large enough for someone small, and…

"Four. Four dead bodies."

She nodded once and hefted her suitcase. There would be an additional corpse under the porch—she was sure of it. The rotted wood and craggy slats made the perfect cover for one final interment.

"You are so weird," muttered Gertrude. Tess's teenaged daughter didn't bother lifting her own suitcase, opting instead to drag it on the ground. The bump of the bag matched the slump of her shoulders. The prospect of sharing her home with a few corpses wasn't doing much to improve a mood that had been questionable to begin with. "Please tell me we at least have Wi-Fi out here."

Tess took a deep breath, taking in the mingled scents of summery pine trees, rich soil, and clean air. "No Wi-Fi. No phone service. No electricity and no running water. This is going to be fantastic."

Gertrude stared at her from underneath the neon pink flash of her recently dyed hair. "That's not true. You're making it up to scare me."

"You're more scared about the lack of Wi-Fi than the possibility of dead bodies? Who's the weird one now?"

Tess didn't wait for an answer. She could hear her daughter cursing her life, her parentage, and her fate all in one mumbled breath. Which, to be honest, was the reaction she'd expected. She'd toyed with the idea of prepping Gertrude ahead of time—warning her that the next month was going to be one of rusticity and a return to basics—but she was no fool. Nothing turned a fourteen-year-old against her mother faster than the threat of prolonged one-on-one time.

"What am I supposed to do for a whole month if I don't have electricity?" Gertrude wailed.

"It's strange, isn't it? How centuries of humans existed without power of any kind? They lit candles and cooked over open flames and survived just fine."

Gertrude turned on her. "No, they didn't. They all died of dysentery."

"Ooh, good call. There are probably five bodies inside. I forgot about dysentery."

As promised by the estate agent, the key to the cabin was waiting for them underneath the doormat. In Seattle, this lackadaisical approach to security would have been a cause

BURIED IN A GOOD BOOK

TAMARA BERRY

Poisoned Pen
PRESS

Published by Poisoned Pen Press, an imprint of Sourcebooks
P.O. Box 4410, Naperville, Illinois 60567-4410
(630) 961-3900
sourcebooks.com

Library of Congress Cataloging-in-Publication Data

Names: Berry, Tamara, author.
Title: Buried in a good book / Tamara Berry.
Description: Naperville, Illinois : Poisoned Pen Press, [2022] | Series: By
    the book mysteries ; book 1
Identifiers: LCCN 2021042277 (print) | LCCN 2021042278 (ebook) |
    (paperback) | (epub)
Classification: LCC PS3602.E7646 B87 2022 (print) | LCC PS3602.E7646
    (ebook) | DDC 813/.6--dc23
LC record available at https://lccn.loc.gov/2021042277
LC ebook record available at https://lccn.loc.gov/2021042278

Printed and bound in Canada.
MBP 10 9 8 7 6 5 4 3 2 1

for alarm, but not here. They were so far north they could practically reach out and touch the Canadian border. Any robbers or murderers would have to battle the wilderness and the elements just to get to them. In Tess's experience, any murderer willing to go that far would find a way inside regardless of locks on the doors.

She was something of an expert on murderers *and* dead bodies, though she'd never seen either one of them first-hand. Her information was culled almost entirely from books, interviews, and the depths of her imagination. On the page, Tess Harrow, renowned thriller writer, lived an incredibly dark and twisted existence. In reality, she was behind on her deadline and needed a serious break from the real world. She had several notepads and a typewriter in her suitcase to prove it.

"This is exactly what the doctor ordered," she said, as much to herself as to her daughter. "A little peace, a little quiet, and—"

BOOM!

The porch rattled and shook underneath them, and Tess's ears thrummed with the sound of the earth cracking in two. In her sudden fright, she dropped the key to the cabin. It clanked and rolled, not stopping until it fell through one of the larger porch slats.

"What's happening?" Gertrude cried, drawing close enough to clutch at Tess's shirt. "Please tell me we're not going to die out here. Ohmigod, we're going to die out here. I can't believe you're doing this to me."

The shaking stopped, and the sound ebbed away, leaving

nothing but the twitter of birds and the rustling of leaves in the distance.

"What *was* that?" Gertrude demanded. She had yet to relinquish her hold on Tess's flowy, peasant-style top. The fabric wasn't going to provide much in the way of protection, but Tess didn't dare point that out. Displays of vulnerability from her daughter were too rare—and too precious—to be squandered. "Mom, what *is* this place? You weren't serious about the dead bodies, were you?"

Tess leaned down to press a kiss on her daughter's hairline. The pink dye job was so new that it was evident in patchy spots on her scalp. "Of course I wasn't serious. My grandfather built this cabin with his own two hands. There's supposed to be a deer trail out back and everything. They come right up to the veranda."

"Really? Deer?"

"If we're lucky, we might even get a moose or two. You've always wanted to see one of those."

Just like that, the moment was gone. The mention of such a childish treat, which would have once transported Gertrude to the moon and back again, now caused her daughter to release her hold and step back, her expression one of carefully cultivated ennui.

"This place is the worst," she said.

Tess knew when to pick her battles and when to give ground, as the pink hair could attest to. "It's not going to get any better here in the next few minutes," she admitted as she pointed a finger straight down. "I dropped the key. You're going to have to climb under there and get it."

This time, her daughter's muttered animadversions on fate were replaced without outright cries of indignity and indecency.

"I know, Gertie, but there's no way I can fit under there to get it. I'm sure the dead body won't mind a little company."

"Mo-om!"

"Just kidding. But there is probably a spider or two, so make sure you pull up your hood before you crawl under."

Tess made a mental note of the look on Gertrude's face as her daughter finally gave in and started to worm her way under the porch. A writer was always working, and there was so much emotion to capture in those flaring nostrils and tightly drawn lips. The next time one of her villains was preparing to bump someone off, Tess was going to make him look exactly like that.

"Do you need a flashlight?" Tess asked. "I packed several. I'll have to grab them from the car, but—"

BOOM!

The second crashing sound caused the trees to shake and birds to take flight. It also caused a similar pounding inside Tess's chest. One random strange noise in the woods, and she was willing to chalk it up to a falling tree or a rolling rock or whatever else happened in isolated places like this. Two random strange noises in the woods, and she was rethinking her stance on that murderer.

"Gertie, don't move," Tess said. Her daughter's legs were sticking out from under the porch, but the rest of her body was safely obscured from view. "I'm going to go see what that was."

"Don't leave me here, Mom."

"I'll just be a sec."

"I'm coming with you."

"No, don't—" she began, but it was a futile effort. An angsty, irritable teenager was still a teenager. Gertrude's youthful movements were swift and agile, and she was out from under the porch in a matter of seconds. She was also incredibly filthy, and Tess was pretty sure she saw a spider skitter down the neckline of her daughter's hoodie, but she wasn't about to point it out. "Fine. But you're holding my hand. I don't know what makes a noise like that, but it can't be anything good."

She was pleased to find Gertrude slipping her hand into her own without an argument—even more pleased when her daughter angled her body close.

"I bet it's Bigfoot," Gertrude said, her voice a low whisper. They began working their way around the side of the cabin. The slatted logs looked like something out of a fairy tale, and the late afternoon light filtered through the canopy of trees, making it feel almost as though they were underwater. If they were going to die, at least it would be a scenic death. "Leo told me they have sightings here all the time."

"If Bigfoot made noises like that, they'd have captured him a long time ago," Tess pointed out. "There's nothing subtle about—"

BOOM!

Both Tess and Gertrude screamed and clutched each other. They were definitely drawing closer to whatever was causing that noise—it was louder and more rattling and, for reasons Tess couldn't understand, accompanied by a sudden burst of five-second rain.

"Maybe we should just get in the car and leave," Gertrude said. Spatters of water had hit her cheeks, making it look as though she were crying. "There was a cute hotel back in that town. You could write from there."

"We're not going anywhere." Tess spoke with a resolve that was strengthened by the sight of those not-tears, which were the closest thing to the real deal her daughter had evinced in months. "I'm sure there's a perfectly rational explanation for all this."

"Didn't you once tell me that, statistically speaking, more women go missing from rural areas than in the city?"

"I did, actually."

"And didn't you also say that the recent opioid crisis has caused a rise in violent assaults?"

"I had no idea you were so interested in crime statistics, Gertie."

"It's literally all you ever talk about. Crimes and murders and whether or not a person can bite through duct tape." Gertrude slipped her hand out of Tess's and pointed. "I bet you wouldn't be able to bite through duct tape if that man was the one doing the taping."

Tess glanced sharply up, following the line of her daughter's finger. Sure enough, it led through the trees to a clearing several yards in the distance. In the back of her mind, she registered the crystal-blue pond that glimmered behind him, sun-dazzled and bobbing with indistinguishable gray globs.

The front of her mind was taken up with more immediate concerns—namely that the man was running full-speed at them.

"Get down!" he yelled.

Tess barely had time to register the order before yet another boom assailed their ears. Without stopping to think, Tess threw herself on top of her daughter, the pair of them crashing to the packed dirt of the forest floor. Tess barely felt the thud of her knee against a rock as she covered her daughter's head and waited for the danger to pass.

In this instance, danger came mostly as a shower of water and an irate man's voice assailing them from above.

"Lady, are you all right?"

No, she was not all right. She was curled up around a girl who was much more fragile than either of them wanted the world to know. Her knee was throbbing in a way that couldn't be good for it. And, to top everything off, she'd just managed to turn her head and look up at the man when something very wet, very slippery, and very foul-smelling thwapped against her face.

"Is that…an arm?" she asked, horrified.

Her daughter noticed the limb at the exact same moment. She sprang up and started flailing around. "Ew. Get it off, get it off, get it off!"

Although the fall didn't seem to have slowed Gertrude down, Tess could feel her own joints protesting the sudden movement as she got to her feet. Still, she endured it. She'd have endured much worse if it meant putting distance between herself and that waterlogged, fleshy lump of an arm.

It had once belonged to a human, that much she could tell. But the fingers were missing, and it wasn't fresh.

"Putrefaction," she said, the words automatic. "Water slows the process, but we're looking at between three and four days."

She had no idea how her audience received this information. Before any of them could make an observation about human arms, strange men, or the fact that Tess's knee was seriously starting to swell, it began to rain fish.

Big fish, little fish, slimy silver lumps—the moment the first one landed, Gertrude started to scream. And Tess, despite her determination to remain calm, did the same. These days, she wasn't an easy woman to scare, but nothing in her years of research into the ways and means of murder had prepared her for dead fish and body parts falling from the sky.

Chapter Two

"Ma'am, I'm going to need you to go over that one more time."

The sheriff of the town of Winthrop was a slow man— not of intellect but of speech and action. It had taken him three hours to get out to the cabin and one more to decide that the presence of several decaying body parts warranted a thorough investigation and a team of his deputies.

In that same amount of time, Tess had calmed her daughter down, unpacked most of their belongings, made the beds, and plotted an entire novel based on the day's events. It helped that the estate agent must have seen fit to give the place a thorough cleaning before they arrived.

She'd expected it to be in disarray, but the cabin had a fresh lemon scent despite the fact that it had sat empty for the better part of the last year. She'd have to remember to tip them for that.

"I don't see why you need to hear it again," Tess said. "I told you already. The person you want to talk to is the man who was throwing dynamite into the pond. Blast fishing, I think he called it."

"Ah, yes." The sheriff, who'd introduced himself as Victor Boyd, ran a hand along his jaw. Tess could hear the scratch of his rough hand against his five o'clock shadow from the other side of the table. "The mysterious stranger."

"He wasn't mysterious. He was five foot ten and of medium build, probably around a hundred and eighty pounds. His hair was red but not the orange kind—it was more of a deep auburn. His eyes were blue, and he had a full beard. I'd put his feet at about a size eleven, but I could be a little off. He wore a red buffalo-check shirt and khaki dungarees with a Carhartt label."

Sheriff Boyd blinked. "That's awfully specific for a man you say disappeared right away."

Tess bit back a sigh and tried to find a more comfortable position on her rustic, wood-hewn chair. Any pleasure she might have found in sitting at the dining table her grandfather had built was lost under the throbbing of her knee. Despite its propped state and one of the ice packs from their cooler, the pain wasn't abating.

"It's an occupational hazard, I'm afraid," she said. "I could summarize your stats and the stats of all three deputies out there gathering up body parts, too. Would you like me to prove it?"

When he didn't answer right away, Gertrude popped up in her defense.

"She really can. She also knows all kinds of weird things, like how to hide a body so no one will ever find it and all the poisons that will be untraceable during an autopsy. Go ahead. Ask her."

Tess shot her daughter a warning glance. "She's exaggerating. There aren't that many untraceable poisons." When the sheriff still didn't seem inclined to reply she added, "I'm an author, so it comes with the territory. Maybe you've heard of me? Tess Harrow? I write the Detective Gonzales series."

"I know who you are."

That, at least, boded well for the progress of this conversation. When she'd opened the door to find a middle-aged, unshaven curmudgeon of a sheriff with jet-black hair and deeply tanned skin, she'd almost betrayed herself by calling him Detective Gonzales to his face. She couldn't have chosen a more likely doppelganger for the fictional detective that had been her bread and butter for years. He even had the same cleft palate scar.

"Oh, good. Then you understand. I could easily pick the man out of a lineup or even sit down with a sketch artist, if you want. He didn't appear to have a vehicle nearby, but—"

Sheriff Boyd raised a hand. "There's no need to get hysterical."

"I'm not hysterical. I'm merely telling you that I'm ready and willing to cooperate. I'll do whatever it takes to find out who he was."

"I already know his identity. He's one of the Peabody boys."

"Oh." Tess sat back and shot her daughter a bewildered glance. Gertrude shrugged and continued unloading the groceries they'd brought with them from Seattle. The kitchen was and always would be her daughter's domain. Tess could barely boil an egg, but Gertrude had been born with gourmet tastes. Even as a toddler, she'd refused to touch chicken nuggets, especially if they'd been shaped as stars, dinosaurs,

or any combination thereof. "That's good, I guess. Do the
Peabody boys often throw sticks of dynamite into other people's ponds and dredge up three-day-old bodies that have
been thrown in them?"

The sheriff must have assumed the question was a rhetorical one because he merely scratched his chin and leaned
back in his chair. "How do you know it's three days old?"

"That's another occupational hazard. I spent quite a bit of
time studying rates of decay in the water."

"*Fury on the Waves*," he agreed.

Tess sat up. The action jolted her knee, but she was too
busy leaning across the table to care. "You know the story?
You've read it?"

"There's no way your detective would have been granted
jurisdiction in that particular case," he said by way of answer.
His scowl, which was already quite pronounced, deepened.
"Even if he did have legal cause, the FBI would have swooped
in and taken it over within hours."

"Oh. I'm sorry?"

"Of course, in the real world, he'd have been fired back in
aught-nine for that little matter with the gun he tossed over a
bridge. You can't throw evidence away like that. Even if they
never found it, he'd have to file a report that his firearm was
missing."

Tess knew the exact scene he was talking about. It had
taken her weeks to write and was generally accounted one
of her best. "But he was doing it to protect his source," she
protested. "Honor at all costs."

The look Sheriff Boyd shot her would have caused even

Detective Gonzales to shrivel up in shame. "I'm not saying you aren't right about that arm in the pond," he said, the words a drawl, "but you don't seem to know very much about how law enforcement works."

Tess took it as a compliment. She knew a fan when she met one.

"I could sign your copies, if you want."

"I'll pass, thanks."

"But you *have* copies, don't you?"

He scowled deeper. "As your property is now considered an active crime scene, I recommend you and your daughter remove yourselves to town. There's a hotel."

Gertrude slammed one of the kitchen cupboards shut. "I told her that already. She won't leave."

Sheriff Boyd narrowed one eye and fixed the other on Tess's face. "That so?"

Tess tried not to let herself be cowed by that look. Like the rest of this man's appearance and demeanor, it was a similar tactic to those used by Detective Gonzales, a hypermasculine attempt at intimidation that put defenseless women and criminals in their place. "If I'm not under arrest, then I believe I'm free to remain and observe, yes?"

"Technically, yes. You're within your rights to do so."

A swell of triumph moved through her. *See?* She knew a thing or two about the legal system. No backwoods officer was going to remove her from her home without a fight.

The swell just as quickly ebbed away.

"Of course, considering the nature of the crime, I could also seize your entire property and remove you pending the issue of a search warrant—which, given how slowly things move out here, could be a while. But, then, you already knew that, didn't you?"

Tess hadn't known that, but she tried not to show how flustered she was at being caught off guard. She might have managed it, too, but Gertrude ruined the moment by snorting on a laugh.

"If she didn't know it before, you definitely won't get her to admit it now." Her daughter had finished with the groceries by this time, so she flopped onto the nearest chair as though she had neither a care in the world nor any bones in her body. "She doesn't like it when people know more than she does."

"Thank you, Gertrude."

Her daughter ignored her. "She doesn't like it when they tell her what she can and can't do, either. It's why my dad left. His favorite thing is to order everyone around."

This was veering into dangerous territory. "Gertrude Alex Harrow, that will be enough."

Gertrude grinned, showcasing her silvery row of braces. "She doesn't like it when people talk about her personal life, either. Did you know you look exactly like the detective in her books?"

In her books, the detective in question would have had no part in this conversation. He'd have endured all of a minute of it before storming away in an introverted panic. Detective Gonzales was amazing at tracking down serial killers, but he didn't do well with people—especially people of the young and female variety.

This was where he and Sheriff Boyd diverged. Not only did the man at the table relax a little, but he actually *smiled*.

Once again rubbing a rueful hand across the dark stubble of his jaw, he said, "Yes, it's been brought to my notice once or twice. Your name is Gertrude?"

At this, Tess was inclined to intervene. She didn't mind the sheriff sitting at her table and giving *her* crap about her legal rights and the authenticity of her research, but she wasn't about to sit by and let him interrogate her daughter.

The thing that Gertrude hadn't said—the thing she *wouldn't* say—was that, when Quentin had dropped Tess like a ton of hot bricks, he'd dropped his child, too. That was what hurt the most. Not the betrayal of their marriage vows. Not the girlfriend who was barely old enough to drink. Six months had passed since the divorce had been finalized, and Tess could count on one finger the number of times he'd called to talk to Gertrude.

Needless to say, she counted it on the middle finger.

"My friends call me Gertie," Gertrude said. "And my mom does, too, but I technically didn't give her permission."

"Well, Gertie," the sheriff said as he rose languidly from the table and stretched, "I'm not going to ask you to move to the hotel in town just yet. But have your things packed so you can go if and when the call comes."

"You know she's fourteen, right?" Tess asked. "And therefore not the primary decision-maker in this family?"

Sheriff Boyd ignored her. "You're the spitting image of your great-grandfather, by the way—minus the pink hair. I never knew a better man."

"I never knew him at all" came Gertie's quick reply. It was followed by an accusing glance toward Tess. "In fact, I didn't even know about my great-grandfather until he died and left us this place."

In her defense, Tess had brought up the existence of her extended family on numerous occasions. Like most children her age, Gertrude showed more interest in YouTube celebrities than an elderly hermit who lived in a cabin without electricity or running water.

The sheriff nodded once. That was all the answer he supplied before making his way to the door. Tess thought, for a moment, he wasn't going to say anything else—not even about the police cars parked around the premises or his deputies swarming about—but he paused at the threshold and looked back.

"If you could be ready in ten minutes, that would be great."

"Ten minutes?" she echoed. In addition to modern comforts, the cabin was also lacking a clock. She had no idea what time it was or where she needed to be right now. "What for? Where are we going?"

Sheriff Boyd sighed and cast a pained look at Gertrude.

"Mo-om, he's obviously going to take you to the station to identify the man with the dynamite. You already promised to help."

"I thought you said he was one of the Peabody boys," Tess protested.

"I did." The sheriff coughed and rolled his shoulder toward the door. "But although Detective Gonzales might be willing to take a witness's word on faith, here in Okanogan County, we do things by the book."

━━━━━━━━

Tess had never spent a more agonizing half hour in her life than the drive to Winthrop in the company of Sheriff Boyd. She'd wanted to bring Gertrude with her to the station, hesitant to leave her impressionable daughter alone near an active crime scene, but both Gertrude and the sheriff had pointed out how unnecessary it was.

"There are like eleven billion cops outside," Gertrude had said. "I'm fine."

The sheriff's contribution had fallen upon more precise lines. "There's no need for both of you to come," he'd said. "I can get her testimony later if it's needed."

Tess still wasn't sure which argument had been more persuasive, but she was tempted to conclude it was the latter. She'd never admit as much out loud, but Sheriff Boyd intimidated her. She was much better at dealing with fictional law enforcement officers than the real thing. The real ones had guns and logic and deeply compelling voices.

"I stayed here once as a child," she said by way of conversation. They'd just passed their six thousandth evergreen tree. Unless she planned on breaking up the monotony, she had the feeling he'd spend the entire trip in taciturn silence. "I must have been, oh, seven or eight years old at the time."

The sheriff grunted. Tess had no idea whether it was

an encouraging grunt or a dampening one, but she forged ahead anyway.

"My mom didn't really get along with her father. She wouldn't have brought me that time, either, but she didn't have a choice. She just pulled up, dropped me off, and promised to come back at summer's end."

She got another of those grunts in reply. This time, she felt there was a strong undercurrent of judgment in there. Toward her mother. Toward *her*.

"It's not easy, you know," she said. "Being a single mother, raising a daughter in a world like this one. She did the best she could."

The sheriff slammed on the brake so suddenly that Tess was thrown against her seat belt. Naturally, Sheriff Boyd was also wearing one, but that didn't stop her maternal instincts from taking over. Her "mom arm"—that beautiful, automatic thing that had saved many a child and even more purses—flung up to prevent him from being dashed into the windshield. The car came to a screeching halt at almost the exact same moment.

The sheriff paused just long enough to look down at the hand pressed against his chest and back at Tess before reaching for his firearm.

"Stay here," he ordered.

Tess was rattled by the stop, but she was able to pick up on the situation fairly quickly. "What is it?" she asked. "What did you see? Is it one of the Peabody boys?"

"Stay here," he said again. "I mean it."

Nothing could have been better calculated to make Tess

unclip her seat belt and slide out of her seat. If he'd said it once, she'd have taken it as an officer of the law commanding a citizen and acted accordingly. The repetition, however, roused all her writerly instincts. He wasn't making an order for her safety; he was trying to avoid having a witness.

"I knew I should have put you in the back," he muttered as soon as he saw what she was about. Throwing perfectly innocent bystanders into lockdown was such a Detective Gonzales thing to do that she instantly forgave him.

"I brought my bear spray." She patted the purse at her side. "Don't worry about me."

He muttered again, this time using terminology that was better left unrepeated. Since he followed it up with a motion for her to be silent before beckoning for her to follow, Tess didn't let it bother her.

The stretch where they'd stopped barely qualified as a road. Once upon a time, someone had seen fit to lay gravel over the dusty red dirt, but it had long since been ground down and covered with potholes. Nothing but rustic isolation extended off at every angle. Most of it was composed of endless, spindly towers of trees, but one section opened up to a field bursting with lacy patterns of white and yellow yarrow.

Unfortunately, they weren't headed toward that safe, sunny field. Instead, the sheriff fell into a crouch and started moving in the direction of the darkest canopy. Tess followed and gently massaged her eyes so they could more quickly adjust to the dark. It was a trick she'd learned white writing *Fury on the Mountain*, in which Detective Gonzales had been trapped in the Sierra Nevada mountains with a troop of missing Boy Scouts. His quick thinking had been all that had saved them from death by cougar.

They moved with deliberate slowness, their feet soundless as they drew further and further into the undergrowth. Tess tried her best to be of use to the sheriff, but she couldn't see anything worth note. She couldn't hear anything worth note, either, and she had a particularly acute sense of hearing. Gertrude and the not-so-secret phone calls she shared with her best friend Leo long into the night could attest to that.

"What are we looking at?" she asked after a somewhat lengthy pause next to a huckleberry bush.

Sheriff Boyd turned to glare her into silence. There was such ferocity in those dark-brown eyes that it might have worked, had Tess not caught sight of his quarry at that exact moment. Against all reason, against all logic, even against the laws of nature, she could have sworn she saw a man in a bear costume standing no more than a hundred feet away.

"Um," she said, unable to find a better way of summing up her feelings. "I hate to sound like a city slicker who's never seen a woodland creature before, but—"

"Quiet," the sheriff barked.

Tess didn't have to point out that her volume was much lower than his. Although the bear-man hadn't moved at the sound of *her* voice, the sheriff's sharp command caught his attention. His head swiveled toward them to showcase a pair of beady eyes embedded in an improbably hairy face. For one long, suspended moment, Tess thought he was going to charge at them, his every muscle poised as if for attack. No sooner had she blinked, however, then the creature decided to take off in the opposite direction.

"He's not getting away from me this time," Sheriff Boyd said and took after him.

Tess toyed with the idea of joining the chase. It wasn't every day that she encountered a costumed man in the woods, and she would have given much to know where he was going and why the sheriff seemed so keen on tracking him down. But her knee wouldn't support that kind of activity right now, especially since Sheriff Boyd and the bear-man were both much lighter on their feet than their large sizes would lead a person to believe.

"This has been a very strange day," she said instead and returned to the sheriff's vehicle to await his return.

She wasn't there long. She'd already tried snooping through the glove box—locked—and had just finished trying to open the trunk—also locked—when he appeared in the clearing, looking sweaty, disheveled, and not the least bit pleased.

"Oh, dear." She suppressed a laugh. The other man might have been wearing a bear costume, but Sheriff Boyd was the one who'd grown surly. "He got away, didn't he?"

The sheriff pointed a warning finger at her. "Don't."

"It's too bad you do things by the book, or you could have fired a warning shot over his head," she pointed out. "That might have slowed him down."

The sheriff drew forward, his hand on his side as he struggled to catch his breath. "I don't fire my gun unless I have to. No halfway decent cop does. If you knew anything about law enforcement and the amount of paperwork it entails, I wouldn't have to tell you that."

Tess allowed the insult to slide. Fifteen years of marriage had taught her a thing or two about the male temperament. Losing a foot chase to a man in a costume could hardly be expected to put the sheriff in a good mood.

She held out a hand to help him over a fallen log, but he merely scoffed and stepped over it himself. She didn't allow that to hurt her feelings, either. Leaning against the car, she tilted her head and mused, "You'd think having a mask over his face would've slowed him down. Not—" she added quickly "—that you're a slow runner. It just seems like it would be dangerous for him to take off like that. I can't imagine he had much in the way of peripheral vision."

Instead of accepting this olive branch, the sheriff stopped and stared at her. It was the first time he'd looked at her head-on, and she was forced to admit that, in these surroundings, he was an attractive man. He wasn't handsome in the conventional sense, and she doubted any amount of good tailoring or a decent haircut would change that, but there was a weather-beaten air to him that matched the setting. He was like the rough wooden chairs back at the cabin. In any other house—or, indeed, in a showroom—those chairs would never look like anything except what they were: handmade, homegrown, and functional. But they fit the space. Looked good there, even.

"Say that one more time," he commanded, blithely unaware that Tess was busy comparing him to furniture.

"Please."

"Please what?"

"Say that one more time, *please*. I'm not some criminal you picked up on the streets. You'd be surprised how much more conciliatory people are when you ask instead of demand."

The intensity of the sheriff's stare didn't abate any, but when he spoke again—albeit through his teeth—it was with a more polite veneer. "Will you please, if it doesn't get in the way of your other plans, explain the meaning of what you just said?"

By that point, Tess had all but forgotten their conversation. "You mean about how you're a fast runner?" she guessed. "I'm no expert, but Detective Gonzales once trained for a marathon, and he had that same way of—"

"Oh, for the love of Pete." The sheriff pinched the bridge of his nose. "I don't have time for you to dredge up everything that man has ever seen or done. That…thing you just saw. You said he was wearing a mask."

She nodded.

"As in, you think he was a man? A human man?"

She glanced around the forest as if searching for a hidden camera. Such a thing wouldn't be unheard of. Deer cameras were often affixed to trees so hunters could use them to discover the best spots to set up a slaughter. In fact, Detective Gonzales once installed one to—

She took a deep breath and forced her mind back to the present. She had a feeling Sheriff Boyd wouldn't appreciate that particular anecdote, even if the detective *had* uncovered a corrupt maple syrup mafia with the setup.

"Of course I think he was a man," she said.

Sheriff Boyd stalked forward, not unlike a man in a bear costume. "Explain your reasoning." Then, with a visible wince, he added, "Please."

"You mean, other than the fact that I'm pretty sure I've seen that costume for sale at those Halloween stores they set up every year in abandoned grocery stores?" She shrugged. "He walked like a man. He ran like a man. What else could he have been?"

She knew the answer to that question before it finished leaving her lips. Recalling her daughter's initial fears about the explosion, she laughed outright.

"You don't mean *Bigfoot*, do you?" she asked.

Sheriff Boyd allowed her to finish her outburst, not moving or speaking until the final trill of laughter left her lips. "That *is* what I meant, actually."

"Yeah, um…" She pulled her lower lip between her teeth to keep from breaking out in giggles again. This was a new one for her. People were known to have some pretty strange fears and theories, but for a rational, level-headed sheriff of the law to believe in cryptids was a bit much. "Bigfoot isn't real. He's a mythological creature, a bogeyman who frightens children. You know that, right?"

"Of course I know that," he said through teeth clenched so tight she could have cracked a nut with them. "Anyone who's studied anything about geography and animal behavior knows that."

"Then why—"

He lost what little patience remained. "That blasted

creature—thing—*man*—has been stalking this forest for months. He's got half the town hiding in their homes and the other half walking around with hunting rifles strapped to their backs."

"Oh, dear," Tess murmured. "Do you want to talk about it?"

"Of course I don't want to talk about it," he muttered, but then proceeded to do just that. With a finger pointed in the direction the Bigfoot had run, he said, "He's taunting me. He always seems to know exactly where I'll be and when I'll be there."

"Maybe he likes you?"

The look the sheriff leveled on her head was designed to turn a woman to stone. Tess, however, was no mere woman. She was a bestselling author in a male-dominated genre. She was a divorcée at a time when internet dating brought out the worst in people. She was the parent of a teenager whose heart and world had recently been shattered to pieces. Stone wasn't going to be enough to stop her.

"Well, if he always knows where you'll be, I'm sure you'll have another opportunity to catch him. He doesn't hurt anyone, does he?"

"Not yet."

"Well, there you go. There's no crime against playing dress-up. Shall we get back on the road?"

Tess could tell that Sheriff Boyd wanted nothing more than to argue with her—likely for the sole reason that he was in a foul mood and needed to argue with *someone*. But he could hardly force her to stand in this forest forever, waiting for the return of a creature that neither one of them believed in.

He kicked ineffectively at a rock and started to make his way back to his patrol car. From the way he eyed the tail end of the vehicle, it was obvious he was toying with the idea of making her ride in the backseat. Well, either that or in the trunk. At this point, Tess wasn't willing to hazard a guess as to which.

"The next time I tell you to stay in the car, you'd better listen," he said. "For all you know, I was going to chase down a murderer."

"If you were going to chase down a murderer, you would have radioed in for backup first," Tess pointed out. And, because she couldn't help herself, "It's not what Detective Gonzales would have done, but then, he's not as fond of *the book* as you are."

Chapter Three

THE WINTHROP POLICE STATION WAS AS CLOSE TO A WILD West jail as Tess was ever going to get in her lifetime.

"It's adorable," she said as she followed Sheriff Boyd through the front door. It didn't swing like an old-timey saloon, but there was a bar next door that promised just such a treat, should she decide to linger. The entire town was like that, a touristy concession to the days of old, when miners crowded the streets and spent all their earnings on liquor, women, and gambling—in that order.

The county sheriff's office might not be as rustic as the saloon, the bank, or the hotel everyone kept trying to get her to patronize, but the wood-paneled walls made a good start. Especially since they held framed daguerreotypes and decorative horseshoes by the dozen.

"You should be wearing a cowboy hat," Tess said as she took it all in. "Or cowboy boots. Or, at the very least, a brocade waistcoat. Gertie is going to love this place."

Her comments went unheeded. Now that the sheriff was on his own turf and away from mythical creatures crashing through the forest, he was obviously back to being in charge. He made no mention of the impromptu chase to the young officer manning the front desk, so Tess politely followed suit.

"Did you get both of them?" the sheriff asked as they walked up to the desk.

"Yes, sir," the young officer replied. There was a curt respect in his voice that confirmed Tess's belief that Sheriff Boyd was a man who knew what he was doing.

"Any trouble?"

The young man winced and rubbed a hand along his jaw. As Tess leaned closer, she noticed a red swelling along one side of his face. His was a cherub-like face, small and unremarkable, with a pair of hazel eyes that sparkled mischievously at this line of questioning.

"A little," he admitted. "Adam was aiming at Zach, but I was standing between them at the time. I thought I could keep the peace."

"Fool." The sheriff spoke without heat. "You should have ducked."

The young officer answered with a smile. Tess had no idea what the age requirements were for police training out here, but that smile made him look all of fifteen years old. "I did. That's why I took the rock to my face. Adam never could hit the broad side of a barn."

The sheriff chuckled and, without a word to Tess—not even one of command—moved past the desk and through a door leading toward the back. Since she wasn't the sort of woman to sit patiently in a waiting room, she didn't hesitate to follow him.

The back portion of the police station was much less exciting than the front. There were no signs of rustic charm back here—there was just one large room crammed with desks.

No one was *seated* at any of them, but Tess imagined that was because most of them were at her cabin searching for clues.

"Adam and Zach are the Peabody boys, I take it?" Tess asked as she rushed to keep pace with Sheriff Boyd's massive stride. She only just managed to avoid banging her bad knee against the metal of a desk that had seen better days.

The sheriff grunted his assent.

"And they're at liberty to assault police officers without fear of repercussion? Interesting."

He stopped mid-stride. Tess had been forced to resort to hopping on her good foot to keep up, which meant she wasn't in a position to stop that suddenly. She barreled into his back at full speed.

It was like slamming into a wall, assuming the wall was a cozy ninety-eight-point-six degrees and had reflexes like a cat. No sooner had she bounced back and begun a perilous topple to the floor than he whirled and gripped her by the upper arms. From the tight press of his fingertips against her flesh, Tess thought she might have preferred hitting the floor, but he let go almost immediately. He snatched his hands away as if they'd been burned.

"Now you listen up," he said, as if she had any choice in the matter. Unless she ran screaming from the police station—which, in her current state, wasn't likely—he could say and do whatever he wanted. "This is my town, and I run it according to my rules. If you don't like it, you can pack up your things and go."

"Are you giving me your official permission to leave? Can I get it in writing?"

Predictably, Sheriff Boyd ignored her. "I'll handle the Peabody boys in my own way and in my own time. Got it?"

"Why?" Tess asked, suddenly suspicious. Although she'd lived in Seattle her entire life, she understood enough about small towns to know how they worked. "Are they the mayor's sons or something? Above the law? Untouchable?"

The sheriff released a long and heavy sigh. "The population of this town is less than five hundred people. Do you really think our mayor is throwing that kind of weight around? Otis runs a bike shop around the corner, and his sons are about the same age as your daughter."

"Oh," Tess said, blinking. A bike shop owner named Otis didn't sound like grounds for intrigue and corruption. Especially if he had teenagers. "Are they nice boys? Do you think Gertie would like to have them over? I've been worried she won't be able to find anyone here who—"

She didn't have the pleasure of hearing what response the sheriff had planned for her. Angry shouting in the distance distracted them both.

"I know, I know." Tess took a hop-step back and held up her hands. "Stay here. And you mean it this time."

A sound remarkably like a laugh escaped the sheriff's throat before he turned on his heel and took off toward the source of the shouting, a sort of holding room behind this one. He was followed almost immediately by the young man from the front desk, who paused long enough to send an apologetic shrug Tess's way. His uniform was much too big for him, and she longed to fix the loose knot of his tie, but he darted off before she had a chance.

She would have crept closer to the holding room in hopes of overhearing something of interest, but a tentative "Hello?" came from the front of the station before she could figure out the best place to conceal herself.

"Just a second!" she called as she wobbled her way through all the desks toward the reception area. She popped her head in and smiled at the older woman who stood clutching a purse in her hands. She was a tiny scrap of a thing, less than five feet tall according to the height strip by the door, and had a pair of glasses perched on the end of her nose. Partly to put the woman at ease and partly because she felt some explanation was necessary, Tess said, "Sorry for being a little slow on my feet. I hurt my knee earlier today."

The woman stared at her for two seconds before replying. "I hurt my knee in nineteen seventy-two. *Both* of them."

"How terrible," Tess murmured as she moved the rest of the way into the waiting room. This put her in a position not exactly behind the front desk, but not *not* behind it, either. "Would you like to sit down? Can I get you a chair?"

The woman released her grip on her purse long enough to push her glasses up her nose and peer at Tess through a pair of owlish eyes. "Who are you supposed to be? You look like a clown."

Tess's hand shot to the mass of brown curls that always seemed to expand the further away she got from the city. There was something about fresh air that put an extra spring in her unruly locks.

"My name is Tess," she said, tactfully ignoring the remark. "Is there something I can help you with?"

"Yes." The woman drew forward, her steps much sprightlier than a pair of damaged knees from the seventies would lead a person to believe. "I'd like to report a crime."

"Oh, dear." Tess cast a glance around, as if expecting help to emerge from behind the potted plant in one corner. She didn't know what the exact protocol was for reporting a crime, but she was pretty sure she could wing it. "If you'll wait just a moment, I'm sure I can get Sheriff Boyd to—"

"Sheriff Boyd is an ingrate and a vagabond. I want to report it to you."

Tess blinked at the woman. The ingrate part she could believe—the sheriff's reluctance to accept her help with that Bigfoot fellow was proof of that—but the vagabond part didn't fit. "I'm not really supposed to—"

"You've got hands, don't you? You can read?" The woman only waited until Tess nodded before she snapped, "Then write this down. I'll wait until you're ready. There's no rush. I'll only be dead by the time you get around to it."

Tess reached for the nearest pad of paper, curiosity and fear getting the better of her. Curiosity, because this woman clearly had something important to share. Fear, because if it came down to a fight between Sheriff Boyd and this fierce old woman, she was putting all her money on the latter.

"Okay," she said. "Go ahead."

"I was attacked on my way home from the grocery store," the woman said and leaned close as Tess lifted the pen.

"And which grocery store was that?"

"The only grocery store we have, you fool. Aren't you going to write it down?"

Tess obligingly wrote down the words *attack*, *grocery*, and *store*, though she didn't know what good that would do if she didn't know the name of the place. "What was the nature of your attack?"

"I was burgled."

Tess glanced up. "Actually, if it was an attack on your person, it's considered a robbery. A burglary is when—"

"I know what a burglary is," the woman snapped. "What did you say your name was?"

"Tess. Tess Harrow, and—"

"What's your badge number?"

Tess had the feeling that to disclose her civilian status now would result in a very unpleasant and stern talking-to, so she rattled off the only badge number she knew by heart: the one belonging to Detective Gonzales. "Ten-twenty-oh-three." She spoke with such a convincing air that the woman believed her.

Channeling her fictional detective imbued Tess with a confidence she'd been hitherto lacking. With a neat click of her pen, she slid to a more authoritative position behind the desk.

"Now, I know it might seem like a waste of your time, but I need to get a few basics before we go any further," she said. "What is your name, your date of birth, and your address, if you please?"

The woman seemed to shrink a full inch in light of Tess's air of authority. She unclasped the handbag she carried and rummaged around before extracting her driver's license. It was expired and had been for about ten years, but Tess let it pass.

"Okay, Edna St. Clair of 1313 Medford Drive." She jotted

the information down and handed the ID back. "If you could tell me exactly what happened, I'll be sure and get this information in the right hands."

"As I already told you," Edna said carefully, "I was burgled. There I was, carrying my bag of oranges and my cat, when out of nowhere—"

"I'm sorry." Tess held the pen poised above the pad of paper. "Did you say you were carrying your *cat*? Out of the grocery store?"

The door behind her burst open before Edna could answer—or Tess could explain what she was doing behind the reception desk.

"What in the devil is going on out here?" Sheriff Boyd demanded. He didn't wait for a response from either woman before whisking the notepad out of Tess's hand. "I thought I told you to stay put."

"You did."

Instead of finding her conciliation soothing, the sheriff's color deepened. "Then why aren't you in the exact location where I left you?"

"Because this nice woman needed my help," Tess explained. She pointed at the paper. "Apparently, she was attacked while coming out of the grocery store. I thought it might help if I got the details down for you."

"It'd help if you did what you were told."

"That wasn't a choice, I'm afraid. I could hardly leave Ms. St. Clair all alone out here." Tess turned to Edna with a smile. "Would you like to finish giving your report to the sheriff, or did you want us to continue?"

The woman opened her mouth to respond, but Sheriff Boyd cut her off.

"This had better not be about that blasted cat of yours," he warned.

"I'll thank you not to use that kind of language in the presence of a lady," Edna said primly. She glanced at Tess and doubled down. "*Two* ladies."

"It *is* about the blasted cat." Sheriff Boyd pinched the bridge of his nose. "Edna, if I've told you once, I've told you a thousand times. Your cat running away isn't a crime."

The old woman stiffened. "He didn't run away. He was taken."

"Did you physically see someone take him?"

"No, but that doesn't mean anything. I don't physically see the air around me, but it's there."

Tess had to muffle her laughter by taking her lower lip between her teeth, and, even then, it was close. Her hand itched to reach for the pad of paper and jot down a few notes about the way the sheriff looked right now—his jaw so tight it could crack stone, his eyes like a pair of black holes—but she didn't dare risk it.

"Oscar wouldn't leave me like that. He was lured away."

"I don't have time for this," the sheriff muttered. "I'll let Animal Control know that your cat is missing again, but I recommend you open a can of tuna and put it outside your door. I'm sure he'll be back by dinnertime."

Edna gave a sniff of dismay. "Well, I never."

"I also recommend that you put a leash on him the next time you take him anywhere. You'd be surprised how much less likely he is to run away when he's attached to you." The sheriff turned to Tess and, taking note of her quivering mouth, only glowered more. "Now, if you'll accompany me, Ms. Harrow, we can get that other matter cleared up."

"Absolutely, Sheriff," Tess said obediently. "Anything you say, Sheriff."

She was prepared to follow through with this, but Edna wasn't done. "Don't let him bully you," she said, pointing a gnarled finger at Tess. "He only won the last election by five votes. His time here is almost over, and he knows it."

They both watched as the older woman turned on her heel and walked away, once again without any sign of lasting knee damage.

"Five votes, huh?" Tess asked as soon as the door swung shut behind her. "You might want to be a little more conciliatory to your constituents if that's the case. The poor woman just wants her cat."

"And *I* want to get back to work," he returned. "Are you coming to identify your trespasser or not?"

Tess thought about arguing, but she wanted to get back to the cabin before dark. It wasn't that she was *afraid* to leave Gertrude alone—not with all those police milling about—but she wanted to be available to her daughter in case she needed her. That was the whole reason for this retreat in the first place.

"Absolutely, Sheriff," she said, echoing her tone and words from before. "Anything you say, Sheriff."

"Is this supposed to be a trick?"

Tess stood in front of a one-way mirror, staring into a room that contained a lineup of exactly three people. One of them was the young man who'd been working at the reception desk when she'd come in; the two on either side of him were twins.

Identical twins, both in matching red flannel shirts and with the same swoop of too-long auburn hair. Their boots were the same and their pants were the same—even the smirk that lifted one side of their lips was the same. The only difference she could see was that one was sporting a black eye, and the other had a cut along his temple.

"If you could just identify the man from your property, we'll get this logged and be on our way." Sheriff Boyd didn't look at her, his gaze fixed straight ahead. "Go ahead."

"You didn't tell me that the Peabody boys were twins."

He didn't say anything.

"And I'm pretty sure you're not allowed to put the man who greeted me at the desk in the lineup. Is this how *the book* does things?"

The sheriff sighed. "Not even remotely, as you well know. But with all my guys on the scene and those two idiots in there starting a fistfight anytime they share breathing space, this is what you get. I can't call Carl out or the Peabody boys will be on top of each another in a matter of seconds. Pick one."

Tess did her best to comply. The sheriff was starting to sound as though he was reaching the end of his metaphorical rope, and she wasn't keen on alienating him too much on her first day. If this town was going to be full rough-and-tumble lumberjack types and little old ladies being robbed outside the grocery store, she wanted to know she could count on the man at the other end of a 9-1-1 call to come running when she and Gertrude needed him.

"Could you have the one on the left say, 'Lady, are you all right?'"

Sheriff Boyd pressed a button the wall and repeated her request. With a sigh, the man on the left said the words. He sounded exactly like the man from her pond, if more annoyed this time around.

"And the other one?"

"Again," the sheriff ordered. "Number three."

"Lady, are you all right?" This one was uttered much more dramatically, almost as though the man was reading a teleprompter on a soap opera. It didn't help matters any. Whether being annoyed or melodramatic, the two were impossible to distinguish.

"Well?" the sheriff prompted.

"What if you had them run at me at full speed?"

"You've got to be kidding."

She wasn't kidding—not really. Without any distinguishing features other than their visible bruises, which had obviously been acquired within the last few hours, she had no way of telling which of the two men had been at her cabin. According to the research she'd done for *Fury in the Big City*, the first book she'd ever written and her personal favorite, it wouldn't even do any good if there was DNA evidence left behind. When you were dealing with twins, even the lab couldn't provide irrefutable evidence—something that had almost cost Detective Gonzales his career.

"I don't see what you expect from me," Tess said. "You could have warned me that they dressed like the dolls my daughter used to play with when she was little. What kind of grown man wears the same clothes as his brother?"

"The kind of grown man who knows he's about to be hauled in for identification." The sheriff sighed with genuine feeling. "I'm sorry. I didn't know they were going to pull this stunt."

Tess gave a decisive nod. Between the Bigfoot chase, Edna's missing cat, and the body parts at her cabin, the sheriff had more than enough work ahead of him. The least she could do was make this easy on him.

"All right," she announced. "I'm going in."

"Going in *where*?" the sheriff demanded, but he got his answer half a second later when Tess turned on her heel and limped out of the room. "Don't you dare. It's not—"

By the book. She knew. She also knew she wouldn't be able to tell these men apart any other way. Needs must, desperate times, and all that.

She yanked open the door to the room where the men were lined up. As she suspected, it was a foul-smelling space, with blood, eau de man, and the briny scent of fish hanging overhead. Carl looked only slightly less surprised than the Peabody twins to see her there, so she used the momentary silence to make her assessment.

Walking quickly to the first Peabody—the one with the black eye—she inhaled deeply. His scent wasn't a pleasant one, but it didn't seem as though he'd recently been rained on by fish parts. As she approached Peabody Number Two—he of the head wound—she knew she was facing her man.

"It's this one," she called. By this time, the sheriff had more than caught up to her. As he'd also caught on to what she was doing, he didn't make an attempt to stop her. "I bet if you check his pockets, you'll find bits of fish in them. They were raining pretty heavily there toward the end."

At first, she was afraid his silence was going to be accompanied by irritation, but when she turned to look at him, he was struggling to suppress a smile.

"Okay, Ms. Harrow," he said, his lips twitching. "You win this round. Carl, go ahead and let Adam go. Put Zach back in holding. He and I are going to have a little chat."

Zach didn't appear to find this plan to his taste. "Just because this lady doesn't like the way I smell? Forget that. I don't like the way *she* smells."

"There's no need for insults," Tess said primly, though she did feel a qualm of concern. She'd had the foresight to change her clothes after her contact with the fish-rain, but her hair had a way of absorbing scents as well as moisture.

"I'll remember this," Zach said. He nodded at his brother. From the look they shared, they seemed to have decided on a temporary truce. "Me and Adam both. We don't forget things easily."

"Yeah." Adam sniffed. "We don't forget."

Sheriff Boyd cleared his throat. "I believe that qualifies as a threat. You're both going into holding now. Anything else you'd like to add?"

Tess put her hand out for a high five. "Nice one."

The sheriff only stared at her hand before ignoring it. Tess was too accustomed to Gertrude leaving her hanging to take it to heart.

"No," Zach said sullenly.

"No," Adam agreed.

Tess stepped back and watched as Carl ushered the two men out the door. "Well, Sheriff?" she asked. "Where are we going to perform the interrogation?"

His stare could have cut glass. "*I* am going to perform the interrogation where I normally do. *You* are going home."

She made a light tsking sound. "You forgot that you're my ride. If I'm stuck here, you might as well get some use out of me. I'm excellent at interrogating."

"Too bad. Carl is taking you home."

Despite her eagerness to get back to Gertrude, Tess was tempted to put up a fight. Now that she was facing the actual perpetrator of the crime, her keen sense of curiosity was taking over. She wanted to know what Zach had been doing on her property, and why he thought fishing via dynamite was a smart thing to do…unless, of course, he was trying to blow up a body at the same time. If that was the case, then it was *very* smart thing to do. Reckless sporting activities as a cover for murder. Blast fishing so that all traces of human matter were mingled with the fish, unidentifiable and useless.

Her writerly senses started to tingle. That wasn't a bad idea, actually. She could use that.

"What is it?" Sheriff Boyd asked, eyeing her askance. "Why do you look like you just swallowed a winning lottery ticket?"

She laughed. "You know what? I think I will take you up on that offer to have Carl drive me back. Thank you."

"Why? What are you going to do?"

She could have told him the truth—that she was going to sit down at her typewriter and start blowing up bodies and fish simultaneously—but that would take all the fun out of it.

"Oh, nothing. Enjoy your time with the Peabody boys, Sheriff. It's been...interesting."

The sheriff looked as though he wanted to sit *her* down in the interrogation room and start demanding answers, but she left before he could make the attempt. It was best to leave your audience wanting more.

Dead bodies, explosions, and a taste of something to come.

That was Thriller Writing 101.

Chapter Four

TESS RETURNED TO THE CABIN TO FIND ALL THREE deputies sitting in the living room eating turkey sandwiches.

"Hey, Mom." Gertrude waved a knife at her from the kitchen. "Do you want Havarti or Muenster on yours?"

Based on the size of the sandwiches currently being enjoyed by Sheriff Boyd's finest, Tess was guessing that Gertrude had used up most of the food meant to carry them through the month.

"Havarti, please," she answered. Edna St. Clair's promise that the town contained a grocery store meant they wouldn't starve. She doubted they'd find much in the way of gourmet cheese stocked on its shelves, but they *were* rusticating. Kraft slices would do in a pinch. "And you'd better make one for Carl, too. He's out parking the car."

Gertrude didn't find anything noteworthy about this request, but all three of the deputies sprang to their feet. Tess had assumed, based on Carl's age and the ease with which he'd followed Sheriff Boyd's orders, that he was some sort of lowly underling. The guilty looks on the deputies' faces, however, put that theory to rest. They obviously didn't want to be caught sandwich-handed.

"Sit," she commanded them in her best mom-voice.

"Finish your dinner. Even Sheriff Boyd can't expect you to catalog a crime scene on an empty stomach."

"Yes, he can," said the only female deputy of the lot. She looked to be in her early thirties and unremarkable in that pulled-back way that women in uniform had a tendency to be. "You obviously don't know the sheriff very well."

No, she didn't, and she might have used this opportunity to pump his staff for information, but there were far more pressing issues on her mind right now. Bodies in her pond, for example.

"What did we discover in my absence?" she asked as Gertrude passed a plate through the window separating the kitchen from the rest of the living space. Her sandwich looked slightly thinner than the ones currently being devoured by their guests, but that was probably for the best. She'd put on ten pounds since the divorce. "The other arm? A leg? A head?"

"Gross, Mom."

"A head would be the logical conclusion."

"We're not really at liberty to discuss our findings," the female deputy said with a sniff.

Tess was eyeing the other two officers to decide which of them was more likely to share confidential information when Carl walked in with his too-big uniform and too-innocent face. He took one look around the room, accepted the sandwich being offered him, and asked, "Well, Ivy? What's the story with our John Doe?"

Tess could have kissed him.

The female deputy, Ivy, sighed but answered. "Well, first of all, she's a Jane Doe, not a John, and not much."

Tess and her daughter shared a knowing look—and by knowing, Tess meant Gertrude gave her the self-satisfied smirk that only a fourteen-year-old who was too smart for her own good could manage. All those statistics about women dying in rural areas were starting to hit a little too close to home.

"Are you sure we should be talking about this here?" Ivy tilted her head at Tess. "*Now?*"

"It was my pond you found her in," Tess pointed out. "And my face she slapped on her way down to earth. I think I have a right to know what's going on."

"*Gross*, Mom," Gertrude repeated. "Why can't you act like a normal parent and take me back to Seattle? I'm scarred. I'm traumatized. I'll never be the same again."

"What if I told you I bought a back-up generator while I was in town and installed a Wi-Fi hot spot in the house?" she countered.

Gertrude perked to a ridiculous degree. "You did? Yesss. Where's my phone?"

Tess wagged a finger at her daughter, who, despite being too smart for her own good, wasn't quite smart enough for her mother. "Gotcha! Save your trauma for your future therapist. We're not going anywhere."

This decree wasn't as cruel as it sounded. She *could* pack up her daughter and all the supplies they'd brought, bundle everything into the car, and head back to the city. Summer in Seattle could be quite lovely, with full days of sunshine and opportunities to picnic on the beach. Unfortunately, being in the city also meant being within reach of her ex-husband, Quentin.

Quentin, who wouldn't call. Quentin, who wouldn't write. Quentin, who wouldn't ask to see his only daughter even once.

Gertrude might be smiling right now, but that didn't mean Tess wasn't aware of what was going on beneath the surface. She saw a glimpse of it sometimes in the haunted expression that would flash across Gertrude's face when she thought Tess wasn't looking. She saw it in the pink hair and the black fingernails and the way Gertrude couldn't open her mouth these days without saying something scathing. She saw it in the way that angular, angry teen would wake up in the middle of the night and crawl into bed with her, a thing she hadn't done since she was a child and used to fear monsters in the dark.

So, yes. It could be argued that it was bad parenting to stay in this cabin when a body had been so recently uncovered out back, but the alternative was worse. At least out here, where phone service was sketchy and Gertrude couldn't check social media twenty times every hour, she could pretend that her father still loved her.

There wasn't much Tess could do to ease Gertrude's pain, but she could—*would*—give her this.

"The coroner already left with most of what we found," Ivy said. She rose and brushed the crumbs from her meal onto the floor. "I'll give you the report on the way."

Carl shook his head. "No can do. The sheriff wants me posted out back until morning."

"What?" Tess spoke through a mouthful of her sandwich, her maternal instincts roused. "All night? But where will you sleep?"

Carl rolled one shoulder in a casual shrug. The action dislodged a lock of his hair, which he wiped away from his forehead only to leave a streak of mustard behind. "It's protocol. You can always take it up with Sheriff Boyd, but…"

He didn't need to finish. Tess could picture that conversation, and it didn't end with her getting her way. She didn't love the idea of this young man being forced to stand in the dark woods for hours, but it would be nice to know that someone with a gun and a badge was on hand. There *was* an ancient rifle mounted above the doorway that might work in a pinch, but most of Tess's gun experience came from a well-controlled shooting range where someone else loaded the bullets for her.

She liked hands-on research as much as the next award-winning author, but bullets made her nervous.

The other deputies got to their feet and murmured their thanks for the sandwiches. Gertrude was busy cleaning up in the kitchen, and Carl was focused on his sandwich, so Tess walked them to the door. She also walked them down the dirt path to where the cars were parked. There was no way she was letting an opportunity like this go to waste.

"If you know the body is a Jane rather than a John, I'm assuming you found the rest of her," she said without preamble. "It was just the one dead person, though, right? You didn't find two left feet or anything weird like that?"

At this line of questioning, Ivy frowned. She also answered, which was the most important thing. "From what we can tell, yes, it's just the one victim."

"And all her…parts have been accounted for?" Tess

coughed and added, "What I mean is, my daughter isn't going to look out her window and see an intestine dangling from a tree? She's tough, but she's not that tough."

Ivy stared at her. Tess wasn't an easily cowed woman—as her interactions with Sheriff Boyd had proven—but there was something about the deputy's confidence that unsettled her. "This is an interesting line of questioning."

"Just being a good parent."

It was clear from the flat line of Ivy's lips that she didn't agree. "Since you brought it up, no, we haven't recovered everything."

For the first time since body parts had fallen from the sky, Tess felt a nervous qualm. Part of it was the matter-of-fact way Ivy answered her question, but it also had something to do with the look of deep foreboding in the other woman's eyes.

Tess swallowed. "May I ask which parts are missing?"

One of the other deputies overheard them. "You might as well tell her. She'll find out soon enough anyway."

Ivy recited her findings as though reading from a list. "No head, no fingers, no teeth."

The fact that Ivy mentioned both teeth and a head wasn't as redundant as it seemed. While it was a given that you couldn't have one without the other, there was a logical connection between them: namely, that they could be used to identify the deceased. Without a recognizable face, fingerprints, or dental records, it would be very difficult to discover the name of their Jane Doe.

"I don't suppose you found any highly distinguishable tattoos?" Tess asked, purely for form's sake.

Ivy's only answer was a hard stare.

"Well, I guess that eliminates an accidental drowning," Tess said.

"I guess so," Ivy agreed.

"Or someone giving their favorite relative a Viking burial," she added.

"Looks that way."

"She must have been murdered."

Ivy didn't respond. She didn't have to. Even if Tess hadn't been well-versed in the nature of murder and all the ways it was carried out, there was no denying the obvious facts. Someone had put that body in the pond in hopes of it never surfacing again.

Tess had dozens of additional questions she'd have liked to ask, but Ivy was proving just as difficult to crack as Sheriff Boyd. The thought that these two would make an admirable couple flashed through her mind, which naturally led her to consider Detective Gonzales's lonely state. She'd given him a few one-night stands over the years—a man did have his needs, after all—but she'd never considered a long-term love affair before.

"Yes, that might work," Tess murmured, her head tilted as she looked at Ivy through fresh eyes. The deputy wasn't a beauty in the classical sense, but there was something about her utilitarian, no-nonsense practicality that would appeal to a man like Gonzales. She was tall, well-built, and solid. With her hair and her inhibitions down—

"What are you doing?" Ivy snapped her fingers in Tess's face. "Hey. You. Come back."

Tess blinked, startled back into awareness. It used to drive Quentin crazy when she did that, meandering off into the recesses of her own imagination, but she could no more stop it than she could prevent the passing of time. He used to accuse her of avoiding reality, of hiding herself away where nothing could touch her.

It's like you don't even know how to function in the real world, he'd say. *The moment things get hard, you disappear into those stupid books.*

Funny how that hadn't stopped him from spending most of the money those *stupid books* brought in.

"Oh. Um. I'm sorry. I was just…thinking."

"About what?"

Since Tess wasn't about to tell this stranger about the way she'd broken her marriage, she focused on the one thing she could control: the story. Always the story. She and Gertrude might be alone in the world, surrounded by murderers and cryptids and who-knew-what else, but she still had a deadline to meet and palimony to pay.

"Is your hair naturally curly or straight?" she asked.

"Straight. What does that have to do with anything?"

Tess considered her. "Would you call yourself more of a pantyhose-and-Sunday-best sort of dresser, or do you prefer a nice pair of slacks when you go out?"

"What's wrong with you?"

"What do you order to drink at the bar? Whiskey neat? You strike me as a whiskey neat sort of woman."

Ivy muttered something about city slickers before turning away and stalking off to join the other two deputies. She cast a look over her shoulder as she did and, seeing that Tess was noting the exact cadence of her walk, quickly jumped into her car.

"Not whiskey neat," Tess said aloud. "Moonshine. She definitely drinks moonshine."

She didn't wait to watch them drive away. She wandered back up to the cabin instead, deep in consideration of the fictional lady love she was about to descend on poor Detective Gonzales. Oh, how he was going to hate that. It was going to turn his life upside down.

Especially when it turned out he needed his lady love's help in order to solve his newest murder: a body with no head, no fingers, and no teeth.

Chapter Five

"IF THEY'RE GOING TO KEEP A REGULAR ROTATION OF deputies posted at the back door, we need to beef up on supplies."

Tess dug around in her purse until she located her Space Needle key ring and swung it around her finger. The gesture was meant to entice Gertrude, but all the teenager did was roll her eyes.

"Maybe we can throw caution to the wind and pick up a pack of playing cards while we're out." Remembering what Sheriff Boyd had said about the mayor and his two sons, she added, "And I think we should rent a couple of mountain bikes, too. That might be fun. There are supposed to be some really good trails around here."

She realized her error too late.

"You hate mountain biking." Gertrude removed the pot of coffee she'd been brewing on the stovetop. She poured a cup into Tess's favorite writing mug, oversized and proclaiming her a member of *Team Oxford Comma*, before willfully— and cruelly, if you asked Tess—carrying it to the deputy posted at the back door.

Not one drop of coffee had yet crossed her own lips. Out of compassion, she and Gertrude had kept Carl supplied overnight. His replacement, a twentysomething young man who had the stature and appetite of a hobbit, had arrived around six o'clock and also seemed to require a steady influx of caffeine. Not to mention first breakfast, second breakfast, and, if the hopeful way he kept poking his head into the kitchen was anything to go by, third breakfast.

"You used to tell Dad that mountain biking was a marketing ploy for aging suburban men who were desperately clinging to their lost youth."

"Me?" Tess carefully avoided her daughter's eyes. "I would never."

"And that you'd rather climb a mountain on foot than go anywhere near one of those torture devices."

"I don't know what you're talking about. Think of all the fresh air and exercise we'll get."

Gertrude passed the cup of coffee to the hobbit deputy and heaved a sigh. "Do I *have* to?"

"Do you have to come to town with me to resupply? Yes." Tess swung the key ring again. "Do you have to rent a mountain bike and all the requisite safety gear? Afraid so, child of my heart. Do you have to like it?"

"As if you care whether I like it or not," Gertrude muttered. She reached for her ubiquitous black hoodie and shoved her arms through it. "Fine. Whatever. At least it'll be hilarious to watch you try to ride a bike."

This was taking things too far. "I know how to ride a bike!"

Gertrude's only answer was a hard stare.

"I used to ride bikes all the time," Tess protested. "Before you were born, I did a lot of fun things, actually. I skied the Alps and swam naked under the full light of the moon and—"

"Gross, Mom. Please don't talk about being naked."

This wasn't the turn Tess had hoped the conversation would take, but Gertrude seemed to have moved past that bit about her hating mountain bikes, so she was willing to see it through to the end. Mountain biking had always been Quentin's thing. *Anything* fun had been Quentin's thing. He was the parent who took Gertrude to amusement parks in the summer and booked indoor water park getaways in the winter. He splurged on whale-watching cruises and bought her one of each kind of candy whenever they went to a movie. Tess was the parent who made her clean her room.

And that had been fine, for the most part. No one wanted to grow up and be the grouch who oversaw the making of beds, but Gertrude was the only teenager Tess knew who understood how vacuum cleaners worked. That had to count for something.

"I used to do a lot of naked things, now that I think about it," Tess said as they made their way to the Jeep. It was bright orange and had never actually been driven through the wilderness before this trip, but it had taken the rutted dirt roads like a champ. "One time, when I was in college, my friends and I streaked the entire—"

"Nope." Gertrude clamped her hands over her ears and practically ran to the passenger seat. "You might be able to make me ride a bike against my will, but making me hear about your crimes against humanity isn't happening."

The first thing Tess noticed when they pulled onto Main Street was a Peabody brother standing in front of the grocery store.

He wasn't *guarding* it, exactly, but there was a disturbed air about him that made Tess take a sharp right and park in front of a row of rental cabins a block away.

"Maybe we should pick up supplies somewhere else," she said. "I think there was a Stop 'N' Snack in the next town over. You love Stop 'N' Snack."

"I also like not driving for three hours every time we run out of butter," Gertrude said. She unbuckled her belt and slithered out of her seat. "Since when are you such a chicken?"

Those were fighting words, and Gertrude knew it. If the Peabodys had been released from their jail cell already, it meant the sheriff had found them innocent of any crimes. Tess might not relish the idea of facing them again so soon, but it was a task that would have to be done sooner or later.

Tess was a woman who *always* opted for sooner.

At least, that was what she strove to do. Sometimes— say, when facing a large, angry man recently identified in a lineup—she admitted to a nervous qualm. Or two.

"Stay behind me," Tess ordered Gertrude. "And do that thing where you dial 9-1-1 and keep your finger hovering over the send button."

"Do you also want me to put your car key between my fingers to use as a knife in case he attacks? I can carry the rape whistle in my mouth and pull out the bear spray, too."

Tess absorbed this sarcasm with a beaming smile. She planted a kiss on her daughter's forehead. "That's my girl. I taught you well."

A chuff of annoyed breath escaped Gertrude's mouth, but Tess didn't mind. Like being the parent who was always in charge of chores, forcing a solid understanding of self-defense was something she could only be proud of.

"Good morning!" Tess called brightly as they approached the grocery store. Now that she was close enough to the Peabody brother, she could see that he sported a gash on his temple. That made him Zach and, according to her scent test yesterday, the man who'd blown up the fish in her pond. "You seem to be doing better today."

In all honesty, the cut on his head looked as though it hadn't been properly cleaned, and he bore the heavily shadowed eyes of a man who'd spent the night in a jail cell, but Tess didn't trust the old key-in-the-fingers trick as much as she let on.

Zach smirked, which didn't do anything to improve his appearance. In another lifetime, he could have been a dreamboat. All that rich, auburn hair, the build of a man who worked with his hands, a decidedly lumberjack-y air—he was basically a walking advertisement for men's cologne.

Alas, it was wasted. The taint of murder would do that to a man.

"Bet you're surprised to see me walking about," he said.

"Not particularly, no. I assume you posted bail?"

His smirk quavered at the edges. "No. I was freed. I have an alibi. Sheriff Boyd can't touch me."

If it had been up to Tess, she would have left things there. Zach wasn't acting in a menacing or threatening way, and thanks to her late-night book plotting, she'd come to the conclusion that he couldn't have been the one who put the body in her pond. Not if he came back three days later to blow it up. Doing *one* of those things made sense—you either buried a body in water without its identifying parts or you blew it up in hopes of making it impossible to find—but both was just overkill.

Literally.

But there was something about his smile, confident and mocking, that raised her bristles. He'd been waiting here for her; she was sure of it. He'd wanted her to see him walking around without a police escort, to know how easily he'd been able to dupe the legal system.

She nudged Gertrude into the store. "Go pick up what we need, honey. I'll be inside in a sec."

"And miss the alibi?" Gertrude countered. "Never."

"*Now*."

Few things in Tess's parenting arsenal had the power to move her child like that particular note in her voice. It took Gertrude half a second to register it and half a second more to grab a nearby cart and head inside. There was a good chance Tess would be punished with things like kale and sardines and other culinary monstrosities, but that was a price she was willing to pay.

She waited only until Gertrude's bright head disappeared through the automatic door before turning to Zach Peabody with all the force of her five feet four inches.

"Now, you see here, young man," she said. The steely note in her voice remained. "I don't know how you're tangled up in this dead body business, or why you're stalking me outside a grocery store, but let's get one thing straight. You don't approach me when I'm with my daughter, understand? She's a minor, and if you say one thing that's even remotely threatening in her earshot, I'll have the sheriff on your doorstep faster than you can say *harassment*."

"But I have an alibi—" he began before Tess cut him off with a warning finger under his nose.

"You might have a hundred alibis, but it still wouldn't matter to me. You were found trespassing on my property, in possession of a deadly and what I'm assuming is an illegal amount of dynamite. That might not be enough for Sheriff Boyd to keep you, but my arsenal of lawyers back in Seattle will be happy to open a civil suit the moment I say the word. I'm a very wealthy woman, and you're not the first man to threaten me."

Zach swallowed before casting nervous eyes in every direction. Tess had no idea what he was looking for, unless it was the nearest exit route. "I don't know what you're talking about lady, but—"

"Ma'am."

He blinked. "What?"

"Don't address me as 'lady.' Address me as ma'am or not at all."

"Yes, ma'am, only—"

"What's the alibi?"

The nervous, darting glance was more pronounced this

time, but Tess angled her body to block off his escape. "You started this," she said. "And you're not going anywhere until we finish it. What's this magical alibi of yours?"

"I...I was on the logging crew," he said, faltering slightly. "Up north a ways. For all of last week."

"You, Zach Peabody, were on a logging crew?"

"Yes, ma'am."

"And was your brother on that crew?"

"My brother, ma'am?"

She inclined her head in a tight nod. "It's not a difficult question. Was your identical brother also on the logging crew?"

"No, ma'am."

It was all she needed to hear. "So only one Peabody was accounted for? Or does Adam have a magical alibi in place for that whole week as well?"

A slow grin crossed Zach's face. She didn't trust it any more than she trusted his motives in seeking her out today, but she allowed him to say his piece.

"Adam was in the next county," he announced as one imparting an important piece of news. "In jail. His alibi is as tight as they come."

At least Tess had been right about one thing: Sheriff Boyd had let the Peabody brothers go because he'd had no other choice...and because it was perfectly safe to do so. Tess didn't like them, and she hadn't been kidding about bringing in her lawyers if the twins showed any aggression toward her daughter, but she was a fair woman. From the sound of it, they were nothing more than your average, garden-variety examples of toxic masculinity.

"There you go, then," she said. "You're all cleared. Did you want to add anything else?"

He blinked. "Anything else?"

She made a vague gesture at the storefront. "I'm guessing you don't hang out at the grocery store because of the riveting social life it affords. You're obviously here to say something to me, so I suggest you say it and move on. My patience is wearing thin."

Zach gave a start of surprise. "I'm not scared of you," he said in a voice that sounded, in all honesty, a little scared.

"And I'm not scared of you. Look at that. We have something in common."

Zach opened his mouth to speak again, but Tess would never learn what he had to say. A shadow crossed over her in the way of a man approaching at her back, but no sound of footsteps accompanied it.

"Sheriff Boyd," she said. "So nice to see you again."

The sheriff didn't greet her, but that didn't stop her from turning in triumph to find him glowering.

"How'd you know it was me?" he demanded.

She didn't answer. Detective Gonzales always walked like that—silent as a cat, sneaking up on bad guys in dark alleyways every chance he got—but she doubted he wanted to hear it. "Zach and I were just searching for common ground," she informed him instead.

"Did you find it?"

Zach answered for her. "You can't arrest me for standing in front of a store. Whatever she says I did, it's a lie. I never threatened her or her stupid kid."

"Gertrude is an exceptionally bright human being, thank you very much."

It took a moment for Zach to digest this remark. By the time he figured it out, his mood had taken a turn for the worse. "I'm an innocent man," he said. "And I have rights. Do you hear me? Rights!"

Zach looked as though he wanted to add something more, but one look at the sheriff had him rethinking his stance. With a few muttered curses and an invitation for Tess to enjoy carnal relations with herself, he took himself off. She watched him go, her eyes narrowing as she took in those long, angrily sloping strides.

"You know, from this angle, I could almost swear he's walking just like—"

"Don't say it," Sheriff Boyd grumbled. "I'm well aware what you're thinking."

She said it anyway. "But that's impossible. Both he and his brother had been rounded up by Carl when we were driving to the station. There's no way he could have been the one in that Bigfoot suit."

"There's no way he could have been the one in the Bigfoot suit," Sheriff Boyd echoed in a level tone. He sighed and added, "Just like there's no way he could have been responsible for the death of the woman in your pond. You might as well know that we got the coroner's report back. Three days of decay. You were right."

"I'm sorry. I'm not sure I heard you correctly. Could you say that again?"

He leaned against a cement block and glared at her. "No."

She didn't let that glare discompose her. "Without any formal training, and with only a cursory glance, I knew exactly how old that arm was."

"It was a lucky guess."

"It was an *educated* guess," she corrected him. "My educated guess also tells me that Zach is hiding something. Alibi or no alibi, he's up to no good."

The sheriff agreed to this with no more than a slight tilt of his head. With a voice just as harsh as before, he asked, "Was he bothering you?"

"Not as much as he seems to bother you."

Sheriff Boyd straightened. Unlike when she encountered him at her cabin yesterday, he wasn't dressed in the official green uniform of a man of the law. Most of the residents around here wore some combination of jeans and flannel, but he was dressed remarkably well for someone who lived in a place where bears outnumbered humans two-to-one. A pressed pair of slacks and a button-down shirt that fit across his chest like a piece of plastic wrap were as out of place around here as a yacht in her pond. His only concession to his surroundings was a pair of cowboy boots that gleamed with a recent polishing.

"I'm on my way to court, so don't look at me like that," he said.

"Detective Gonzales wouldn't be caught dead in a shirt that tight."

"Detective Gonzales is a figment of your overactive imagination. And my shirt isn't tight. It's fitted."

She ignored this to focus on the more pressing issue at

hand. "You *do* think Zach is your Bigfoot—well, either him or his brother. Was Adam really in jail last week, or is that just a story Zach fed me to keep me off the scent?"

Sheriff Boyd's answer came as a finger pointed in warning. "I don't need your help solving this case. I only came over here to make sure Zach wasn't harassing you."

"What was Adam in jail for? Drunk and disorderly behavior? I feel like it might have been drunk and disorderly behavior."

"You're not an investigator, and I'd appreciate it if you'd stop pretending otherwise."

Tess nodded once. "He has all the classic signs of alcoholism. His hands were shaking when you had him in the lineup yesterday, and I thought I detected a bit of yellowing in his sclera." She paused. "That would explain the aggression, too."

"Oh, for Pete's sake!" The sheriff pushed himself off the cement block. For a moment, it looked as though he was going to tackle Tess, but he didn't make a move toward her. "I've already rearranged my team's schedule so you have a deputy posted at your house at all hours. I cannot and will not assign you a private guard to go with it."

That surprised—and, if she was being honest, alarmed—her. "Do I need one?"

He glanced at the vintage leather watch on his wrist and cursed. "If you keep alienating everyone you encounter, yes. This isn't a place that takes kindly to meddlers."

She was just about to protest this—she didn't meddle; she was *inquisitive*—but the sheriff didn't give her a chance.

"I'm going to be late if I don't get going," he said. "You sure you're all right?"

Tess cast a glance around her—at this quaint historic town, this place where she and Gertrude were supposed to lay low and lick their collective wounds for a month—with a bemused air. "I was until you asked me that question. Why shouldn't I be all right? What aren't you telling me?"

His answer surprised her. "If you see one of the Peabody boys again, don't engage him in conversation, got it? And if, for whatever reason, you come across another Bigfoot..."

She waited, curious what he thought she could possibly do to a costumed bear roaming the woods. "Take a photo?" she suggested when he didn't make an attempt to finish his sentence.

"No." He grimaced. "*Run.*"

Tess didn't fill her daughter in on the gory details.

"Sorry, Charlie," she said as Gertrude wheedled and begged and otherwise tried to pump her for information. She'd never admit it, but that conversation with Sheriff Boyd had unsettled her. She might not be afraid of the Peabodys, whom she was ready to write off as a pair of bullies with too much time and not enough imagination, but that bit about Bigfoot had done the trick. "Some things aren't meant to be shared with impressionable teenagers."

Gertrude made a face and tossed a can of artichokes into the cart. As Tess had feared, there were a lot more vegetables than she cared for—most of which looked as though they'd been in this store for more years than she'd been on the planet.

"That just means he didn't tell you anything," Gertrude said.

"He told me enough," she countered. Casting a sideways glance at her daughter, she added, "What do you know about cryptids, Gertie?"

A dusty can of hearts of palm clanged against the metal of the cart. "Cryptids? You mean like the Loch Ness Monster?"

Tess feigned nonchalance. "Yeah. Stuff like that. Nessie, El Chupacabra…Bigfoot."

The cart came to a screeching halt. "Mom!"

"What? Don't they teach that sort of thing in school anymore? When I was a kid, they were always trying to cram mythology down our throats. Well, that and a bunch of boring books by old, outdated white guys—although I suppose that still accounts for ninety percent of the curriculum. I keep meaning to write a letter to the superintendent."

Gertrude dismissed the bulk of this with a wave of her hand. "You made fun of me for being scared of Bigfoot yesterday."

"I didn't *make fun* of you."

A jar of pickled beets made their way alongside the artichokes. Tess plucked it out and put it back on the shelf. She had to draw the line somewhere.

"We're here for food, Gertie. Not beets. Beets are an abomination."

Gertrude grabbed the jar and dangled it over the cart.

"Let me get the beets, or I won't tell you what I know about Bigfoot."

"This is a trap. You don't know anything."

Gertrude shook the beets, which jiggled in a way that seemed alarmingly lifelike. "There's only one way to find out."

The jar had a bright orange sticker offering a fifty percent discount, so Tess gave in. "Fine. Get them. But you'd better have scientific names and exact locations of sightings, or I'm going to feel cheated. And I refuse to eat a single root vegetable."

Gertrude laughed. It was such a rare and delightful sound that Tess would have promised to eat nothing else for a full month if her daughter would only do it again.

"Well?" she demanded as they started the cart up again and headed toward the checkout lane. "What do I get for your blood price?"

"From me? Nothing." Gertrude started loading up the food on the slick black conveyor belt. Tess would have protested this, but her daughter paused long enough to point toward the large glass window. It took her a moment to realize that Gertrude wasn't ordering her out to the street. Instead, her finger landed on an oversized blue delivery truck with a painted logo of encyclopedias and the word BOOKMOBILE on the side.

"You're the one who's always telling me I should spend more time in the library. I think you should start there."

Chapter Six

To call the bookmobile a *library* was pushing things too far.

"Knock knock!" Tess called as she and Gertrude mounted the metal steps. She peeked inside to find that the vehicle had been hollowed out of everything except a driver's seat and an oversized stick shift that rose up from the center console like the sword in the stone. Instead of whatever mechanics were supposed to be in there, the walls had been lined with shelves.

Lots and lots of shelves.

"Oh, wow," Gertrude breathed as she pushed her way past Tess and entered the vehicle. There was just enough headspace for them to stand, but a taller person would have to hunch.

In fact, that was exactly what a taller person *did* have to do. No sooner had they announced their presence than a woman unfolded herself from a corner in the back of the truck. Tess had never seen a woman that tall before. She was long and lanky and had the kind of neck that belonged on a swan.

That was where all comparisons to graceful birds ended. Before she made it more than two steps, the woman tripped over a box of books, sending its contents flying.

"Blast and botheration!" she cried as she hit one of the shelves on the wall, rattling a row of weathered paperbacks. "Quick—catch the Quixote."

Tess noticed a particularly large book toppling on the edge of the shelf and dove for it. She managed to save it from falling, though not without straining her already-strained knee.

"Thank you." The woman righted herself without causing any more books to go flying. "I've been manning this bookmobile for a year now, but I still haven't gotten the hang of moving around in it. Anyone who tells you that living in a tiny house is glamorous is lying."

Tess was bent over her knee, gently massaging it, but that caused her to look up. "Don't tell me you *live* in here?"

The woman laughed. It was a light, tinkling sound at odds with her tall frame, and Tess liked it. "Goodness gracious, no. Can you imagine? Trapping me in here is like caging a giraffe."

Gertrude must have liked her laugh, too, because she giggled and immediately set about putting the box of books back in order. "This is a library, isn't it?" she asked. "One of those mobile ones that goes from town to town to reach people who don't live close enough to the real thing?"

Tess couldn't help shooting her daughter an admiring glance. "How do you know about those?"

"Books are literally the only thing you ever taught me about."

"That's not true. We had that nice talk about puberty a few years ago."

The woman released another of those trilling laughs, but Gertrude's face screwed up in a tight ball. "Mom! Don't bring up puberty in front of strangers."

"I'm pretty sure she's already gone through it. I think we're safe." She straightened and extended a hand to the woman. "Nice to meet you. I'm—"

The woman took her hand and crushed it with a strength that cracked Tess's finger bones. "There's no need to introduce yourself. I know who you are."

"Oops. Small town. I keep forgetting."

The woman shook her head. Her hair was cropped close to her scalp, but she had long, dangling gold earrings that swung across her shoulders. In addition to being preternaturally tall, she had the kind of looks that could have been found on the catwalks of Milan. Rich, dark skin, perfectly arched brows, and a jawline that puffy-chinned Tess couldn't help but admire gave her the appearance of a supermodel.

"It has nothing to do with the size of Winthrop." The woman stabbed a finger over her shoulder. To Tess's surprise, an oversized photo of her own face was tacked on the far wall. It was an out-of-date headshot with nary a crow's foot in sight. Underneath it sat a row of recognizable hardbacks—the complete *Fury* set. "You're Tess Harrow. I'd have known you anywhere. We can barely keep your books on the shelves. Everyone wants to know what Sheriff Boyd—I mean Detective Gonzales—will get up to next."

Tess couldn't help grinning. "That explains why the sheriff is familiar with my work."

The woman smiled back. "*Everyone* here is familiar with

it, but I'll let you in on a secret. I have a deal with Victor. He gets first dibs to check out every new Tess Harrow release. In return, I can park the bookmobile wherever I want."

Tess laughed. "He loves me. I knew it."

"Actually, he says it's because he needs to know what nonsense to prepare for next, and he refuses to spend a single cent on such trash." The woman's eyes went wide, and she clapped a hand over her mouth. "Oops. Forget I said that. I have no filter."

Tess was inclined to demand more information on Sheriff Boyd's miserly habits, but Gertrude intervened.

"My mom is a big supporter of the library system," she said, a stern warning in her eyes. "Aren't you, Mom?"

"Of course I am. Books should be accessible to everyone."

"And you're always saying that readers who borrow your books are as important as the readers who shell out thirty bucks a pop to get it on release day."

It was true. She *had* said that, and she *did* believe it. Her library readers were among her most loyal fan base. But would it have killed the sheriff to pre-order a copy every now and then?

"I'm Nicki, by the way. Nicki Nickerson, Okanogan County librarian and bookmobile driver extraordinaire." The woman straightened as she spoke, her head grazing the ceiling of the truck. With a grimace, she gestured toward the door. "And much too tall for this old clunker. Do you mind if we talk outside?"

Tess was starting to feel a little claustrophobic herself—especially with that huge picture of herself staring at her through youthful, happy eyes—so she agreed. Her knee made the stairs a bit tricky, but she did her best.

"That's better." Nicki drew a deep breath, her arms spread wide as she stretched in the open air of the sidewalk. "Now. What can I help you with? Did you want a library card? I'll need a piece of mail with your name and address on it, but that should be pretty easy."

Tess blinked. It had been so many years since she'd had to sign up for a library card that she forgot you couldn't just roll up and demand access to the full collection. "Actually, it might not be easy at all. We don't get mail service up at the cabin."

"That's okay. Anything sent to the store will work, too."

"The store?" Tess echoed. On instinct, she glanced toward Gertrude, but her daughter had elected to stay inside the truck to peruse the shelves. "What store?"

Nicki blinked at her behind attractively owlish black frames. "Uh oh. Did you not inherit that from your grandfather along with everything else? I *assumed* but…"

The woman really did look worried that she'd made a muddle of things, so Tess was quick to reassure her. With a hand pressed warmly on Nicki's arm, she said, "I'm not upset. Just curious. Do you mean the old hardware store?"

A look of such profound relief crossed over Nicki's face that Tess was hard-pressed not to laugh. So far, everyone in this town had treated her with, if not hostility, at least some variety of disdain. It was nice to know there was at least one kind soul in the place.

"So you *did* inherit it," Nicki said.

"Well…no." Tess wrinkled her nose and cast her memory back to the one summer she'd visited her grandfather. She remembered a lot of canned beans, a stack of old *Time* magazines that had been the only thing to read, and hours spent dangling her feet in the pond because she'd been too scared to slip all the way in to its slimy depths. She also remembered a few trips into town, when her grandfather had bought her ice cream and held her hand as she crossed the street.

Toward his hardware store.

"I'd completely forgotten about it." Tess shook her head as she recalled those dusty shelves and barrels full of nails. "But that was how he made his living, wasn't it? I only saw the inside of it once or twice, and I remember being unimpressed. It smelled like motor oil and taxidermy."

Nicki laughed. "What does taxidermy smell like?"

"When it's done well, nothing."

"Uh oh. And when it isn't?"

Tess shuddered. "Imagine a half-rotting mummy that's been doused in Agent Orange before being dressed up in your grandmother's favorite nightgown."

To Tess's surprise, Nicki responded to this description with a long, appreciative sigh. "I always knew it would be something, meeting an author, but I had no idea it would be like this," she said. "You're the real deal."

"I'm afraid so."

"And your grandfather *didn't* leave you his hardware store?"

"I don't know, to be honest. The lawyers didn't mention it, but we haven't completely wrapped up probate yet." Tess scanned Main Street, trying to recall exactly where the hardware store had been located. Somewhere near the dodgy end, if memory served, where the local bar and a second-hand store specializing in end-of-times prepping had stood.

"Well, you can use the address to get a library card, at any rate. I won't tell anyone if you don't."

Gertrude hopped down the bookmobile stairs, a stack of graphic novels in her hand and a smile splitting her face. When she grinned like that, Tess could see the gap where the last of her baby molars had recently given way. "They have the whole Nightwave series, Mom. Can I check them out? If I promise to rent a stupid mountain bike and only cook things you like from now on?"

"I thought you were looking for stuff on Bigfoot," Tess said, but mostly for form's sake. The one thing she'd never denied her daughter was reading material. These days, it was mostly graphic novels, but there had been a time when Tess had been perilously close to purchasing the entire Scholastic catalog.

"There isn't anything on cryptids in the bookmobile." Gertrude, whose interest in murder was easily set aside in favor of antiheroes who dressed from head-to-toe in black, clicked an impatient tongue. "Please, Mom? I don't know what else I'm supposed to do all day. I've already read the entire stack of *Time* magazines I found under my bed."

Tess held back a laugh. It was just like her grandfather to have thrown nothing away in the thirty-something years since she'd visited. "It's fine with me. I'll need to look up the address to get the library card, but—"

"122 Main Street, postal code 98862. You'll find the applications in the top desk drawer."

Tess was startled to find the librarian so quick with an answer, but Nicki just grinned and tapped a finger against her temple. "If it's an address anywhere in this county, I can not only locate it for you, but I can tell you exactly how much they owe in late fees. Your grandfather, I'm happy to say, is debt-free. Mostly because he never used the library, but it still counts."

Tess eyed the librarian with renewed interest only to find that Nicki was looking at her in the exact same way. They both opened their mouths to speak and, realizing what was happening, closed them again. It had been s long since Tess had met someone for whom she felt such a natural affinity that she grinned.

"You go first," Tess urged.

"I was just going to say that if Bigfoot interests you, I can find some books for you the next time I'm at the main branch. I stop by a few times a week to pick up patron requests and restock the truck, so it won't be a problem."

"That would be great, actually," Tess said. "I'd normally dive into the depths of the internet to get my answers, but we don't have electricity up at the cabin, and I'm trying to teach Gertie the importance of self-reliance."

"Consider it done."

Nicki's enthusiasm went a long way in making Tess feel better about making her next request. It was one thing to beg a library-related favor from a virtual stranger; quite another to ask for the kind of assistance she really wanted.

"Well?" Nicki prompted. "Now it's your turn."

Tess peeked to make sure Gertrude had ducked back into the truck to fill out the application before she spoke. "The reason we're so interested in Bigfoot is because there have been some…sightings around here."

"Oh, I know." Nicki didn't seem the least bit surprised by Tess's confession. "I haven't seen anything during my rounds, but I'm usually watching the road instead of the forest. My friend Marvin saw him once, though. He was scratching his back against a tree."

Tess wrinkled her nose. She'd been hoping for something a little more blood-curdling than that. "That doesn't sound very Bigfoot-y."

"It is. Bears do it all the time. They can't reach otherwise."

That made a disappointing amount of sense. Still, Tess pressed on. "You visit all the towns around here, though, right? You hear things?"

"If you mean, do I know that Rupert Jones is probably going to lose his foot to gangrene thanks to his feud with Doc Fulsom or that Purdy Garrett has been checking out an alarming number of books on household poisons for a woman who just took out an insurance policy against her husband, then yes. I'm remarkably well-informed."

If Tess hadn't already been on her way to adoring this woman, that clinched the matter. Female friendships had been the one thing lacking in her life for far too long—if divorcing a cheating husband of fifteen years taught her nothing else, it was that. When everything went sideways, she'd have given almost anything to have someone to unburden herself to.

"I have no idea who those people are, but I love them," she said. And, because it wasn't in her nature to play coy, she added, "I think I might love you, too."

Nicki giggled. "Anyone who says living in a small town is boring has obviously never lived in one. You haven't seen what petty looks like until you've watched neighbors of twenty years fight for the top begonia title at the agricultural fair."

Tess heaved a happy sigh. "Petty people are my kind of people."

"Do you want me to see what I can find out? Nose around, tap into the grapevine, keep my ear to the ground?" Nicki grinned and added, "I've been reading a lot of noir detective novels lately. Please say I can."

Tess could hardly believe her luck. "You wouldn't mind?"

"Are you kidding? The great Tess Harrow is asking *me* for help with book research? It's a dream come true."

Tess felt a pang of remorse. While there was still a chance Bigfoot might make an appearance in her novel, she wasn't ready to commit herself to that subplot just yet. After all, readers expected there to be *some* element of believability.

"I should probably admit that it's not for a book. Not really."

Nicki raised a skeptical brow. "Just for fun, then?"

"To tell you the truth, I'm helping Sheriff Boyd with a murder investigation." It wasn't strictly the truth, but Tess salved her conscience with the promise that she'd tell him anything she discovered. "You heard about the body found in my pond, right?"

Nicki nodded. "It's all anyone can talk about."

"Well, what you don't know is that the sheriff and I ran across someone who looked an awful lot like Bigfoot in the woods near my cabin. Sheriff Boyd says he's seen him several times already, but he always manages to get away before he can catch him."

Tess could easily recognize the light that flashed in Nicki's eyes. It was interest and appreciation and a determination not to let a good story get away without a fight.

With a nod of her head that set her earrings rattling, Nicki said, "That's it. Tell me everything you know. And don't leave anything out."

Chapter Seven

Tᴇss ᴡᴀs ᴇxʜᴀᴜsᴛᴇᴅ ʙʏ ᴛʜᴇ ᴛɪᴍᴇ sʜᴇ ᴀɴᴅ Gᴇʀᴛʀᴜᴅᴇ eventually got back to the cabin. The early evening sun still shone brightly, and her typewriter sat on her desk demanding attention, but she couldn't bring herself to sit down and get to work.

As it turned out, solving *real* crimes took a lot more effort than writing about them. In her books, Detective Gonzales just showed up where he needed to be, when he needed to be there. He could go weeks without a shower and get through a whole day on a single piece of beef jerky.

Tess, on the other hand, desperately needed to wash her hair. And Gertrude, despite all her promises to the contrary, seemed to be making a meal that included the entire jar of discounted beets.

After a quick glance in the hand mirror tucked in her purse, Tess decided that her hair took precedence. If she was going to be recognized every time she walked out in public in this town, she was going to have to seriously step up her personal grooming. The last thing she needed was to go viral because she looked like something Edna St. Clair's missing cat dragged in.

Tess stepped onto the back porch to find Ivy standing at

attention. "Oh, good. It's you." She handed the deputy the large metal washtub that hung by the back door. "As long as you're keeping watch, you might as well be useful."

Ivy stared at the washtub through narrowed eyes. "What do you want me to do with this?"

Tess gestured toward the edge of the tree line, where an in-ground spigot provided the cabin with access to a well. "I've already used so much dry shampoo I look like Marie Antoinette on a bender. If I don't give my hair a deep clean soon, I'm going to have a colony of spiders taking up residence."

Ivy dropped the tub with a clatter. "I'm not your servant. Fill it yourself."

Tess laughed. "I figured it was worth a shot. Dinner should be ready in about an hour, by the way. Gertrude's whipping up a feast."

The mention of home-cooked food went a long way in making Ivy relax. Tess took note of it with interest. She might not be getting much done in the way of *actual* writing, but she was laying a lot of good groundwork. Maybe she should make her fictional Ivy an amazing chef. She could melt Detective Gonzales's hard exterior by making his favorite baked goods and delivering them to his crime scenes. If all the poor man was getting was the occasional piece of beef jerky, the least Tess could do was give him a girlfriend who'd feed him some cookies every once in a while.

Her stomach rumbled its wholehearted agreement.

"How long are you on duty, by the way?" Tess asked. "I'm having a hard time keeping track of everyone."

"The sheriff should be here to replace me around midnight."

"Really?" Tess stopped in the act of dragging the washtub toward the stairs. "I'm surprised Sheriff Boyd put himself on the rotation. Doesn't he have more important things to do? Like...solve a murder?"

Ivy shrugged. "I expect he wants to take a look around. You sometimes see things at night that you miss during the day."

"How? It's pitch-dark."

"Exactly. There's no better time to catch something out of the ordinary. A beacon in the woods, maybe, or a path that's only visible by the full light of the moon. He thinks the deer trail out back might sometimes be used by people taking a shortcut to the road."

Tess had to admit that made a certain kind of sense. She'd always assumed it was the other way around—that daytime was what exposed the cracks and rifts in a crime scene— but this worked, too. If the body had been dumped at night, it would be important to know what kind of ambient light there was, or how easy it would be to access this area without being detected.

"Drat the man," Tess said. It had never occurred to her to have Detective Gonzales investigate at night. "Sheriff Boyd's really good at this, isn't he?"

Ivy looked surprised. "His job, you mean?"

"Yeah. You'd think a small-town sheriff wouldn't have much experience with murder, but he seems to have a good handle on things. Unless people die here all the time?"

Ivy snorted. "He wasn't always a *small-town* sheriff. Before he moved back home, he worked in a big metropolitan department. Some of the things he's seen…" As if suddenly aware of how forthcoming she was being, Ivy stopped and pointed a warning finger at Tess. "And don't you go repeating that all over town, got it? I don't know why I'm telling you this, unless it's so you don't make the mistake of asking the sheriff about it. He doesn't take kindly to meddling."

That was the second time someone had accused Tess of meddling today, and she didn't like it now any more than she had the first time. These people were investigating a crime on *her* property, where her daughter was basically providing craft services for the lot of them. She was allowed to have questions.

"Oh, fine." All at once, Ivy took the other handle of the washtub and yanked it. She almost threw Tess off balance in the process. "It's going to take you three years to get that tub down to the spigot by yourself. But I'm *not* washing your hair."

"Noted." Tess was too happy to have a helping hand to argue. She was also keen to get back on the topic of the sheriff. "So the sheriff hasn't been in office for very long? Interesting. He certainly acts like he owns this place."

"I'm done giving you information for free, so don't even try."

"Why, Ivy. Are you asking for a bribe?"

"I don't want your money."

"Information, then?"

Ivy chuffed on a breath. They'd managed to get the tub

down to the spigot by this time, so Ivy began ruthlessly pumping water into it. A few wayward droplets warned Tess that her bath wouldn't be a warm one, but she refused to be daunted. Her grandfather had lived like this for forty of his eighty-three years on this planet. She could handle it for one month.

"Any information *you* have is useless," Ivy said. "There's nothing you can tell me that I don't already know."

Tess was running out of options. "…my friendship?"

That one caused Ivy to snort outright. She also put a hand on Tess's shoulder and shoved her to the ground. With a severity that shocked Tess into immobility, she began ruthlessly washing her hair. The cold dunk of water was painful, and she was pretty sure Ivy used way too much shampoo, but it wasn't long before she started to enjoy herself. The rake of the other woman's nails against her scalp was like a soothing massage for her head.

"If none of those things are enticing, what do you want from me?" Tess asked.

Ivy's fingers stopped just as they were working along her temple. "You're a writer."

"True. What gave me away?"

"This isn't easy for me, so you could cut the sarcasm. The thing is…I'm a writer, too. Well, *trying* to be one, anyway."

Tess bit back a groan. The number of aspiring authors she'd met during the course of her writing career numbered in the literal hundreds. Unlike being a surgeon or, say, a deputy in a remote Washington county, there was no starting hurdle. Anyone with a computer or a journal and a well-sharpened pencil could create a story.

Whether or not those stories were worth reading, however, was another matter. The first few times someone had solicited Tess's opinion on their work, she'd been more than happy to help. After all, she'd been a raw, newbie writer herself at the time. The manuscript she'd written while sitting in the car at Gertrude's toddler gymnastics had been plucked straight from the slush pile.

By the time she'd been sent the third thousand-page sci-fi novel with a hero who was a thinly disguised facsimile of the writer, she'd changed her tune. The only way anyone was getting their writing in front of her now was by sending in a packet of divorce papers.

"Good for you," Tess said, not entirely politely. "If you ever want a list of writing resources and publication tips, there's one on my website. I'd be happy to send you the link."

"The sheriff was born and raised here, but he ran away when he was sixteen. It was the talk of the town at the time—something to do with his sister. He only came back a few years ago, and not everyone was happy to see him again." Ivy's tone wasn't entirely polite, either, and her fingernails transitioned from soothing to painful.

Tess barely registered the pain. She bolted upright, water dripping down her neck, and twisted to face the deputy. "What are you telling me? Is this about that woman who said he only won the last election by five votes?"

"I wrote a sci-fi novel," Ivy said. Negotiations were clearly underway. "It's a good one, too."

Of course she had. It would have been asking too much for Ivy to dive deep into literary fiction or—God forbid—an explicit romance. *That* would have been something worth reading.

"How many pages is it?" Tess asked.

"One thousand, two hundred, and ninety-two," Ivy said proudly. She pushed Tess back and began scrubbing her head again. "It took me four years to finish."

Tess ran over a mental checklist of her options and decided that her best bet was to hand this one off to her agent. What was the point of paying Nancy fifteen percent of her earnings if she wasn't going to make herself useful every now and then?

"Email it to me, and I'll pass it along to my agent," she said. "I can't promise she'll get to it right away, but—"

"Email it?" Ivy echoed. "You want me to scan every single page? Do you have any idea how long the copier at the station takes to do anything?"

Tess's heart, already starting to regret its kindness, started to sink. "You only have a typewritten copy?"

"No." Ivy drew a deep, proud breath. "I wrote every word by hand."

At this point, the sheriff would have to be a serial killer for Tess to feel she was getting a fair shake out of this deal. In one of her books, Detective Gonzales would have pulled Ivy up by her lapels, hauled her down to the station, and threatened the truth out of her. Tess doubted she could get anywhere near Ivy's lapels without losing a limb.

But she was onto something here, she was sure of it. No one ever said that solving real-life crime would be easy.

"Okay, I'll take a look," she said, trying not to wince

at Ivy's excited whoosh of air. It was a truth universally acknowledged—the amount of confidence a budding author had in their manuscript was inversely proportionate to its quality. She held up a hand and continued. "I'm not saying I'll read the whole thing. But I'll give the first fifty pages or a ~~so a~~ perusal and let you know what I think."

"That's all I ask," Ivy said and handed her a towel.

Tess rubbed her hair dry, pleased to find that her head no longer felt as though it had recently been used as a scrubbing pad. "And in return, you're going to tell me what Sheriff Boyd's deep, dark secret is, right?"

"Not that. I have something better."

"What's better than a sordid past?"

Ivy glanced around the forest as though checking for eavesdroppers. The cabin was situated on high enough ground that it would be easy to spot intruders, but her deputy training made her do a double sweep *and* lower her voice before she spoke.

"The truth is, Ms. Harrow, we already know who killed that woman."

———————————

One thousand, two hundred, and ninety-two pages crammed inside a cardboard box was no light burden.

"Jeez, Mom. This thing must weigh ten pounds. What is it?"

Tess peered inside the box and groaned. *Cursive.* Ivy had written in cursive—the scrawling, spidery kind.

"It's a book," Tess said.

Gertrude perked up. "Are you going to start buying manuscripts on the black market so you don't have to write them yourself?"

Tess glared at her daughter, but that was mostly because Gertrude handed her a plate that looked to contain some kind of beet salad. "I thought we agreed I wouldn't have to eat this." She eyed the slimy root vegetables and clumps of wet, white cheese with disfavor.

"You have to at least take a 'no thank you' bite," Gertrude said.

Tess fought the urge to roll her eyes. When Gertrude had been little and much less gastronomically adventurous, she and Quentin had implemented a "no thank you" bite rule. No dish, however unsavory or how strongly it reeked of seaweed, could be passed over until it had at least been tasted.

Which was all well and fine when introducing a toddler to the delights of sushi, but not so great when faced with a teenager intent on exacting vengeance.

"I'll take *one* bite, and no, I'm not buying black market books." Tess carried both her plate and the manuscript to the table. "Although it's not a terrible idea. James Patterson built an entire empire that way."

Gertrude joined her at the table. She'd already taken a plate out to Ivy, who'd devoured the meal as though she'd never seen food before. "Then what is it?"

"Ivy wrote it. I promised I'd take a look at it for her."

Gertrude reached across the table. "Oooh, can I read it?"

"No, you may not. She wants a *professional* opinion."

Tess hoped that would be the end of the conversation, but Gertrude was much too smart—and too stubborn—to drop things there. "You hate reading other people's stuff."

"Not *everyone's*."

"You wouldn't even help my teacher judge that creative writing contest last year," Gertrude pointed out.

"I was on a book tour. That doesn't count."

"And when Dad wanted you to look over his screenplay that one time, you threw a fit."

Tess paused in the act of bringing the fork to her mouth. It was true. Quentin *had* asked her to offer a critique on the screenplay he'd worked on for a large chunk of their married life. What Gertrude didn't know—and never would, if Tess had anything to say about it—was that it had taken Tess all of five minutes to recognize several plagiarized passages.

Maybe it was cowardly of her, but she'd been unable to confront her husband about it. They'd already been having marital troubles by then, and Quentin had never been one to take criticism well. Rather than risk the sulking outbursts that would be sure to result, Tess had decided to maintain a tight-lipped refusal to go anywhere near it.

"I know." Tess speared the salad with her fork and lifted it to her mouth. "I should have been more patient with him. With you, too, a lot of the time. If it means anything, I'm sorry for it now."

Gertrude stared in open-mouthed wonder as Tess chewed her salad. She had a glass of wine ready to wash it down, but a surprisingly delicious burst of flavor broke out over her tongue. She stabbed another bite and ate it.

"What?" she demanded around a mouthful of kale. "It's not as bad as I thought it would be. I don't know what you did to these walnuts, but they taste like candy. I can eat a salad with candy."

Gertrude waved her off. "Did you just apologize? To *me*?"

Tess didn't like the way this conversation was headed. "I've apologized before. I apologize all the time."

"Not once. Not ever. Not for anything."

A stab of guilt forced Tess to put her fork down and look—really look—at her daughter. She done something playful and spiky with her hair today, giving her a punk-rock aura that matched the oversized band T-shirt she wore. The shirt had once been black and had also once belonged to Quentin. Neither of those qualities was lost on Tess, especially since she could occasionally detect a whiff of Quentin's favorite cologne. Some days, she could almost swear the ghost of Creed Aventus haunted the cabin. If she didn't know any better, she'd almost think he'd been living here before her.

"I know I haven't always been the best mom, but I'm trying to be better, Gertie. I really am. You hate this place and you hate me, and that's okay, but—"

"I don't hate it here," Gertrude was quick to say.

"What?"

"This cabin. This town." She hunched a shoulder and refused to meet Tess's eyes. "It's not as bad as I thought it would be. I like that library lady. And solving a murder is fun. How come you're reading Ivy's book all of a sudden?"

For a long, embarrassing moment, Tess had to fight a

wave of tears. Gertrude had been very careful about saying it was the *cabin* she liked rather than her mother, but it was the closest she'd come to a declaration of affection in a long time.

Tess would have done the unthinkable to keep continuing on that path. So she did.

"I had to promise to read it so I could get information out of her." She leaned across the table. "Apparently, they already have a suspect."

Gertrude's eyes gleamed. It was all the confirmation Tess needed to know that she was taking the right course. Was it wise to draw a precocious fourteen-year-old into a murder investigation unfolding right outside her door? Probably not. Was Tess going to do it anyway? If it meant that her daughter was willing to sit at the dinner table and talk to her, the answer was an unequivocal yes. Tess couldn't remember the last time Gertrude had been this animated about *anything*.

"No way," Gertrude breathed. "Did she tell you a name?"

"Not exactly." Tess had begged and even—horror of all horrors—promised to read the book in its entirety, but Ivy refused to budge. "Ivy said they can't talk about it until they gather more evidence. But she *did* say it was likely he'd be in town at some big event tomorrow. If we go, we might be able to figure out who he is."

Gertrude's eyes grew wide. "He's walking around? Free to murder anyone else he wants?"

Tess nodded. It wasn't unusual in cases like these. Until the police gathered enough evidence to make a charge stick, it was often too risky to arrest someone. The suspect might lawyer up or bring the police up on discrimination charges or, worst of all, flee the country before they could be caught. Tess had a recurring villain in her *Fury* series who was always hopping off to Indonesia when things got too hot.

Too late, Tess realized that while *she* might have a deep understanding of the law and how criminals sidestepped it, Gertrude was just an impressionable child.

"You mean…he might even come back and murder *us*?"

Tess dashed a hand across the table and grabbed her daughter's hand before the teen could pull away. "We can go stay in the hotel, if you want." Gertrude opened her mouth to respond, but Tess rushed on. "I know I was against it at first, but with everything going on, I totally understand if—"

Gertrude snatched her hand back. Instead of looking frightened, her customary smirk of outrage and annoyance was back. "Are you kidding me right now?"

"Um…no?"

"You made me abandon all my friends. You dragged me out here. You took away my internet." None of these were uttered as a question. Gertrude took a deep breath and kept going. "You exposed me to dead body parts and made me rent a mountain bike, and now that things are *finally* starting to get interesting, you want to pack up and run away?"

It was all Tess could do not to grab her daughter by the shoulders and pull her into a hug. *This* girl—the fearless, intelligent, determined one—was the one she'd been so afraid she'd never see again. To know that Quentin hadn't quashed those qualities…to know that *she* hadn't quashed them…

"I'm just putting the option out there," Tess said as nonchalantly as possible. "The moment you're ready to go, just say the word, and we're outta here."

"Ugh, Mom. You're the literal worst." Gertrude pushed back from the table and gathered up her plate. "I'm going outside to eat with a *real* detective."

"She's only a deputy!" Tess called after her, but it was no use.

As Gertrude slammed the door, Tess could hear a muttered, "That's way closer than you'll ever get," behind her.

Chapter Eight

"COFFEE."

As if by magic, mention of the word conjured up a blue enamel cup underneath Tess's nose. Without hesitation, she tried her luck again.

"A pink lemonade cupcake. One from that bakery we like near Pike Place."

"Nice try, Mom. We're having oatmeal." Gertrude waved the cup again. Tess took it and inhaled once more before taking a sip. Gertrude had always known her way around a dark roast. "I made it extra strong. You were up late last night."

It was true. Tess had stayed up well into the wee hours, her head and the typewriter buzzing with all the new threads to weave into *Fury in the Forest*. So far, Willow—as she'd named Ivy's counterpart—had baked Detective Gonzales a coconut cream pie, a batch of shortbread cookies, and brownies. She was also a budding novelist who slipped a page of her book into each pastry box. So far, the detective had refused to read a single one.

"Should I take one out to Sheriff Boyd, too?"

Tess finished sitting the rest of the way up in bed, the scent of the freshly laundered quilt mixing with the coffee to wreak havoc on her senses. She had no idea what time it was, but considering how bleary her eyelids felt, she was guessing it was pretty early. "What? He's still here? Doesn't he have to sleep?"

"He can sleep when he's dead," Gertrude said, parroting one of Tess's favorite expressions when trying to pry her daughter out of bed to go to school. "Is that a yes to the coffee?"

"Yes. No. I don't care." Tess took a deep drink, the caffeine going a long way in perking her up. She tried again. "Yes. Make it with four sugars and three tablespoons of cream. *Exactly* four sugars and three tablespoons of cream."

Gertrude didn't miss a beat. "He's not going to think that's funny."

Tess smiled into her cup. *He* might not find anything amusing in receiving a cup of coffee the only way Detective Gonzales would drink it, but it tickled her sense of humor. "Hang on—I'll take it out to him. I didn't get a chance to talk to him last night, but I have questions. Lots of them."

Tess waited just long enough to throw a blanket over her shoulders before heading down the path to where the sheriff crouched next to the pond.

"Good morning," she called cheerfully. She held out the cup of coffee, surprised when he took it and sipped without a single remark. "What's on the agenda for today? More evidence-gathering? A press conference? Dredging the pond for additional clues?"

Tess wasn't sure what the normal uniform for standing watch over a wooded forest during a long summer night looked like, but the sheriff had opted for worn black jeans, a fisherman-style sweater in dark-gray wool, and a black toque crammed over his head. He looked like he was about to go on a wilderness heist.

"I'm not going to discuss this case with you," he said, his mouth a flat line. Either the sheriff wasn't a morning person or spending all night staring into the abyss left him a little cranky. "But thank you for the coffee."

She waited for him to remark on the cloying sweetness of it, but all he did was inhale the forest air.

"What's your favorite dessert?" she asked.

His eyes narrowed. "Why? Are you going to put it in your dratted book?"

The speed with which he guessed her intentions only made her smile. He really *was* good at his job. "I'm thinking about it. It'll add an air of authenticity."

He turned to look out over the pond. "Then I'm not telling you anything. Make something up."

"Good thing that happens to be my specialty," she said. Since she obviously wasn't going to get anything out of this man through direct means, she tried another tack. "Gertie and I were thinking of heading into town today to watch the spectacle. Would you like a ride in?"

His glance was sharp. "Is that supposed to be a joke?"

"You don't plan on attending?" she asked as innocently as she could manage.

With one menacing step, he was inches from her. Under any other circumstances, she might have felt intimidated by such a large, pulsatingly angry man trying to stare her down, but curiosity won out.

"I warned you not to push too hard, Ms. Harrow," he said. "I can't protect you if you continue to poke the bear."

Enlightenment started to dawn. She'd angered many a man in her lifetime, but only two had any relevance to this situation. *The Peabody boys.*

"The bear or...the Bigfoot?" she asked.

The sheriff tossed the rest of his coffee into the pond. The milky liquid made splotches in the water before quickly dissipating under the surface. "I can't stop you from appearing in a public place during the full light of day, but if you knew what was good for you..." He trailed off and shook his head, apparently finding no need for a response. "Who am I kidding? Of course you're going to be there. I'm just surprised you're not leading the whole parade."

Tess felt an odd ping of disappointment. A parade through the streets of Winthrop was hardly the slam-dunk solution to this mystery she'd been hoping for. Still—if Ivy promised there'd be a murderer present, it was her duty to go. Especially if anyone by the name of Adam or Zach made an appearance.

"Can I help you with something else?" he asked as he handed her back the empty cup.

She stared into it, hoping for some sort of sign among the dregs, but all she could see was the faint outline of a circle. If she was going to help solve this murder—and she was—she'd have to rely on more concrete methods.

"Did the toxicology report come back yet?" she ventured.

"Yes."

"And?"

He didn't appear to want to share the findings with her, but he must have decided that there was no harm in indulging her just this once. "And she wasn't poisoned, if that's what you're asking."

Tess nodded. "Blunt force trauma to the head, then. Or a gunshot wound. I suspected as much."

His glance was sharp, his expression anything but pleased. "How do you know that?"

She knew it the same way she knew that she'd better hightail back up to the cabin before Sheriff Boyd indulged in some blunt force trauma of his own: with a little bit of instinct and a whole lot of common sense.

"Her head's still missing, right?" Tess asked.

Her only answer was a narrowing of the sheriff's eyes.

"Then there you have it. The killer hid the identifying body parts and his M.O. in one fell swoop." Tess sighed with something almost like satisfaction as she turned back toward the cabin. "I've always appreciated a man who can multitask."

———

"Mom, is it okay if I go watch the parade from the bike shop with Tommy and Timmy?"

Tess glanced over at her daughter, whose excitement over a rural parade was, understandably, right up there with a trip to the orthodontist. "You lie. Those can't possibly be their names."

Gertrude sighed. "You're the one who wanted me to make friends with the mayor's kids. It's not my fault if their parents have a bad sense of humor." She didn't wait for a response. With something approaching excitement, she added, "Please? They said we can throw popcorn into the back of the fire truck if we sit in the top window."

"That sounds kind of fun, actually. Mind if I join you?"

"*Yes.*" Gertrude practically spat the word out. She paused and added, in a kinder tone, "I promise to let you know if we see any murderers, but I wouldn't hold your breath."

Gertrude ran off in the direction of the mayor's bike shop, where the two of them had managed to score a couple of rentals the previous day. One look at this parade—which so far contained a fire truck, a lackadaisical high school band, and a cavalcade of horses leaving steaming piles behind them—and Gertrude had come to the same conclusion Tess had.

This is no place to find a murderer. Unless you counted the rodeo clown or the vendor hawking kettle corn, everyone here looked perfectly ordinary and even more perfectly bored. She was starting to suspect Ivy of yanking her chain.

"What's the point of all this?" Tess wondered aloud.

Although several locals had gathered to watch the lackluster proceedings, she didn't expect a response, which was why she was all the more surprised to hear a loud, clear voice.

"He'll be coming around the corner any second," Edna St. Clair said at her elbow. A look of delighted anticipation curved her lips. "Watch."

Tess did watch but not until she'd surveyed the older woman for any signs of her cat. Other than a dusting of yellowish hair all over her clothes, there wasn't any.

"He who?" she asked.

"The sheriff's competition." Edna pointed at a black sports car rounding the corner. The vehicle was flashy in the way that would have impressed Quentin, but Tess had never been a fan of convertibles. Her hair was hard enough to control without sixty-mile-an-hour winds whipping it up into a frenzy.

"Wait a minute..." She leaned forward, eyes sharp as she scanned the man sitting on the ledge of the car's backseat. He smiled and waved like a politician bent on making a good appearance—which would have been fine, only Tess could have sworn she'd seen that face before.

"Is that one of the Peabody boys? Why is he being trotted out as a candidate for sheriff? He should be in jail!"

Edna cackled. "That's not just any Peabody, you ninny. That's Mason."

Tess could hardly believe her ears—or her luck. Twins always made for good crime fiction, since there was something inherently tricky about dealing with two potential villains who were indistinguishable from one another. Triplets, however, were a whole different kind of plot twist. *Especially* if one of them was running a campaign to become the next sheriff of a small town plagued by murder.

"No way," she breathed as the car drove by. A sign proclaiming *Mason Peabody, The People's Choice* dangled from one side. As though he could hear her, the man in question turned and offered her a wink. It confirmed everything she'd thought about Zach Peabody when she'd run into him on the street yesterday: he could be attractive, if only he let himself.

Mason Peabody was, without a doubt, a man willing to let himself.

In terms of face and build, he was indistinguishable from the other two Peabody boys, all muscle and homegrown lumberjack goodness, his hair a gleaming auburn and a devilish smile on his face. But there were no recent injuries marring his features, and he was impeccably turned out in a suit and tie, his hair cut in a style that Tess knew from Quentin's hair salon bills cost no less than two hundred bucks a pop.

"We'll get him this election!" Edna yelled in a rallying cry as the car passed.

Mason Peabody grinned. "That's the spirit, Edna. Vote for me, and you'll never lose your cat again."

That seemed like a bold—and unusual—campaign promise, but it spoke volumes that this man knew both the woman's name and the exact words she needed to hear to secure her vote.

Tess released a low whistle. "Sheriff Boyd has his work cut out for him."

"You're telling me. I wasn't here for the last election, but they tell me it got ugly toward the end." Nicki appeared at her other elbow, a smile on her face and what looked like a pair of tiny bird's nests dangling from her ears. "I didn't know you were into local politics, or I'd have invited you to come watch from my truck."

Tess glanced behind Nicki to find the large blue bookmobile parked some distance back, a lawn chair and a radio propped on the top.

"It's a great place to take in the festivities. Sometimes, the fire truck passes so close that I can throw popcorn in the back."

Tess laughed. "I think I'd rather throw popcorn at Mason Peabody. How come no one thought to tell me there are three of them?"

"If by no one, you mean Sheriff Boyd and his crew, I should think the answer is obvious. They like to pretend Mason doesn't exist."

Tess wasn't sure she agreed with that. With the exception of Edna St. Clair, who didn't have the strength to remove a woman's head and toss her in a pond, and Nicki Nickerson, who was quite possibly the friendliest person Tess had ever met, she hadn't met any potential murderers at this event. Ivy *must* have been talking about Mason Peabody.

Besides—all the pieces fit. The sheriff had lost no time in hauling both Adam and Zach in for questioning as soon as the body had been found, a thing you'd definitely do if you suspected their brother of murder. He'd also pointed out the similarity between the way Zach moved and Bigfoot moved—which, considering the family resemblance, could easily carry over to Mason.

Mason, who as far as Tess knew, had no alibi for four days ago.

Mason, who as far as Tess knew, had been roaming free and at large when they'd spied Bigfoot in the woods.

She barely held back a squeal of excitement. A rival sheriff candidate made the *perfect* murderer/faux Bigfoot. Tess couldn't have written a neater solution herself.

"Why do you look so excited?" Nicki asked.

Tess grinned. "A cutthroat rival in the ranks. An officer's livelihood on the line." Already, her fingers were itching to get to the typewriter to introduce her new villain, a hotshot detective who stopped at nothing—including removing the heads of his victims—to give himself an advantage over Detective Gonzales.

That was the kind of storyline that won awards, the books that movie deals were made of.

Oh, yeah. She could work with this. "Detective Gonzales will never see it coming," she breathed.

"I have no idea what you're talking about, but I like your enthusiasm. How can I help?"

Tess turned eagerly toward her new friend. "I need you to tell me everything you know about Mason Peabody."

Nicki arched a perfect brow. "I can do you one better than that."

"You can?"

"Didn't you know?" Nicki jerked a thumb over her shoulder. "He's the whole reason I exist in the first place. I was hired on after he donated a truck to the county library system. Okanogan is the only town big enough to support a physical library, so it's up to me—and Mason's bookmobile—to fill in the gaps."

"This gets better and better. You mean he has money?"

Nicki grinned. "I mean, he practically prints it. Come on. I'll introduce you."

––––––––––––

After fifteen minutes in Mason Peabody's company, Tess knew she had her man.

Not necessarily her *murderer*, since anything approaching evidence or motive had yet to materialize, but definitely her villain. Never, in the many writer's conferences she'd attended and awards shows she'd presided over, had she met such a pompous bag of wind. And that was saying something. Give some of those guys a microphone and a spotlight, and there was no getting out of there awake.

"And that's why it's so important to have boots on the ground. You have to dive deep, leverage local resources, and embrace a paradigm shift to get results." Mason sipped his coffee with a self-satisfied slurp. "There's a real natural synergy between a community like this and a bright economic future, as long as you're ready to think outside the box."

Tess glanced over to find that Nicki's eyes were as glazed over as her own. If she'd had any idea what she was getting into when she'd sat down at the coffee shop with Mason Peabody, she'd have spiked both their coffees with whiskey. This entire conversation would have made an excellent corporate buzzword drinking game.

"Which is why I'm so glad you invited me for coffee," Mason continued. "Getting my message out there is the most important thing. Which newspaper did you say you write for, again?"

"Oh, I'm not that kind of writer."

Mason sat back, a flicker of human emotion crossing his face for the first time. The fact that the emotion was annoyance wasn't lost on Tess. "What do you mean?" he demanded. "What kind of writer are you?"

"Fiction, mostly," Tess said, unperturbed. "I occasionally dabble in personal essays, but it's a dying medium."

Mason looked back and forth between Tess and Nicki, his consternation growing. It was accompanied by a lowered brow and a darkened expression that made him look much more like his brothers than he probably cared for. "If this is for an exposé, you'd better lawyer up, and fast. I don't take kindly to meddlers."

Tess bit back a sigh. There was that word again.

"Nicki? Did you know about this?"

Tess intervened before Mason could take out his wrath on the librarian. God forbid she be responsible for him taking the bookmobile back—and Nicki's job along with it.

"I'm a *novelist*, Mr. Peabody. An author. I have no intention of writing about you, exposé or otherwise." Since this was skirting the truth a little—she had every intention of immortalizing this pretentious blowhard in print— she amended this statement with, "If you must know, I'm living out at the cabin where the body was recently found. After spending so much time with the current sheriff, you can understand why I'm interested in learning about his competition."

And just like that, Mason Peabody returned to his smiles. He began a long diatribe on the current administration's lack of transparency, citing a list of grievances that seemed to arise mostly from his personal experiences with Victor Boyd.

"He had the audacity—the *audacity*, I tell you—to shut down my entire operation yesterday, and on no more pretext than a bailey nail hole he found in that dead woman's thigh."

He paused and made a quick motion of the cross over his chest. "May God have mercy on her soul."

"A bailey nail?" Tess echoed. "What's that?"

"They're found on the end of logging tape measures," Nicki explained. She crooked her finger and held it up. "Wonky little spikes that stick into the tree and hold the tape in place. I'd hate to take one of those to my leg. I've always thought they looked like a health hazard."

That caught Tess's attention. "Logging?" She cast a sharp glace at Mason. "You're a logger? Like Zach?"

Just like that, the annoyed look was back on Mason's face. Tess was starting to feel a little disappointed by how evident his emotions were. A true master villain wouldn't be so easy to read.

"Of course I'm not a logger," he said. "I own the company."

A whoosh of air left Tess's lungs as she sat back. There was so much to unpack here that she was starting to feel dizzy. If Mason owned the logging company, then he was the alibi Zach had thrown so gleefully at her head. *Legally*, there was nothing wrong with a family member providing an alibi; your chances of being with a relative or close friend on any given date were pretty high compared to the rest of the population.

But it didn't always hold up in court. And to be perfectly frank, it was sketchy as all get-out. A man like Mason would do anything to avoid the aura of murder hanging over his brother's head. Even lie.

"So...my Jane Doe took a logging nail to the thigh?"

"A *bailey* nail," Mason corrected with a glower. "They're

made from horseshoe nails, so it could have come from anywhere. You can buy anything online these days."

"He's not wrong," Nicki said. "I bought three pounds of gourmet cream cheese the other day, entirely by accident."

Tess stifled a laugh, but Mason seemed less than amused. Of course he'd be lacking a sense of humor on top of everything else.

"While Sheriff Boyd was there, he checked your entire logging operation to look for clues?" She paused, considering. "He had a warrant and everything?"

"Of course he had a warrant. I wouldn't have let him in otherwise." Mason leaned across the table. He looked as though he wanted to grab Tess's hands, but she was careful to leave them in her lap. Her skin crawled at the thought of this man making contact. "I followed him to make sure he didn't plant any evidence, but there's no saying what he might have done. That man is as corrupt as the day is long."

Tess would have liked to hear more on this subject, but Gertrude and her two new friends burst through the door of the rustic café. They carried with them the noise and energy that could only come from a group of teenagers who'd decided, after an hour of hanging out together, that they were soul mates.

"There you are, Mom! I thought you left and went back to the cabin without me."

"I considered it, but it's a long walk, and I wasn't sure if you were wearing the right shoes."

She was just about to make the introductions when Mason pushed back from the table, his whole body stiff. He tossed a hundred dollar bill on the table. It might have been a bribe to buy Tess's silence—which, if it was, would only buy about five minutes—or it might have been him throwing around his weight. Either way, Tess took note.

"I'm not sure how else I can be of assistance to you," he said, his words back to its earlier formal pomposity. "But if you find yourself in need of a logging company—or if you're ready to start discussing how you can help my campaign— Nicki knows where to find me."

With that, he took himself off. Tess watched his footsteps closely, but nothing about them matched either his brother or Bigfoot. He walked with long, confident steps, the gait of a man who believed himself to be superior to all other mortals. He probably walked like that even when he was with someone else, forcing them to jog to keep up.

"Mom, is that—?" Gertrude cocked a head at Tess, her eyes wide as she took in Mason's full Peabody splendor.

"Yes. Don't ask. It's a long story." She turned her best and brightest smile on the two boys. One looked to be about thirteen, undersized and all too aware of it, while she placed the other at around sixteen. A bit old for Gertrude, but he seemed pleasant enough. He took his hat off and called her ma'am, at any rate. Someone had seen fit to instill him with manners. "Mom, these are Tommy and Timmy Lincoln. They invited me to spend the night at their house, and I'll die if you don't say yes."

Tess was about to protest, but Gertrude wasn't done pleading her case.

"*Please?* They have a PlayStation 5. And internet. And

electricity. And their mom said I can even take a shower if I want. A hot one."

With such treats as these in store, Tess knew she didn't stand a chance. Besides, she'd met Otis at the bike rental store yesterday and had liked both him and his wife. It would do Gertrude a world of good to be around a nice, normal family for a bit.

"How could I possibly say no to such inducements as those?" she asked. "You didn't pack a bag or anything, but—"

"It doesn't matter. I can just sleep in these clothes, and Mrs. Lincoln says she has an extra toothbrush I can use." Gertrude was already halfway out the door, both boys a step behind her. "Okay, bye!"

Nicki laughed as she watched the three push through the door and sprint down the sidewalk. "They're good kids," she promised. "Tommy's a little too fond of *Catcher in the Rye* for my taste, and Timmy has doodled in the margins of every book he's ever checked out, but I know their family well. Otis and Mya are good people. They've been dabbling in organic backyard farming lately."

"You really *do* know everything about everyone around here," Tess said. "I can't decide if I'm more alarmed or impressed."

"Oh, you should definitely be alarmed." Nicki grinned. "Especially since I have a good idea how that poor woman got impaled by a bailey nail."

"Nicki!"

"If I'm right, I'm also pretty sure I know her identity."

"We should go to Sheriff Boyd with this information," Tess said, but she made no move to get up. "But only *after* you tell me everything you know."

Chapter Nine

"A one Wilma Eyre, age twenty-two, height five-foot-seven, weight around a buck-fifty."

Tess's face fell as Sheriff Boyd rattled of the statistics of their Jane Doe with the ease of a man who'd known them for days.

"She suffered a workplace injury at Peabody Timber last week and wasn't expected back on the job until Monday, which is why no one reported her missing. She was treated at the local clinic with a tetanus shot and antibiotics. From the way the wound was starting to heal, I'd say the medication was doing its job. Until, of course, someone saw fit to remove her head, identifying body parts with a serrated kitchen knife."

Instead of taking comfort from this display of capable policing, Tess frowned. She could feel Nicki doing the same next to her.

"How long have you known?" Tess demanded.

"Since about five minutes after the coroner showed me the injury report." The sheriff pushed a photo across the top of his bare desk. His workspace was surprisingly neat, especially when compared to the haphazard stacks of papers that cluttered the rest of the station. Carl sat behind a box piled so high with files that only the top of his head was visible. "This is from her Facebook page."

Until she saw that picture of the woman's face, Tess hadn't realized how real all this could feel. When the body was just a hypothetical and anonymous person, it had been easy to treat everything as a puzzle to be solved—a clue to discover. It was no different than the mythical bodies that littered her own books, casualties in name only, forgotten as quickly as they were disposed of.

Seeing the woman's smile, realizing just how young and alive she once was, changed everything.

Neither she nor Nicki touched the photo.

"A kitchen knife?" she asked, her voice trembling. "Who could have *done* such a thing?"

"That, Ms. Harrow, is precisely what we're trying to figure out." The sheriff whisked the picture away and tucked it back in his desk. He glanced back and forth between her and Nicki before adding, "Is there any other information you feel I've overlooked in my *official* capacity as the *official* head of this investigation, or can I get on with my work now?"

Tess didn't appreciate his heavy emphasis. "If you'd rather we kept any future discoveries to ourselves, then by all means say so. We're happy to continue under a shroud of secrecy."

"You shouldn't be continuing at all," he said.

She blithely ignored this. "It's strange that Mason didn't mention the woman by name." She turned to Nicki. "Right? He must have known that it was his own employee who was injured by the nail and, therefore, found in the pond."

"What do you know about Mason Peabody?" the sheriff demanded.

"I know you were careful to keep his existence a secret from me. I wonder why that is?"

She didn't get an answer. The sheriff turned to Nicki instead. "Why are you encouraging her?" he asked. "Don't you have anything better to do?"

Nicki heaved a mournful sigh as she got to her feet. "Afraid not. I'm bored silly. No one ever checks books out when the weather is nice. They're all too busy enjoying the sun. This seemed like a good way to pass the time." She paused and added, "I wasn't wrong. I haven't had this much fun in ages."

"If you want my advice, take up a hobby."

"Scouring the woods for signs of Bigfoot *is* a hobby."

Tess hissed a warning, but it was too late. The words had already reached the sheriff's ears.

"Scouring the woods for *what*?"

"Bigfoot," Tess said. There was no backing down now. She pulled out the book Nicki had procured for her and pointed at the first page. At some point in the book's history, it must have fallen into Timmy Lincoln's hands, because there was scrawling, illegible writing all over the margins. "Sasquatch. Yowie. Yeti. Grassman. I haven't made it past the second page yet, but I imagine there are lots of other things we can call him. I'll make you a list."

"Out."

The word was uttered with such vehemence that Tess found herself getting to her feet. She didn't leave, though.

Her submission to authority only went so far. "It's not illegal to search for wildlife."

"Out."

This time, Tess took two steps back. "There's so much natural beauty around here. You can hardly blame Nicki for taking it all in."

"Out."

A discreet cough caused both she and Nicki to turn around. Carl poked his head up over the stack of files and grinned. "I'd listen, if I were you. When he turns monosyllabic, it's best to beat a hasty retreat."

Nicki laughed. "You know who else does that?"

"For the love of everything, if you say that man's name inside these four walls, I'll have you arrested," the sheriff said. "And before you ask me on what charges, I have my pick of contempt, disorderly behavior, and interference, so don't try me."

"What happens when he turns *multi*syllabic?" Tess asked as both she and Nicki started to retreat toward the door.

"Come back in an hour and ask again," Carl said, grinning good-naturedly in the face of his superior's mounting ire. "If I'm still alive to tell the tale."

———————

"That poor woman," Tess said as she and Nicki made their way down Main Street to where their respective vehicles were parked. All signs of the parade had been packed up and put away. Only a few stray streamers played about in the wind. A man in a hunting jacket scooped up a few of them before ducking into an alleyway. "Did you know her?"

"I knew *of* her," Nicki said. "Wilma wasn't a reader, and the logging camp isn't one of my regular stops, so she didn't come my way much."

"She didn't have any family?"

"Not locally. Most of the loggers don't. It's seasonal work, so we get quite a lot of out-of-state workers. Wilma was one of them. I wouldn't have known about her at all, only Mason doesn't hire women very often. Something like that spreads fast."

Tess stopped. Men who didn't respect women professionally generally used them for other purposes instead. "Do you think he was sleeping with her?"

"I wouldn't put it past him to try. I don't know if you've noticed, but there aren't a lot of attractive, unattached females wandering around here." Nicki heaved a sigh. "Believe me—I've looked. I'd have a better chance scoring a date with your...what did you call him? *Grassman*?"

Tess laughed and started walking again. "That one wasn't in the book. I just added it to annoy the sheriff."

"You seem to do that a lot."

"I get the feeling it's not difficult to do."

Nicki shook her head, sending her bird's nest earrings flying. "It is, though. He's normally the calmest, most level-headed man in a room. Something about this case must be bothering him."

Tess believed it. On the surface, the case made a certain kind of sense: a woman who worked in a logging camp for a misogynistic rival sheriff candidate went missing only to show up in a pond without any identifying marks. It was all the rest that she was having a hard time making sense of. The misogynistic rival sheriff's brother blowing the body up was an odd twist—not to mention the Bigfoot sightings that seemed to make Sheriff Boyd turn purple with rage. Add in the fact that no one seemed to have any idea where the woman had been killed or why she'd ended up in Tess's pond, and all you had was a pile of clues that didn't fit.

"Well, I'm kid-free for the next twenty-four hours," she announced. "I don't suppose there's a swanky martini bar somewhere around here where you and I could kill some time?"

Nicki clucked her tongue. "I make a mean appletini, but I've already spent too much time in Winthrop. I need to hightail it down to Methow before it gets dark. I've got a couple of patrons there who are dying to get their hands on my signed copies of the newest Tess Harrow book."

Tess eyed her friend askance. "But you don't have any signed copies of the newest Tess Harrow book."

Nicki grabbed her by the hand and tugged. "Not yet, I don't. But if you want me to keep my eyes peeled for your Grassman, it's the least you can do in return."

Chapter Ten

Tess found the cabin much too quiet for writing.

Quiet was nothing new to her. At home, she always slipped on a pair of noise-canceling headphones when she wrote. It was necessary to drown out the sounds of the house and her family and the ceaseless pitter-patter of Seattle drizzle on the roof. But there was something about *this* kind of quiet that felt different.

It was isolated. It was lonely. It was *alone.*

Tess jolted to her feet, unwilling to dwell too much on that particular word. She didn't like the way it felt, like a sweater that was too tight around the neck. She didn't regret her divorce—and, with a kid like Gertrude to call her own, she *definitely* didn't regret the marriage that led to it—but she hadn't expected being on her own to feel this way.

It was supposed to be liberating and full of potential, her future a dazzling array of new people to meet and new experiences to enjoy.

Instead, she mostly felt lost.

"I should go help Ivy," she announced to no one in particular. Her typewriter sat motionless and mocking, so she pulled a plastic cover over the top. "I can't be expected to work under these conditions. There's a murderer on the loose, for crying out loud. If that doesn't get me an extension on my deadline, I don't know what will."

Before she could talk herself out of it, Tess tugged on one of Gertrude's oversized black hoodies and headed outside.

Sunset in the forest wasn't much to write home about. The trees overhead blocked most of the sky, and although some of the sun's final rays filtered down, it wasn't enough to light her path. She stumbled over a few rocks and tree branches before reaching the area where Ivy was once again posted on night duty.

"It's just me," she called. "Don't worry—or shoot."

Ivy snorted in derision. "You don't need to warn me. A drunk mongoose would be able to hear you coming."

Tess crunched to a halt next to the other woman, who stood with her arms wrapped around herself against the rapidly chilling night air. That was another thing the forest didn't let in—heat. Even though the temperatures today had soared well into the nineties, this part of the woods felt like walking into an underground cavern.

"I thought I might keep you company for a bit," Tess said.

"Shouldn't you be working?"

"My muse is taking a nap."

"Then shouldn't you be *reading*?"

It took Tess a moment to realize what Ivy was talking about. Her untouched sci-fi manuscript still sat in its box on the rough wooden table. "I read best in the morning," she lied. "When my eyes are fresh."

"Hmmph."

Understandably, this didn't put Ivy in a conciliatory

mood, but Tess was nothing if not opportunistic. "I went to the parade today, by the way," she said. "It's Mason, isn't it? Mason Peabody is the murderer."

"Shh. Did you hear that?"

"It has to be him," Tess continued. "Not only was there no one else there worth note, but I talked to Sheriff Boyd about that poor woman's identity, so I know she worked for him. The thing I can't figure out is the motive. Were they seeing each other? Is he a serial killer who can't help himself?"

Ivy flapped a hand at her. "I'm serious. Be quiet."

Tess promptly clamped her mouth shut. She didn't hear much of anything except the usual rustle of leaves and twitter of birds, but she was willing to accept this woman's word for it. Ivy's solid build, tight bun, and gun holster were vastly comforting in that respect.

Less comforting was the ease with which Ivy pulled the gun out.

Tess jumped. "Oh, jeez. Are we about to die?"

"Not if I have anything to say about it," Ivy said, her expression grim. She began moving forward with a gesture for Tess to stay where she was. Tess disobeyed, but not because she was feeling particularly contrary. Mostly she just wanted to be where the gun was.

"What did we hear?" Tess whispered. "Man or beast?"

A rustle overhead answered that question for her. If it was a man, it was a man in a tree—a thing Tess was pretty sure would result in the death of them both. There was a pair of binoculars hanging back in the cabin near the rusty old shotgun, but it hadn't occurred to her to grab them. It also hadn't occurred to her to bring the bear spray.

"The first branches are like twenty feet up," Tess whispered. "Who could climb something like that?"

"We're about to find out."

Tess and Ivy watched, both tense, only one of them poised to shoot, as the branches swayed ominously, rustled loudly, and then...burst into color?

"Wait—what?" Tess stood up straighter. "Is that a *toucan*?"

Her answer came as not one, not two, but three identical birds with huge, bright orange beaks soared over their heads and deep into the forest. Ivy's gun fell heavily to her side, and she stared, perplexed, as the birds disappeared into the darkness.

"Well, I'll be," she said. "Those *were* toucans."

"But why...?"

Tess wasn't sure how to finish that question, but she had no shortage of options. Why were there toucans in a coniferous forest? Why had they soared overhead like it was just another day in tropical paradise? Why wasn't Ivy immediately calling this in to Sheriff Boyd?

"Well, that's odd." Ivy secured her gun and scratched her chin. "That's right up there with the time I spotted a three-horned elk near Perrygin Lake."

With that, she returned to her post at the edge of the pond. Tess struggled to stay next to her this time, her head so busy that her legs were slow to keep up.

"Is that all you're going to say?" she demanded. "That you once saw a three-horned elk?"

Ivy cast a quizzical look at her. "Have you ever seen one? It was all the town could talk about for months. Every hunter with a license—and a score of them without—was on the watch for him, but he was a wily beast. I like to think he's out there somewhere, living his best life with his three giant horns."

"Ivy!"

Ivy sighed. "Look—what do you want me to say? They're *birds*, Ms. Harrow, not murderers. I can't go after them."

"You could call for backup."

Ivy just stared at her.

"Or Animal Control. Don't tropical birds carry weird diseases? What if this is how the zombie apocalypse starts?"

"What makes you so sure they were tropical toucans? Maybe they were someone's pets. Maybe they escaped from a cereal ad campaign a few counties over."

Tess wasn't sure how to feel about the deputy's blasé acceptance of what seemed to her a very strange, very unsettling circumstance. As a kid, she'd often been accused of having an overactive imagination, but that was pretty much a requirement if you wanted to grow up and become an author. It was literally Tess's job to ask the questions that no one else wanted to ask, to push until she discovered the story behind it all.

She had a lot in common with Detective Gonzales—and, yes, Sheriff Boyd—in that way. The only problem was, she had a typewriter instead of a badge and the full force of the law at her back.

Tess toyed with the idea of going after the toucans herself, but dark was starting to take over by now, and she didn't relish the idea of getting lost on her own. As if on cue, an owl hooted in the distance. Ivy heard it the same time she did.

"Uh oh. There's another large bird trespassing on your property." Ivy grinned. "Should I shoot him for you? Do you want me to put out a warrant for his arrest?"

"Laugh all you want, but there's something seriously strange about these woods," Tess said. She hugged her daughter's sweatshirt close. "I came here to rest and work, not..."

Words had always been her forte, but she was having a hard time coming up with the right ones. What she wanted to say—that she hadn't come here to get caught up in a bunch of drama not of her own making—wasn't true. In all honesty, that was *exactly* what she'd come here for. A new scene, a change of pace, a chance to think of something other than Quentin.

Well, she'd gotten her wish. Instead of worrying about deadlines or Detective Gonzales or even her daughter, Tess was suddenly ankle-deep in murder. And Bigfoot sightings.

And birds.

Birds, of all things.

Chapter Eleven

"You know, this book of Ivy's isn't half-bad."

"Gertie, not right now." Tess leaned a rickety, highly unstable ladder against the roof of the cabin. Like most of the tools around here, it had been made by hand sometime in the middle of the twentieth century. For a man who had once owned a hardware store, her grandfather had been stringently opposed to upgrading his own supplies. "I need you to hold this so I don't fall to my death."

Gertrude glanced up from the manuscript, which she was plucking page by page from the box. She lay sprawled in a hammock, looking the picture of a teenager driven to such extremes of boredom that even homespun sci-fi was entertaining. "What are you doing?"

"I need to get up on the roof to see if I can get a cell signal."

Gertrude didn't move. "I thought we were rusticating."

"We are."

"Then why do you need your phone?"

"Because I need to call my agent," Tess said. "I have an important book question."

"Liar. You only call her when you want more money."

"Fine. I need to call the probate lawyers and see if I'm allowed in the hardware store. We need a new ladder."

That didn't get Gertrude to move, either. "You're using an unstable ladder for the sole purpose of getting a ladder upgrade?"

There were times when having a brilliant, observant, hard-edged child was a source of inordinate pride for Tess. This was not one of those times.

She threw up her hands. "You win. I want to call the sheriff and see if he's checked in on those toucans for me. This is getting ridiculous. It's been two days, and no one has said a word. I can't be the only one who's bothered by them."

That got Gertrude to unfold herself from the hammock. With only minor grumbling, she grabbed either side of the ladder to stabilize it. "If it makes you feel any better, *I* think the toucans are pretty cool. Do you think they'd come back if I put out birdseed for them?"

"I don't think toucans eat birdseed."

"They're birds, aren't they?" Gertrude countered. "I'm gonna pick some up the next time we're in town. At least it'll give me something to do."

Tess's brow furrowed at the thought of purposefully luring the birds back to the cabin, but she tried not to let her worry show. So far, the only person who'd seemed even remotely impressed by her toucan sighting was a fourteen-year-old child who'd once shown the same amount of awe over a rotary phone. She appreciated the support, but she'd been hoping for a little more assistance of the official, state-funded variety.

As if reading her mind, Gertrude spoke up. "What did Carl say about them?"

Tess glanced over at where Carl stood on watch. It had been so long without any kind of incident or headway on the case that there was talk of ending the rotation. She fervently hoped they wouldn't. The problem with having a twenty-four-hour armed guard was that you very quickly got used to having a twenty-four-hour armed guard. Being alone out here would feel weird now.

"He said that anyone living in the woods with no one but Ivy to talk to was bound to start seeing things sooner or later." She chuffed a hard breath. "But Ivy corroborated my story. She knows I didn't imagine them."

"You shouldn't be mad at Carl because you don't have any more excuses not to write your book," Gertrude said.

"That's not what this is about. It's about justice. It's about seeing a project through to the end. It's about..." She sighed. In all honesty, it *was* about not wanting to sit down and write. She'd been staring at the dratted typewriter all morning, wondering what to do with the flock of flamingos that had suddenly appeared at the edge of Detective Gonzales's camp.

Nothing she tried to do made any sense. No twist of the plot, no turn of the screw fit the complexities of the story—particularly now that it included flamingos. A daring escape from the zoo occurred to her only to be immediately cast aside—a zoo escape would be highly publicized. News stations loved stories like that, not to mention people looking for entertaining pictures to post to social media. Besides, what would be the point? Detective Gonzales was on the hunt for a killer, not a PETA vigilante.

She'd also brainstormed hallucinogens in the water, a villain who felt about flamingos the way Batman felt about bats, a twisted hunting party who released tropical birds only to hunt them down again, and, in a moment of desperation, demon birds from another dimension.

Needless to say, she'd hit something of a wall. It didn't help that no arrests had been made and that all three Peabody boys were wandering around at large. A woman was dead, her identity now established, and they were no closer to finding her murderer than they were before. According to all reports, Wilma had been a quiet woman, private in the way that a female lumberjack would have to be among all those men. The most Tess had been able to get out of anyone was when a waitress at the diner in town said she'd tipped well.

Gertrude coughed and shook the ladder, jolting Tess back to the present. "Are you going to do this or what? I don't have all day."

It was on the tip of Tess's tongue to point out that she literally *did* have all day and that the burdens of being a teenager on summer break were nothing compared to those of an author with a flock of fictional flamingos and no idea what to do with them, but there was every chance Gertrude would storm off in a huff and leave her stranded on the roof.

Even with Gertrude holding on, the ladder wobbled precariously, but Tess made it to the pitched roof and picked her way up to the highest point. She held her phone out as far as it would go, but no magical bars of connectivity appeared.

"Whose bright idea was this?" Tess demanded as she got

up on tiptoe and tried again. "Humans aren't meant to live so far away from civilization. It goes against our nature."

Gertrude offered a reliably sarcastic reply, but Tess was too far away to hear her. If she extended her arm toward the side, where the lean-to met the roof's slope—

BOOM!

With a start, Tess stumbled and fell to her knees. The rough texture of the roof shingles scraped away her top layer of flesh, but at least she hadn't fallen off.

"Mom!" Gertrude's head poked up over the edge of the roof. Her eyes were wide with fright. "It's happening again!"

Tess glanced out over the pond to find its sparkling surface serene and untainted by dynamite. "No, it's not. I'm sure there's a rational explana—"

CRASH!

Tess fell again, but, since she was already on all fours, she didn't have far to go. Gertrude, on the other hand, scampered the rest of the way up the ladder to join her mother on the roof. When yet another loud sound filled the forest air—this one of Carl telling someone to stop in the name of the law—Gertrude kicked her leg out and caught the edge of the ladder. Tess could only watch, horrified, as it clattered to the ground below.

She also watched with horror as Carl took off into the forest with his gun drawn. Acting on instinct more than anything else, she scanned the skyline for signs of her tropical bird friends, but there were no toucans or flamingos anywhere. There was just Carl dashing off into the underbrush, the sound of branches snapping and leaves falling as he gave chase.

"Did you see what Carl—?" Tess asked as her daughter huddled under her arm.

Gertrude shook her head. Her whole body was shaking, but her voice came out loud and clear. "A blur of something, maybe. A man in a dark coat. Maybe it was just a hunter or something?"

Tess nodded and pulled her daughter closer. "I'm sure that was it. A hunter or a scientist or even a bird-watcher. Carl will realize his mistake and be back any minute to help us down."

What she didn't say—but what was taking alarming possession of her mind—was the thought that a hunter or scientist wouldn't, when commanded to stop by the law, start running away.

That was an action preserved for Bigfoot.

Or a murderer.

———————

"It's not that far." Tess gauged the distance to the nearest branch of the nearest tree through narrowed eyes. "If I got a running start, I'm sure I could make it."

Gertrude laughed, but there was no humor in it. Three hours trapped on a hot roof with one's mother would do that to a girl. "I dare you to try it. Go ahead."

Tess stepped back as far as she felt comfortable and pretended to run toward the roof's edge. Her "running start" was four feet at most, and a sloped four feet at that.

"I don't hear you coming up with any bright ideas," Tess

said, defeated. "Besides, you have younger legs than I do. You might be able to make it."

Gertrude scowled and picked at the chipped polish on her fingernails. She'd already used up the battery on Tess's phone playing solitaire and had sung "The Song That Never Ends" for forty-five minutes. Picking off her nail polish was the only fun left to her.

"Sure thing, Mom. And when I fall and break my legs, what will you do then?"

"Your screams will be sure to bring someone running," she said. "Remember that time you got stung by a bee on Alki Beach? You cried so loud someone called an ambulance. They thought you were dying."

Despite herself, Gertrude laughed. "You're not exactly tough, either," she pointed out. "You cry at Hallmark movies."

"I don't cry *at* them," she protested. "I cry *with* them. It's different."

She slumped onto the roof next to her daughter, struggling to come up with another way to distract her. Tess was determined not to let Gertrude think too much about their current predicament, but it was getting more and more difficult as the hours wore on. She wasn't worried about being rescued—the next deputy would be here to relieve Carl's post in another few hours—but she *was* worried about what could be keeping him. Three hours was an awfully long time for an armed man to disappear into the woods.

As if thinking along these same lines, Gertrude suddenly said, "Tell me a story."

"What story?"

Gertrude hunched one shoulder. "I dunno. *Any* story. Maybe the one with the lamb that you used to tell me when I was a kid. I don't want to think about—"

Tess didn't need to hear more. Verbal storytelling had never been her forte—what came out of her fingers wasn't even remotely close to what came out of her mouth—which meant Gertrude must be desperate. Especially if she was willing to hear about Lamby Lambkin at the ripe old age of fourteen.

BEEP BEEP!

At the sound of a friendly honk, both Tess and Gertrude shot to their feet. Tess stumbled and had to grab her daughter to keep from plunging over the edge of the roof, but that didn't quell her excitement at the sight of a familiar blue bookmobile rumbling up the drive.

"Yoo-hoo!" Nicki's voice called. "Is anyone home?"

Nicki parked the truck at an angle in front of the cabin and leaped out. Tess had always heard people say that librarians were the *true* superheroes of the world, but she never felt it in her bones until this exact moment.

"Oh, thank goodness," Tess said. "We're up here, Nicki!"

Nicki held a hand to her eyes and scanned the tree line. "Did you build a tree house? How fun."

Gertrude giggled, but Tess raised her voice and tried again. "No—on the roof. The ladder fell, and we got stuck."

"Oh, dear. That doesn't sound pleasant." Nicki picked the ladder up off the ground and held it to the edge of the roof. Tess had never been so happy to see someone in her whole life—and with a pair of gorgeous silver peacock earrings dangling from her lobes. "How long were you up there, poor things?"

"*Hours,*" Gertrude said as she leaped down the last few rungs of the ladder. It took the girl a moment to orient herself to being on the ground again. "I've never been so bored in my life. Did you bring me the next Nightwave book?"

Tess had to laugh at the resiliency of youth. Only a teenager could go from demanding childhood stories from her mom to demanding gory YA graphic novels from a librarian without batting an eyelash.

"Even better—I've got a new series for you to try." Nicki tilted her head toward the truck. "They're stacked behind the driver's seat. I think you'll like them. There's lots of murder. With swords. And ghosts."

"Murdering sword-ghosts?" Gertrude's eyes lit up. "I'm in!"

Tess took her time coming down the rickety ladder, but she was no less enthusiastic to see Nicki. In fact, the moment her feet touched solid ground, she pulled the woman into a fierce hug.

"Thank you." Tess made no move to release Nicki from the embrace. "You must be our guardian angel."

"You won't say that once I give you the bad news."

"There's nothing you can say that will make me love you less right now. Come on in." She paused as curiosity got the better of her. There were too many unsolved murders around here to make any kind of bad news palatable. "Wait—the bad news about what?"

Nicki pulled a grimace. "You know those books on tropical birds you asked for?"

She did. So far, the book Nicki had brought her about Bigfoot wasn't proving too fruitful. It was much too old and much too apocryphal, more like a story about bogeymen to frighten children than an instructional tome. Toucans, however, had seemed a much safer bet. Anything she could learn about their migration patterns would be sure to come in handy.

"You found some?" Tess asked eagerly.

"Nope. And it's the weirdest thing. Our catalog says we have three different books on the topic of toucans, but I couldn't find a single one."

Tess stopped. That wasn't *good* news, obviously, but it wasn't what she'd categorize as bad. If people were beefing up their reading, that was only good news for the world—and for Tess's future in it.

"According to the computer, they *should* be available, but they're missing." Nicki drew a deep breath, unable to hide her sudden excitement. "And not just missing. Tess, considering how many of the books on that shelf had been pulled out and rearranged, I'm pretty sure they've been stolen."

Chapter Twelve

"If I had to take a guess, I'd say the toucans got him."

Tess sat across her grandfather's table from Sheriff Boyd and Ivy, playing with the crumbling edges of a cookie. For what was probably the first time in her life, she wasn't hungry. Although it had taken Sheriff Boyd hours to get his team together to investigate the dead body in the pond, it had taken a mere half hour for them to arrive after Nicki put the call in about Carl. There were already a dozen people outside scouring the woods and calling Carl's name; according to the sheriff, another dozen would arrive within the hour.

"That's not funny, Ms. Harrow." Sheriff Boyd yanked the cookie out of her hand and chucked it into the corner. "A man is missing. *My* man is missing. This is no longer a game."

If the sheriff had known Tess better, he'd have realized that her descent into irreverence was a coping mechanism. Cracking jokes might not be the best way to deal with fear, but Tess's only other option was to start crying.

"I'm not trying to be funny," she protested. "I'm just pointing out that there have been a lot of strange things happening lately. How far away is that logging camp from here?"

The sheriff and Ivy shared a look that did little to make Tess feel better.

"As the toucan flies?" Sheriff Boyd shrugged. "About twenty miles."

A startled laugh escaped her. "I thought we weren't making jokes."

"We're not. All evidence to the contrary, I *have* been looking into your stupid toucans. No one else has reported seeing them, and no one seems to be missing any from their local zoo. That was the first thing I checked."

Tess had to fight a shout of triumph. She'd *known* that was a good theory. "Did Nicki also tell you that the library has been robbed? There's nary a tropical bird book to be found."

The sheriff's lips formed a flat line. "She told me."

"Don't you find that…interesting?"

"Not particularly, no."

Ivy cleared her throat. With a heavy sigh, the sheriff pinched the bridge of his nose and started over again. "It's interesting but not my priority right now. I'm sure that if the library did a full inventory, they'd find lots of books either missing or misplaced. I'm calling it a coincidence, nothing more."

This made a disappointing amount of sense, though Tess wasn't about to admit it out loud. One of the things that being a writer had taught her was that coincidences could and did happen all the time in real life. It was only in fiction that every random clue had to tie in to the resolution. Otherwise, editors got heavy-handed with the red pen.

"So, that's it?" she asked. "We drop the lead?"

"*We* aren't doing anything. My team and I will continue looking into the toucans, but don't expect anything to come out of it. In the meantime, I highly suggest you and Gertie spend the night in town. Until we know what it was that drew Carl into the forest…"

Even though the temperature in the cabin was the same as it had been all day, Tess wrapped her arms around herself. "You want us to stay at the hotel, you mean?"

The sheriff nodded, looking both surprised and relieved to find Tess willing to comply. She wanted to tell him that he didn't have anything to worry about—that, deep down, she had an abiding respect for the law and its officers—but he didn't give her a chance. Rubbing a thoughtful hand across his jaw, he said, "If you don't want to stay there, don't forget that you could always hole up in the hardware store. It's close enough to the station for us to keep an eye on you."

"Oh, um…" Tess glanced helplessly at Ivy, but the woman was watching her with unsettling intensity. "I don't know if it's mine. The lawyers didn't say anything about it when they called, so I don't have access to the keys."

"Your grandfather always kept them hanging by the door." Sheriff Boyd pointed toward a rusted keyring that dangled from an equally rusted nail. "And of course it's yours. Who else would the store go to?"

Tess wished she had an answer for that. The longer she spent in this cabin, the more she realized how little she knew about it—or the man who'd lived here for the majority of his life. She probably should have made *some* effort to get to know him all these years, but like so many relationships in her life, she'd let it slide. There was always another book to write, another conference to attend. She'd gotten so used to putting things like grandfathers and husbands and *daughters* aside in the name of her career that she'd inadvertently normalized it.

Thinking of her daughter now, Tess took a worried lip between her teeth and said, "Gertie isn't going to like packing up when things are starting to get exciting."

"My deputy is missing," he said without inflection. "Disappeared without a trace after chasing someone into the woods a stone's throw from your back porch. Is *exciting* the word you want to use right now?"

Tess heaved a sigh. Exciting was as good a word as any to use in this situation, but she knew when she'd been beaten. Besides—if they went to the hardware store, she could always pick up that new ladder she had her eye on.

"Nope. I'm out."

Gertrude took three steps into the hardware store and immediately turned around.

"Don't be dramatic," Tess said. She placed her hands on her daughter's shoulders and propelled her through the door. "It's just a bunch of tools. It can't possibly be that bad—"

She cut herself off mid-sentence and stared around the store in horror. It was, in fact, *that bad*.

"This can't be right," Tess said as she took in the smashed shelves and scattered tools, a tangy, chemical scent undergirding it all. She pressed a hand to her nose and peered deeper. "I remember it being a bit crusty, but Grandpa *loved* this store. He always took good care of it."

Gertrude gagged. "What's that smell, Mom? Oh, God. It's a body, isn't it? We found your stupid five dead bodies."

Tess shook her head. The scent was strong and unpleasant, but it wasn't decay—of that she was sure. It smelled more like urine than anything else. "I think…" The power had long since been turned off inside the building, so she found the flashlight function on her phone and crept forward. Her feet crunched over broken glass and crumpled newspaper, but she forced herself to keep going. Soon enough, the glass gave way to something much softer—and more pungent. "Oh, yeah. That's what I thought."

"Ugh!" From behind her, Gertrude made a retching sound. "What *is* that?"

Tess crouched and ran her finger across the old linoleum floor.

"Don't touch it, Mom! It could be poison."

"It's not poison." She held up her finger so Gertrude could see the dirt clinging to the tip. "It's fertilizer. *A lot* of fertilizer."

A sweep of her flashlight along the back of the store confirmed this. At one time, a row of fertilizer bags must have been stacked against the far wall, but they'd been slashed open and spilled everywhere. It matched the rest of the hardware store, which looked as though someone had taken a baseball bat—or worse—to every single item on the shelves.

Gertrude stepped forward to take a closer look, but Tess

held her back with one hand. "No—don't. There might be footprints."

"Oh, jeez. Do you always have to look for clues?"

In Tess's defense, this was one situation that called for it. Unless she was mistaken, someone had burgled this hardware store. Considering how strongly scented the fertilizer was—and that it was still damp to the touch—it was a recent burgling, too.

"Look right there." Tess stabbed a finger toward one edge of the mess, where she could make out the clear imprint of a man's shoe. Several small animal prints, which looked as though they might belong to a dog, were also scattered haphazardly about. "And there."

A pair of hands clutched at her shirt. "Um, Mom?"

"I've never heard of a burglar bringing a dog to a break-in, but I don't see why you couldn't. A well-trained animal could serve as a guard. I wonder if Detective Gonzales has ever thought of that."

"Mom!"

Tess turned to find Gertrude staring behind the checkout counter. It was only a slab of wood affixed to the wall on one end and propped up with a sawhorse, but Tess remembered it well. There had been two spots worn into the floor where her grandfather's feet had rested.

"Well, that's odd," Tess said. Instead of the time-weary linoleum, there were a bundle of blankets and pillows shoved into the corner. They were huddled in a way that formed the clear outline of a body.

"I think there's someone in there," Gertrude said, her voice wobbling. "Should I go for help?"

"There's no one there," Tess said confidently. She strode over to the blankets and yanked them back. Gertrude cried out as Tess exposed the contents, but there was nothing worth noting. Just a rumpled sleeping bag and several empty bags of blue cheese potato chips. "If there's one thing I know, it's how to tell the shape of a person underneath a comforter. The trick is to make clear outlines of both legs. No matter how you lay under a blanket, you can always see someone's legs."

"I'm gonna have so many problems when I grow up," Gertrude muttered, but her interest was caught. "Do you think someone was living here? In all this...mess?"

Tess wasn't sure *what* she thought just yet. The sleeping bag and pillows hinted at a squatter living inside the store, but she knew for a fact that the brand of potato chips on the ground wasn't a cheap one. At the specialty grocer she used to buy them from in Seattle, they'd come in at over ten bucks a bag. Add in the noxious smell of the spilled fertilizer and the fact that you couldn't even walk inside without encountering piles of glass, and it didn't seem like a particularly habitable place.

"I guess we'd better call in the sheriff," she said, not altogether displeased with this plan. For once, this crime had nothing to do with her. Sure, it was *her* grandfather's hardware store, and, yes, she and Gertrude had been the ones to discover the mess, but Sheriff Boyd was the one who'd suggested they stay here. If anyone was to blame for this newest turn of events, it was him.

"One hour." The sheriff walked into the hardware store, dropped a floodlight, and cast the whole place into harsh illumination. "That's all I ask. One hour without trouble. One hour without a crisis that centers on Tess Harrow."

Lighting up the hardware store did little to improve its appearance. In addition to the recent breakage, it looked as though the place hadn't been properly cleaned in years. Tess ran a finger along the edge of one of the few shelves that hadn't been ransacked, leaving a long line in the dust.

"Stop that," the sheriff muttered. "Are you *trying* to contaminate the scene?"

"I think it's a bit late for that." Tess nodded down at the clear signs of her earlier visit. Both she and Gertrude had left fingerprints, footprints, and who knew what else behind. "Besides, I can already tell you everything you want to know."

"I doubt that."

"These footprints are size nine," Tess said as she fell into a squat near the fertilizer. "I don't recognize the pattern, which is telling in and of itself. Detective Gonzales can identify the imprint of almost every man's shoe in existence, which means I can, too."

The sheriff grunted, but not in a disparaging way. "Why am I not surprised by that?"

"If the shoes come from overseas or were made at a smaller boutique, they might slip my radar. It's rare, but it happens." Tess sighed. "I'm also having a hard time with the animal prints. They're the right size for a dog, but the indentations aren't right."

The sheriff crouched next to her. There was something intimate in the still, careful way he held himself. Tess wasn't a restful person, so it was always alarming to her to find someone who could be so solid and unmoving.

"What makes you say that?" he asked. There was such a note of genuine curiosity in his voice that Tess was taken aback. The sheriff noticed it with a laugh. "Being born on a reservation doesn't automatically make me an animal tracking expert, Ms. Harrow. I don't find a lot of cause for hunting down dogs in my line of work."

"That's not what surprised me," Tess said, though not without a slight flush. To be perfectly honest, the thought *had* occurred to her.

"Then what did?" Sheriff Boyd asked.

"I'm not used to you asking my advice, that's all," she said. She pulled out her phone and snapped a quick photo of the animal prints. Instead of remaining in a crouch, which was starting to seriously tweak her sore knee, she referenced the photo instead. "Most dog tracks have claw marks at the tips, but these ones don't. And look—the pad is wider than it is tall and has three little bumps here at the bottom."

The sheriff leaned close, his brow furrowed. "*Fury on the Mountain,*" he said with a nod. "I remember now. But these aren't nearly big enough to belong to a cougar."

Tess was inordinately pleased to find his ready understanding. Most of the time, her random store of knowledge was met with boredom, perplexity, or—in Quentin's case— exasperation. It wasn't often that someone was both able and willing to follow along.

"A *baby* cougar?" she suggested.

The sheriff's snort told her what he thought of that idea. "If you can come up with a scenario in which a baby cougar broke into your grandfather's hardware store, tore into all these bags of fertilizer, and then took a nap next to whoever was sleeping in that pile of blankets over there, I'm ready to hear it."

Tess shook her head with a sigh, once again finding herself facing a creative obstacle. Like the toucans in the forest, she couldn't seem to make the pieces fit.

"Any news on Carl?" she asked, since it seemed there wasn't much more to say about the footprints. The fact that the shoes were a size nine and not an eleven hadn't been lost on her. One of the Peabody boys *might* have been able to squeeze into a ten in order to throw off suspicion, but nine was taking it a bit too far. And she was pretty sure someone would have noticed a baby cougar running through the streets. As far as she could tell, these were as much of a dead end as everything else.

"No. We might have to bring in the search and rescue choppers."

That surprised her. "It's that serious?"

The sheriff's eyes fixed on hers. They were clouded with trouble in a way that made Tess feel cold all over—well, cold*er*, anyway. The second he'd walked into the hardware store, he'd seen fit to send Gertrude to Otis and Mya's house to spend the night. Nothing appeared to have been stolen from the store, but the disarray hinted at some kind of trouble taking place within its four walls. Now he was calling in helicopters and looking at her as though she was covered from head to toe in iron spikes.

"Carl is one of the most capable and talented officers I've ever had the privilege to work with," he said, and with a tone as icy as Tess's creeping flesh. "Don't be fooled by how young he looks. He grew up in this forest, knows the area better than anyone. If he hasn't found his way back yet, then things are a lot worse than you can imagine."

Considering just how far Tess's imagination was capable of carrying her, these were frightening words indeed.

"There's only one thing for it, then," Tess said with a glance around the hardware store.

The sheriff's gaze transformed from cold to wary. "Why do I get the feeling I'm not going to like what you're about to say?"

Because he was a man and she was a woman. Because he was a sheriff and she was a writer. Because once Tess decided on a thing, no one could move her from it.

"If Gertie and I can't stay here, I might as well leave her with the Lincolns and make myself useful." She dug through the piles of upturned tools until she found a flashlight and a hammer. She tucked both into her jeans. Luckily, the waistband fit so snugly that they didn't immediately fall down to her ankles. "Let's go find your missing deputy."

Chapter Thirteen

"THE REAL PROBLEM IS, I DON'T HAVE ANY GOOD SUSPECTS."
Tess walked alongside Nicki, the pair of them sweeping their
flashlights in an arc as they followed a narrow path through the
forest. Tess had always seen search parties on television and
found it ridiculous that everyone walked shoulder-to-shoulder
at a snail's pace, but the idea was starting to make sense. The
undergrowth was so thick, and the night so inky dark, that it
would be easy to overlook something—or someone—lying
on the ground.

"What are you talking about?" Nicki said. "I thought
Mason Peabody did it."

"Sheriff Boyd and Ivy say Mason Peabody did it," she
countered. "But all we have to go on is that he's smarmy and
Wilma used to work for him. That's not much of a motive."

"Didn't we decide on a torrid love affair?"

Tess rolled a shoulder. She still liked that theory, but she
was willing to admit it lacked depth. "That's no reason to
kill a woman. Not for a man with as high a profile as Mason.
There'd need to be a secret baby, at the very least."

"Or maybe a deep, dark kink he didn't want getting out?"
Nicki suggested.

"I doubt it." Tess shook her head. "I'm pretty sure every

public official has whips and chains in their closets these days. There's barely room for skeletons anymore."

Nicki laughed—a sound she immediately hushed once several other members of the search party glanced over. You weren't supposed to find a midnight search party entertaining, but Tess and Nicki were doing their best to make light of it.

"I'm serious," Tess said in a voice that was anything but. If they stopped chatting about potential murderers, they'd have to think about what they were doing—searching for a nice, friendly, missing young man in a case already dripping with blood. *Anything* was preferable to that. "Let's assume Mason isn't the one who killed that poor woman. Who else do we have?"

Nicki held up a hand and started counting. "Adam and Zach Peabody."

"Alibied."

"Sheriff Boyd."

"A bit of a stretch."

"Ivy?"

Tess laughed. "That's what I mean. We have all these bits and pieces of a puzzle but no idea how they fit together. *Think*, Nicki. Put all those noir novels to good use. A woman is dead. Despite all attempts to hide her identifying marks, her name was easily discovered because of an injury suffered on the job—at a logging site where both Mason and his brothers have ties." Tess sighed. That was where things started to get tricky. "Despite knowing who she is, no one has stepped forward with any information about her final days or what sort of things she might have been into."

"Maybe she was the one sleeping in your grandfather's hardware store," Nicki suggested.

It wasn't the worst idea Tess had ever heard. Sheriff Boyd's words from earlier—about how every crisis was somehow tied to her—were starting to make a certain amount of sense. It was *her* pond where the body had been found, and *her* hardware store that had been burgled. The forest on *her* property was where Carl had chased after a mystery man and gone missing, and *her* trees had seen a flock of mystery toucans whizzing by. As much as she hated to admit it, he was right. The only thing connecting all the strange happenings around them was Tess Harrow, thriller writer without a clue.

"But why would she have been sleeping in there?" Tess demanded. "Why would anyone?"

"I don't know..." Nicki eyed her askance. "You and Gertie were about to do the same. It's not *that* odd."

Tess stopped where she stood. Not only was that alarmingly true, but she and Nicki appeared to have wandered some way from the rest of the search party. Since she could still hear the sounds of the group pushing through the forest, she focused on the first of the two concerns.

"We were only planning to stay there because the cabin was no longer safe. We needed to be somewhere with people around. Somewhere we could easily scream for help."

Nicki tapped her temple. "Exactly. Because you didn't want to be murdered in your beds. Who else might have shared that fear?"

"Nicki, you beautiful genius!" Tess could have kissed the other woman. Say what people might about librarians being a dying breed, Nicki was proving to be worth her weight in gold. As soon as she got back to Seattle, Tess was going to donate heavily to her local library system. "Wilma must have been hiding out from someone. Maybe that bailey nail in her thigh was a warning. Maybe she knew she was in trouble and wasn't sure how to get out of it."

"So she moved into the hardware store with her loyal dog to protect her." Nicki's enthusiasm for their story almost outstripped Tess's. "Only someone came in and attacked her. And...stole her dog?"

Tess couldn't help laughing. "It wasn't a dog, of that I'm sure. Sheriff Boyd thinks it might have been a—"

"Cougar!"

At the sound of Nicki's shout, Tess gave a startled jump. "How do you know that was what we were talking about earlier?"

Instead of answering, Nicki lifted her flashlight and pointed it into the forest. "No—look. There's a cat out there. Only...it's not the right size for a cat. It looks more like a—"

"*Baby* cougar!" Now it was Tess's turn to cry out. She also moved her flashlight toward the forest, but there was no need. Nicki's light had caught the animal right in the eyes. Its brilliant tapetum flashed blue and green. Understandably annoyed by the direct shot to the eyes, the cat started, darted, and ran off into the underbrush.

"Quick!" Tess cried. "We have to follow him."

Tess ran off without waiting for Nicki's response. She wasn't sure what propelled her except the realization that what she was chasing wasn't a cougar—baby or otherwise.

She'd done quite a bit of research into the animals while writing *Fury on the Mountain*, even going so far as to visit a big cat rehabilitation center with Gertrude. She'd wanted to capture how the animals moved, all feline grace and massive, powerful muscles. It had also seemed like a good way to entertain an eleven-year-old Gertrude, who hadn't yet decided to be ashamed of her mother in public.

There had been a litter of cubs when they'd visited, a pile of soft, spotted bodies that looked like oversized kittens tumbling over their too-big feet. The animal she and Nicki had seen was different. It had the sleek build of an adult cat, with black-tipped ears and way more speed than seemed possible for a living, breathing thing.

In other words, it looked more like a bobcat.

"Wait up!" Nicki called as she rushed after Tess. "I'm coming with you."

Tess's hand shot up to stop Nicki dead in her tracks. The other woman came to a skidding halt.

"What is it—" she began, but there was no need for her to finish.

Standing no more than three feet away, a limp bobcat in its arms and a tranquilizer gun strapped across its chest, stood Bigfoot.

"He's real," Nicki breathed. Her voice came out as a long, disbelieving pant. "You weren't making it up."

On the contrary, there was nothing *real* about the creature—man—they both faced. From a distance, the costume had looked convincing, like Chewbacca at a comic book convention. Up close, Tess could see the ragged seams where the fabric had been torn and sewn back together, a line of white T-shirt at the back of the man's neck where the hood didn't quite reach.

Then again, what he lacked in authenticity, he more than made up for in firearms. Tess didn't think the tranquilizer dart that had taken out the bobcat would kill her, but she wasn't willing to wager any money on the outcome.

"Five foot ten," she said aloud. "Medium build."

Her gaze shifted down as if of its own volition. What she saw scared her more than all the rest put together. "Size nine shoes."

The Bigfoot's head swiveled to hers. She had no idea how the man was able to see through the plastic beads for eyes, but she would have sworn that there was something almost like loathing staring out at her.

And then he was gone. No sooner had Tess opened her mouth to scream for Sheriff Boyd than the faux Bigfoot turned and dashed off into the forest, his footsteps making almost no sound in the deep, dark night.

———

It had always been a dream of Tess's to sit in front of a book of criminal mug shots, turning page after page as she attempted to point out the villain responsible for committing a terrible crime. In fact, she liked the idea so much that she'd put it in every single Detective Gonzales book she wrote—a thing that both her editor and Sheriff Boyd weren't slow to point out.

"As you can see, we don't use a physical book." Sheriff Boyd stabbed at the computer screen, which flashed a series of images for her identification. "That practice has been out of date for at least twenty years. Everything is digitized now."

Tess sighed and propped her head on her hand. "Crime fiction hasn't been the same since the invention of the computer," she said, clicking slowly through the images. She wasn't, as might be expected, looking through mug shots so much as Bigfoot costumes from online retailers, but the idea still held. "Or smartphones. You have no idea how hard it is to build up a convincing mystery when every cop with a shady hacker friend can just tap into a cell tower and track everything."

Sheriff Boyd, who'd been leaning over her shoulder so close that she could smell the coffee on his breath, turned to stare at her. "How many cops do you think have shady hacker friends?"

"All of them *should*," Tess said, not unaware of his irony. It would be difficult not to be. It dripped from his voice like an icicle coming loose. "With all the legal channels you have to go through, it seems like an ideal shortcut."

"Ms. Harrow, you can't access cell phone data without probable cause."

"I know."

"And if you do access it, what you find isn't admissible in court."

"I *know*," Tess said, more irritably this time.

"Then there you go. You shouldn't be writing about a rogue detective who breaks every law known to mankind;

what you need is a cop who understands privacy laws and sticks to them." He laughed. He still leaned so close to Tess that the rough-edged sound shook her. "Your stories would practically write themselves."

Tess held herself perfectly motionless, unwilling to shift by so much as an inch. She wouldn't give Sheriff Boyd the satisfaction. He was, of course, perfectly right. It was a lot easier to solve crimes when you didn't have to bother with things like rules and regulations—when you weren't prevented by a badge and an oath of honor from nosing around where you didn't belong. It made for *terrible* fiction, but that wasn't the point. For once in her life, she wasn't thinking about her book. Sheriff Boyd, a cop who unquestionably understood privacy laws and stuck to them, wasn't what this case needed.

She, however, was.

The sheriff noted her sudden stillness and peered at the computer screen. "Is that the one? The 'macho wilderness beast' from Costume City?"

Tess blinked, startled to find herself looking at a scraggly Bigfoot knockoff costume with holes where the eyes should go.

"Oh, um. No. No, it's not this one." She scrolled through a few more images for form's sake. "I'm sorry, but I don't think we're going to find it. The one the man wore was several years old. It might have even been homemade. The workmanship left much to be desired."

The sheriff heaved a sigh and straightened. His back cracked in several places, making Tess feel a twinge of guilt for keeping him hunched over while she sat in his chair.

"It was a long shot anyway," he admitted. "At least now we know we're dealing with an actual human being. And a bobcat. That's closer than we were yesterday."

Tess couldn't tell if it was worry over Carl's disappearance or plain ordinary fatigue that accounted for it, but the sheriff was treating her like a rational, helpful human being for the first time since it had rained body parts. And instead of pressing the point, like she might otherwise have done, she put a hand over his and squeezed it.

"I'm sure he's out there somewhere," she said gently. "We'll find him, and we'll bring him home. I don't care how long we have to keep searching."

The sheriff didn't slip his fingers out from under hers right away.

"I don't like it," he said.

She didn't ask him which part of it he was talking about—mostly because it didn't matter. Once he found out what she was about to do, he'd have something entirely new to hate.

Chapter Fourteen

TESS WASN'T SURE WHAT SHE EXPECTED A LOGGING CAMP to look like, but she was disappointed by how much it resembled any other large, expensive enterprise designed to lay waste to the planet.

She'd grown so used to the old-timey theme in Winthrop that she half-expected there to be canvas tents and men in faded dungarees, pipes dangling from their lips as they felled trees with two-handled saws. Instead, huge machines were revving to and fro around a bare scab of the earth, a mass of temporary buildings huddled off to one side. She parked her Jeep near the largest of the buildings and stepped out to the not-altogether-unpleasant scent of lumber and gasoline.

"It's something, isn't it?" Mason Peabody appeared on the porch of the largest building and took a deep inhale. "Most people go their whole lives without ever experiencing that smell."

"It's what I imagine Hell's like once they run out of brimstone," she replied, but with a smile to show she meant no harm. She *did* mean harm—and lots of it—but she didn't want Mason to know that. "Thanks for agreeing to meet me today."

"It's my pleasure, my pleasure," he boomed as he gestured

for her to follow him inside. "To be honest, I didn't think I'd hear from you so soon."

Neither had she, but that was before she'd discovered that the dead woman in her pond had direct ties to this place. Sheriff Boyd might have done a full search of the logging operation and found nothing worth note, but Tess had her own way of going about things.

Especially since she'd realized she wasn't bound by all those pesky rules that held the sheriff in place. She might not have any cool hacker friends, but she wasn't without resources.

"You said I could come find you once I was ready to help your campaign. Well, I'm ready." Tess entered the office in Mason's wake and blinked. Nothing about the tin-can exterior led her to expect the seventies-era explosion of decadence that awaited inside. The wood-paneled walls were matched by a shag carpet in an alarming shade of mustard yellow, the whole of it tied together with furniture that seemed entirely composed of wicker. The wall behind his desk held a detailed map, but that was the only thing approaching artwork on display.

"I know." Mason sat behind a metal desk that Tess remembered well from her elementary school days. "A bit of a relic, isn't it?"

"I wasn't going to say anything."

"It's not worth updating. I don't spend much time in here."

This surprised Tess. At the coffee shop, Mason had struck her as a pompous man—the kind who demanded the best table at every restaurant he went to, who'd send the steak back if it was the tiniest bit overdone. That he'd willingly—and cheerfully—spend so much as an hour inside this monstrosity seemed wrong, somehow.

This feeling only grew when he steepled his fingers on top of the desk and smiled in a way that made Tess's skin crawl.

"Well, Ms. Harrow? What did you have in mind for my campaign?"

Tess's normal go-to move whenever she supported a political effort was to throw money at it. Time was one of the few things she didn't have much of, and the thought of picking up the phone or going door-to-door to solicit votes made her almost as uncomfortable as Mason's steepled fingers. However, there was no way she was giving this man a single penny. If the number of bared, scraggly hillsides on the drive up here was any indication, he was doing just fine for himself.

"I'd like to write a piece on the feud between you and Sheriff Boyd," she said, resorting to the only other thing she had to offer: her words. "An exposé about corruption in small towns and what the locals are doing to combat it."

"I thought you said you wrote fiction."

"I do, but you planted the seed for something more." She reflected somewhat ruefully that it was likely the *only* thing he'd ever planted in his life. "Considering my ties to this place, it seemed like a good way to give back to the community."

"Your ties?" he asked. A note of genuine curiosity touched his voice.

She nodded. "My grandfather lived in Okanogan County

for most of his adult life. I visited once when I was kid, and it seems to me that everyone here has some sort of link." She weighed her next words carefully. "Sheriff Boyd, for example. I heard he grew up here before he left to become a big-city cop. Are you and your brothers also fixtures?"

She held her bright smile so long it started to crack her face.

"I don't see what my brothers have to do with anything," Mason said, but his shoulders came down. "Where will this exposé run?"

"The sky's the limit," Tess said with an airy wave of her hand. "I have a friend who's an editor with the *Seattle Times*. He's always looking for human interest stories. Especially if there's a systemic corruption element on the side."

She knew the moment Mason was caught. It was her mention of the big-name newspaper that did it. She didn't feel it necessary to mention that her friend was the *food* editor and that he cared no more for small-town politics than he did culinary sea foam. Some things were more important than the truth.

"What would you need from me to get the ball rolling?" Mason asked.

Tess barely managed to keep the grin from her face. "For starters, what I'd really like is a tour."

If Tess never watched another tree crack at the base and come crashing down to earth, it would be too soon.

She enjoyed toilet paper and affordable housing as much as the next modern woman, but there was something devastatingly harsh about the entire process. She'd spent so many years of her life building something out of nothing—crafting entire worlds every time she sat down at her desk—that she'd forgotten the rest of the world didn't always operate that way.

"You get used to it after a while," the man on her right said. He handed her a pair of sound-canceling earmuffs, but she refused to put them on. If she was going to hold a secret investigation into Wilma's disappearance, she needed to hear what was being said around her. "And it looks bad now, but there's a team that sweeps in and replants everything once we're gone."

Tess blinked. "There is?"

"Oh, yeah." The man pointed at a hillside some ways in the distance. He looked as little like a logger as Mason did, only instead of sporting an expensive haircut and an even more expensive suit, he was a tiny, balding scrap of a man with thick glasses. Tess also noted that he had size seven feet. "See that land over there?"

She nodded. The area he was pointing at was lush with green trees and even greener undergrowth. It reminded her a lot of the area behind her cabin.

"Ten years ago, that hillside looked a lot like this one. In another ten, we should be good to start thinning it out. Twenty years after that?" He waved his hands like a magician revealing a trick card. "We can clear the whole thing out and start over."

Tess could only stare at the man. "Do you mean…sustainable logging?"

He nodded and rubbed his stomach like a proud Santa. "Peabody Timber was one of the first companies in Washington to adopt the practice. It's not as easy as just blasting through and taking what you want, but it's much better for the planet—and for our pockets. Lots of companies will pay top dollar if they can be guaranteed eco-friendly wood and wood pulp products."

Mason appeared next to Tess as if from nowhere. "I wish I could take credit, but it was my father's brainchild. I can remember hearing him talk about it as a kid, when Zach and Adam and I used to run around playing swords with the sticks we found. I'll have my assistant fax you over a fact sheet. Some of the statistics about regrowth will blow you away."

Tess's heart sank. *Not* because Peabody Timber wasn't ravaging the earth of its natural resources but because that sounded like a practice she could get behind.

In fact, everything Mason had done today was something she could get behind. Instead of taking her on a tour of the premises himself, he'd excused himself to attend to a tearful employee who was behind on his house payment. He'd handed her over to this nice man, telling him to let Tess go wherever she wanted and talk to whomever she pleased. So far, she'd met several employees who were devastated by the news of Wilma's death, who waxed poetic about all of Mason's virtues, and who generally behaved like well-paid employees who were proud of the work they did.

If she hadn't been the one to instigate this visit, she might almost have accused Mason of staging his business like some kind of North Korean propaganda village.

Then again, she *had* telephoned ahead of time to let him know she was coming…

"It's pretty dangerous work, isn't it?" she asked, determined not to leave this place empty-handed. "What with the falling trees, big machines, and bailey nails flying about."

Mason couldn't pretend to misunderstand her. "What happened to Wilma Eyre was unfortunate."

"Do you mean the workplace injury or the fact that someone murdered her and dumped her in my pond?"

The small man cleared his throat uncomfortably, but Mason only sighed and shook his head. "Both. She was caught in flagrante the day of her alleged incident with the nail. I'm not saying the injury was related, but she wasn't exactly following protocol out there in the forest."

"Neither was the man she in flagrante-ed," Tess pointed out.

Mason blinked, startled. "I beg your pardon?"

"You said she wasn't following protocol. Neither was the person she was caught trysting with. Why should she be the one to take all the blame?"

The small man's coughing picked up in earnest.

"I don't see what this has to do with your article," Mason said. His eyes narrowed in suspicion. "What did you say the name of your editor friend was, again?"

"I didn't." Tess did her best not to sound smug, but she couldn't help it. She *felt* smug. It seemed that she and Nicki had been right about the love affair. To be fair, they'd assumed Mason was the one Wilma was seeing, but a stranger in the forest was just as good—and just as predictable. Almost every crime, fictional or otherwise, could be boiled down to money, power, or sex.

Tess would have been disappointed at the banality of it all if she wasn't so pleased to finally have a lead. If she could just find out who Wilma had been seeing, who'd met her in the woods to enjoy a hefty log or two, she might have something concrete to build the next leg of her investigation on.

"Now, see here," Mason said, filling his chest so expansively that it strained the buttons of his jacket. "I've been fully cooperative every step of the way—just ask anyone."

"Of course you were," Tess agreed.

"You can't try and pin this on Peabody Timber," he continued as though she hadn't spoken. "We had nothing to do with Ms. Eyre's death."

Tess highly doubted it, but she wasn't about to say so. If she wanted to get anything more out of this session, she needed to return Mason to the self-aggrandizing pomposity of his earlier confidences. Unfortunately, she was prevented by the sight of a tall, angry, redheaded man striding across the packed dirt toward them. Realization hit her the same time that she recognized who it was.

"Zach," she breathed. "Your brother Zach was the one who was caught with Wilma."

No one bothered to confirm her theory. They didn't need to. One look at the way Mason's contorted face told her everything.

"What's the meaning of this?" Zach came to a halt in front of his brother. They were strikingly similar in appearance but not demeanor. Mason held himself like a man who wielded all the power; Zach was reduced to nothing but twitchy anxiety. "Are you seriously firing me? You can't do that."

"I'm not firing you. I'm putting you on leave. *Paid* leave." Mason rolled his eyes in Tess's direction, as if to remind his brother that they had an audience, but Zach took one look at her and sneered.

"I don't care who hears me. I have nothing to hide."

"How long were you and Wilma Eyre seeing each other?" Tess asked before someone could think to kick her off the premises.

Zach's mouth formed a flat line. "I didn't kill her."

"I didn't say you did."

"I have an alibi, remember?"

Tess almost laughed out loud. That alibi was starting to feel awfully thin. Even if someone could place him at this logging camp the day of the murder, that only raised *more* questions. Was Wilma here that day, too? Was it a question of in flagrante gone wrong?

And—most important of all—did Sheriff Boyd know about any of this?

"You can't put me on leave, Mason," Zach said. He sounded less angry and more pleading this time. "Not now. Not like this. Not when we still have to—"

"Be *quiet*, you fool." Mason's voice rumbled so loud that it covered the sounds of a nearby excavator. He didn't look over at Tess, but she knew that she was the reason for this sudden lapse into discretion. "Jerry, will you please escort our guest to her car? I think the tour is over."

There was a distinct coolness to Mason's voice now, but Tess didn't regret her questions. Oftentimes, what people *didn't* say was a lot more powerful than what they did. That was a lesson Tess had learned a long time ago. The things Quentin didn't say to her—the things he *still* didn't say to Gertrude—spoke louder than all the rest.

"There's no need to escort me," Tess said, smiling blandly to show she meant no harm. "I've got everything I came for...and then some."

Chapter Fifteen

"WHAT ARE THE CHANCES YOU CAN FAKE A LIBRARIAN emergency to gain access to a woman's private residence and snoop around without anyone finding out about it?"

Nicki proved herself to be a paragon of a sidekick by requiring no explanation. She immediately broke out in laughter. "Slim to none. There's no such thing as a librarian emergency."

"That's not true." Gertrude sat cross-legged on the end of her bed, Ivy's fat stack of a novel on her lap. Against all odds, she'd set aside the ghost sword books in favor of the hand-written tome. Against even more odds, she and Tess were once again living in the cabin. With the hardware store out of the running and a search party in constant motion outside, the sheriff had agreed to let them return home.

Tess suspected he mostly wanted her here in hopes Bigfoot came back. If that man-beast showed up again, he wanted to make sure she was available to serve as bait.

"What's not true?" Nicki asked.

Gertrude glanced up. "There *are* librarian emergencies. What if it's an ultra-rare book in danger of being lost to humanity?"

"Ooh, I like that," Tess said, jumping on board. "A first

edition Shakespeare would demand a break-in. For the sake of literature."

Nicki stared at her over the top of her glasses. "You think there's a first edition Shakespeare roaming around unattended in Okanogan County?"

Tess couldn't help laughing. "There are bobcats and toucans roaming around unattended. It's not that much of a stretch."

Nicki shook her head. Today's earrings were long, gossamer silver threads that tickled her clavicles. "It won't work. If you want to get into Wilma's house, you're just going to have to break in the good old-fashioned way."

"What *is* the good old-fashioned way of breaking in?" Gertrude asked. "Hypothetically, I mean."

Tess tapped her teeth. "Hypothetically, I'd go for the ol' smash-and-grab. Make it look like a break-in. Punch a window, unlock the door, and do your worst."

"No one around here would do that," Nicki protested. "It's too risky. Three-fourths of the population carries a gun, and you never know who's sitting at home in the dark just waiting for a chance to use it. Everyone would know it's a hoax."

"And by *everyone*," Gertrude said, laughing, "she means—"

"I know who she means, thank you very much," Tess said. She tilted her head and considered. "So we'd need to do it in a way that wouldn't set off any of Sheriff Boyd's red flags. Would Wilma have left a key under the doormat?"

"It's possible."

"Cellar access?"

"I've never been to the house she was renting, so I couldn't say."

Tess grunted. "Drat. I was hoping that one would be it."

"Ohmigod, you guys." Gertrude sighed and unfolded her legs from the end of the bed. Tess could have sworn that those legs had grown at least two inches since they'd arrived. "If it was a rental, just go to her landlord and ask to look around. Pretend you want to rent it now that it's empty. No one will think that's weird."

Tess and Nicki's eyes met in a moment of shared excitement—and chagrin. The latter was mostly on Tess's side. Not because her daughter had just outsmarted her, but because drawing an impressionable teenager into her criminal enterprise wasn't going to win her any parent of the year awards.

"And don't even think about telling me I have to stay here," Gertrude said, forestalling the protests that were about to spring to Tess's lips. "It was my idea. I'm coming with."

"As you see, there ain't any blood inside." The landlady of Wilma's house, which was a generous term for a single wide propped up on cement blocks, led the way as one giving a palatial tour. "In fact, ain't no one can prove she died here. Far as I know, she kilt herself in that pond where they found her."

It was on the tip of Tess's tongue to point out that she could hardly have killed herself without her head, but she restrained herself. Her line didn't come next—Nicki's did. They'd come up with a whole script for how to proceed, and it wouldn't do to diverge too much from it.

"The whole thing's a bit spooky, don't you think?" Nicki asked with a wary glance around. "Even if she didn't die here, a part of her must remain."

Tess felt a little guilty at the deception, but not much. It was all well and good to be *inside* Wilma's house, but what Tess really needed was a few private minutes to snoop around. If Wilma was like other women, there'd have to be *some* evidence proving she'd been sleeping with Zach Peabody. A receipt for dinner, a selfie of the two of them, his name carved into the wall with a heart around it...she wasn't picky.

"I don't like it, Mommy. It's too scary." Gertrude sniffled and rubbed at her eyes. That *mommy* bit hadn't been practiced ahead of time, but Tess had to admit it added a certain something. "What if she's still floating around?"

"I'll take fifty bucks off the first month," the landlady promised. "A hundred if you get rid of her stuff for me."

Tess wasn't sure what the going rate was for a place like this, but the hundred dollar discount seemed generous considering how sparse the furnishings were. A rickety dining set, a couch that had seen better days, and a hand-knitted throw blanket were all that were evident to Tess's naked eyes. Wilma Eyre had obviously been a neat person.

"Mommy! I can feel her ghost—I know it."

Tess nodded once. "You're absolutely right, Gertie-pie. I'll have to burn some sage and see if that helps."

"There ain't any smoking in here," the landlady warned. "Or pets. That's on the lease."

"I'm afraid the sage is non-negotiable," Tess said as she reached into her handbag. "It purifies the air of negative energies and lingering spirits."

She extracted a fat bundle of dried leaves, none of which were technically sage. That was one of the few spices Gertrude hadn't packed in her kitchen supply box, and they hadn't wanted to waste any time hitting the grocery store. They'd managed to pull together a collection of dried grasses, a few twigs, and some bay leaves to round out the parcel.

"See?" Tess waved it under the landlady's nose. "It's herbal and all-organic."

The landlady examined it through narrowed eyes. "And you jest…light it up? You don't smoke it or nothin'?"

Tess had to laugh. No one who came near this noxious bundle would want to inhale too deeply. "It's not that kind of herbal."

"I s'pose that's okay."

"Thank you," Tess said and started to light up.

"If you're going to be in here exorcising ghosts, I'm waiting in the car," Gertrude said, backing toward the door. That was part of the act, too, but Tess could have sworn there was real terror in her daughter's eyes. She'd had no idea Gertrude was such a phenomenal actress. "Remember what happened last time? That evil one attached to me, and I couldn't get rid of him for months."

"Wait a minute—" The landlady looked back and forth between the three of them.

"It sounds worse than it was," Nicki rushed to add. "All it took was a little holy water and a few midnight trips to the cemetery, and we got rid of it, easy-peasy. Don't be so dramatic, Gertie. I'm sure we'll be fine."

"I'm still waiting in the car," Gertrude said and dashed down the steps. As Tess had hoped, the landlady wasn't too far behind her. She called something over her shoulder about needing to check her emails and promising to return once the ritual was over.

"And that's how it's done," Tess said, laughing. She lit the edges of the bay leaves to add a convincingly smoky cloud to the air before tossing the whole thing in the sink. "Now let's find some clues."

———

"She was definitely sleeping with *someone*." Tess held up a black lace thong that looked painfully scratchy and peered at Nicki through it. "Nobody would wear these monstrosities otherwise."

Nicki snatched the underwear and tossed it back in the drawer. "Would you please focus? We have about sixty more seconds before that landlady realizes we're up to something"

"I'm just saying." Tess poked around a little more before giving up. She'd been hoping for a secret diary hidden under Wilma's delicates, but the woman didn't appear to have kept one. "My ex-husband used to eat that kind of thing up, but I always ended up with a rash. There are some places lace was never meant to go."

Nicki snorted but didn't slow down. Of the two of them, she was proving a much better—and more professional— investigator. She'd started at one end of the trailer and directed Tess to start at the other. They were more or less in the middle and no closer to an answer than they'd been when they started.

"It's not unusual for a woman to have a social life, even in these parts," Nicki said.

"I suppose not." Tess heaved a sigh. She was just about to give up when she decided to risk a peek under the sink. Even if the landlady did walk in, she could pretend to be checking out the cupboard space.

"Well, that's odd," she said as soon as she pulled the door open.

Nicki was at her back in an instant. "What is it? What did you find?"

"Cat food."

"So? Lots of people keep cat food under the sink."

Tess twisted to peer up at Nicki. "Yeah, but the landlady said no pets, remember? And I don't see any other sign of an animal. No bed, no pet hair everywhere…"

"Everything is really tidy in here. Maybe she vacuumed a lot."

Tess shook her head. People with cats could never get rid of all the hair, no matter how hard they tried. Even after the pets were long gone. One look at Edna the day of the parade proved that. Her cat, Oscar, hadn't yet returned, and she still looked as though she'd rolled him all over her like a lint brush.

"Well, I give up." Nicki rubbed her hands together in a gesture of finality. "Unless you think Wilma was secretly hiding the rogue bobcat in here, I don't see what you hope to discover."

Tess couldn't help being intrigued by this line of reasoning. "Considering how tied up Bigfoot is in all this, it's entirely possible," she said. "Either that or Wilma cat-napped Edna St. Clair's beloved Oscar, and the old woman did her in for vengeance."

Nicki laughed obligingly. "As much fun as that story would be, the timing doesn't fit. You said the cat went missing the day you came to town, which was a full three days after Wilma had been killed." Nicki noticed that Tess had gone perfectly still and was quick to add, "What? What did I say?"

"You don't think—" Tess cut herself off with a shake her head. *No.* It wasn't possible. There was no way that old woman could have mistaken a bobcat for anything other than a wild animal…and yet, *that* timing fit just fine.

"You figured something out," Nicki said. "Tell me."

Tess knit her brow and cast her mind back over that first meeting with Edna in the police station. She'd assumed that Edna had been exaggerating about Oscar the same way she'd exaggerated about her knees—an old woman indulging in hyperbole for the sake of a good story.

But what if she'd been telling the truth? What if Oscar really had been lured away? Not by an evil cat-napper but by someone so determined to find him that they'd don a Bigfoot suit and roam the woods with a tranquilizer gun to do it?

"That's enough, Tess. What is it?"

There was so much force in Nicki's voice—an aura of command that reminded Tess of Sheriff Boyd at his most autocratic—that it pulled her immediately back into the moment.

"Nicki, do you know if anyone ever *saw* Edna St. Clair's cat? Like, in the flesh?"

Nicki blinked at her. "I personally never saw him, but I can't speak for anyone else. She's had that cat for months. Why?"

Tess would have explained, but the handle of the trailer shook before the door swung open. The landlady peeked an anxious—but not unhopeful—head inside.

"Well? What'd you think? Y'all want it? I'll wave first and last month, but the deposit's fixed at two hundred."

Even at such an enticing price—and with electricity, to boot—Tess found she preferred her grandfather's little cabin. It might not look like much on the outside, but she was already starting to consider it home.

"We'll have to think about it, thanks," she said.

"But I let you burn the ghost out and everything."

"And we promise not to charge you for it," Tess said. As long as she had the landlady in front of her, she decided to make one last push. "Provided you tell us whether or not you can remember Wilma bringing any visitors around."

"Visitors?" the landlady echoed.

"*Male* visitors," Nicki said. "Especially late at night."

The woman shook her head. "She was always a good, quiet little thing. Never did anyone a bit of harm."

The fact that she had a secret, mystery lover and that someone had seen fit to remove her identifying body parts suggested otherwise, but Tess didn't press the issue. For one, she doubted this woman could tell them anything they didn't already know.

For another, she had a much more pressing interrogation to undertake.

Chapter Sixteen

"MS. ST. CLAIR! EDNA, PLEASE LET ME IN." TESS POUNDED on the door of 1313 Medford Drive, a ramshackle little house surrounded by one of the most beautiful gardens she'd ever seen. Whatever else she might say about Edna, the woman had taste. Wildflowers and billowing green climbers turned an otherwise unremarkable home into a veritable Garden of Eden. "It's about your cat, Oscar."

A hand pushed aside a pink gingham curtain, followed almost immediately by the older woman's narrowed, puckered eyes.

"I also brought cookies." Tess held up the plate of peanut butter cookies that Gertrude had whipped up that morning. They were one of Tess's favorite foods in the whole world, so the fact that she was willing to share meant something. "They're peanut butter."

"I'm allergic to peanuts," Edna shouted through the glass.

Oh, dear. She hadn't thought of that.

"I'm also allergic to milk, eggs, soy, shellfish, and penicillin. So I hope you didn't bring any of that with you, either."

As Edna rattled off this improbable list, Tess had to fight a smile. It was on the tip of her tongue to declare that she had bottles of penicillin in her purse just waiting for an unsuspecting passerby, but she refrained. Antagonizing an old woman wasn't going to get her any closer to what she wanted.

"That must be very uncomfortable for you," she said in what she hoped was a conciliatory tone. And, since she was starting to suspect that all Edna really wanted was someone to upstage, she added, "I'm allergic to bees."

The door creaked open. "*I'm* allergic to pollen."

"Latex," Tess said, thinking fast.

"Mustard." The door swung wider. "Not to mention any kind of silver. It gives me hives."

"Sulfites do the same to me," Tess countered. "Mosquito bites, too."

"Ha!" By this time, Tess was already halfway into the house. "*Everyone* is allergic to mosquito bites. That one doesn't count."

In truth, Tess didn't fall prey to any kind of allergy but the occasional bout of hay fever, but she salved her conscience with the thought that she'd achieved her aim of getting an interview with Edna—and she hadn't had to resort to calling in Sheriff Boyd to do it.

The green overgrowth on the outside of Edna's house extended well into the interior. The dingy walls could have used a fresh coat of paint, and the floral furniture looked to be as old as Edna, but the overall effect was quite lovely.

"You must need a lot of fertilizer to keep these plants thriving," she said. Edna's glance was sharp but gave nothing away.

"I don't use anything but water, sun, and love," Edna said. "I'm allergic to fertilizer."

Tess couldn't help it—she laughed. She'd slain her fair share of dragons in her day, but Edna St. Clair wasn't a woman she'd care to cross unarmed. "Are you going to invite me to sit down, or should we keep standing like this?"

"You said you found Oscar," Edna said, but she led the way to the floral couches, so Tess counted it as a win.

"I didn't say I found him," she said as she sank into the cushion. Despite their age, they were surprisingly comfortable. They were also, she noted, covered in a light smattering of the same yellowish hair that had been on Edna's clothes the day of the parade. She ran her fingers along the velvety fabric and discreetly gathered as much of the hair as she could. "I said I had some questions about him."

"You're as bad as that sheriff." Edna sniffed. "Getting an old woman's hopes up only to dash them down again."

Tess let that pass. "Do you happen to have any pictures of him? I've been doing some detective work on your behalf— strictly pro bono, you understand—and it'd be so much easier to locate your darling Oscar if I knew what he looked like."

"He looked like a cat."

Tess took a deep breath and tried again. "Would you say he was a small cat or a large one?"

"Oh, he was a big boy, no question of that."

"And his coloring? Was he all one color, or…?"

The old woman lit up from within. "Are you going to draw a picture of him? Like one of those sketch artists?"

Tess's drawing skills were negligible at best, but she was willing to play along for the sake of answers. Extracting the pad of paper she always carried in case inspiration struck, she started drawing the outline of a stick cat.

"Keep going while I sketch," Tess said. "Sheriff Boyd might not care about your missing cat, but he's my number one priority. Tell me everything you remember about him."

The drawing didn't improve much as Edna talked, but Tess's mood perked to a ridiculous degree. Everything Edna said confirmed her suspicions about Oscar's true form: short, wiry hair; black stripes and dots; a white-tipped tale; and, most important, those signature ears with wisps of black at the top.

Instead of showing Edna her drawing, Tess did a quick google search on her phone and pulled up an image of a bobcat. "Is this what Oscar looked like, Ms. St. Clair?"

Two large tears formed in the older woman's eyes. "You found him?"

Guilt and triumph warred within Tess's breast. It was cruel to build up Edna's hopes only to dash them back down again, but this was a serious breakthrough. And it was *hers*.

"I'm afraid not." Tess tucked the phone away again. "But there have been...sightings of him in the area."

"What do you mean, sightings?"

"He was seen prowling around my grandfather's old hardware store," she said with a slight adjustment to the truth. "And a few nights back, in the forest near my cabin."

Edna struggled to her feet—and Tess struggled with the urge to help her. She had a feeling she'd take a cane to the head if she made the attempt.

"You let him go?" Edna demanded. "You didn't catch him?"

Considering that Edna's beloved cat was a wild predator with sharp claws and a penchant for eating house pets, Tess didn't have plans to go anywhere near him—even if she *did* know where the Bigfoot-man had dragged him off to.

"I tried, but he was very fast," she said with an even bigger adjustment to the truth this time. "Can you tell me where you got him? He's very…unusual for a cat."

The mulish set of Edna's mouth didn't bode well for the conversation to follow. "I found him. He's mine."

"Yes, but *where* did you find him? A pet store? Craigslist?" She tried to make the next one sound perfectly natural. "A daring escape from a zoo?"

She must not have done a very good job of it. Edna's eyes narrowed, and she crossed her arms over her scraggly chest. "Where's your badge?" she demanded. "Show it to me."

If there was one thing Tess knew, it was when to beat a hasty retreat. "I left it at home, but don't worry. I'm committed to finding Oscar at all costs."

"I don't think you're a real police officer. You aren't wearing a uniform."

"I'm undercover," Tess said, backing carefully toward the door. It wasn't that she was *physically* afraid of this woman, but she didn't care for that look in her eye.

"Undercover as what?" Edna asked with a snort and an obvious look at Tess's clothes. True, the long linen skirt and men's button-down wasn't much of a fashion statement, but Tess had always preferred comfort over fashion. Anyone who sat at a desk for eight hours a day deserved a relaxed waistline. "I don't know you. I don't trust you. I bet you're not even allergic to latex."

Tess was unable to help laughing at that last one—a disaster in terms of getting on Edna's good side but a great way to get herself out the door in one piece. Careful to grab her plate of cookies in case Edna had been telling the truth about her peanut allergy, she thanked the old woman for her time and ducked under a long tendril of ivy.

"I found him under my porch," Edna said before Tess was even halfway down the front steps.

She whirled, but Edna was already closing the door.

"He was scared and hungry, and I had no choice but to take him in. And that, young lady, is all you're getting out of me."

Chapter Seventeen

"LET ME GUESS." TESS HELD HER CELL PHONE TO HER EAR, the tinny sound of Nicki's voice sounding as if from a hundred miles away. Which, to be fair, she probably *was*. She'd said something about heading up to the border today to drop off a stack of maternity magazines for a woman's shelter that was housed there. Since Tess was perched on top of her Jeep in the middle of Winthrop, straining to get a signal of her own, their conversation wasn't going to be a long one. "There aren't any books on bobcats in your library."

"It's the weirdest thing," Nicki said. "They've been stolen with all the rest. Who robs a *library*?"

Someone who didn't want anyone to know what they were up to, obviously. And who wanted to know everything about the care and feeding of bobcats. And possibly toucans.

"Did you check on the rest of the ones I asked for?" Tess persisted.

There was a delay for a moment before Nicki's fuzzy voice spoke up. "Yep. I've got plenty on garter snakes but nothing on king cobras."

"And the monkeys?"

"Gone."

"Cows?"

"Tons."

Even though Nicki couldn't see her over the phone, Tess nodded. It was exactly as she'd expected. The books on ordinary animals—boring animals like garter snakes and cows—were safe in the library's care. It was only when the animals started to get a little…exotic that things became complicated.

"Well, that settles it," Tess announced. She could have wished for more fanfare for a moment like this one, but standing on a Jeep in the middle of a Wild West town would have to do. "I've finally figured out what's going on around here."

"Really?" Nicki asked excitedly. "What did you—?"

The phone cut out before Tess could share her newest—and most plausible—theory. Which was for the best, really, because this was news she wanted to share with Sheriff Boyd before she brought anyone else in.

Mostly because he was going to *hate* it.

———

"It's an illegal exotic animal smuggling ring."

The sheriff looked up from the papers on his desk, his glance sharp enough to cut glass. "Absolutely not. Ivy—get her out of here."

"No, wait!" Tess darted to the side as Ivy took her boss at his word and attempted to grab Tess's arm. "Hear me out. I think I might be onto something."

When the sheriff still showed alarming signs of having

her forcibly removed from the building, she put her hands up in a pleading gesture. "Five minutes is all I ask. Five minutes to tell you everything I know. If you don't believe me after that, I'll walk out without any argument."

"Without *any*?" the sheriff asked doubtfully.

Tess had to fight a gurgle of laughter. "Well, only a tiny bit. But I had a *very* interesting conversation with Edna St. Clair yesterday. After Nicki checked on a few things for me, I came to the most rational conclusion for all our toucans and bobcats and missing library books."

"Which is an exotic animal smuggling ring?"

"An *illegal* exotic animal smuggling ring," Tess corrected him. By this time, Ivy was starting to show signs of interest. "It's the next logical step after missing zoo animals."

"No, it's not," the sheriff said flatly, but he gestured for her to sit.

She perched on the edge of her seat and pulled out her phone with the image of the bobcat she'd shown Edna yesterday. "This is Edna's cat, Oscar."

The sheriff's nostrils flared. "Now, see here—"

"I'm serious. Not a *literal* photo, obviously, since this is from Wikipedia, but you know what I mean. I showed it to her yesterday and asked her if this is what Oscar looks like. She said yes."

"Edna St. Clair is—"

"An ornery old woman, I know," Tess finished for him. "But she loved that cat as much as I love my daughter. She wouldn't forget what he looked like."

The sheriff stared at her. "Proceed."

Tess didn't wait to be asked a second time. "From everything I could gather, she found the cat under her porch and took him in. Then he was lured away—" At the sheriff's warning throat clearing, she took a breath and tried again. "Then he *ran* away, and he hasn't been seen or heard from since. Only there were all those footprints in the hardware store, not to mention the torn up fertilizer bags."

"So?"

"So, I went to the store and checked." She reached into her purse and pulled out a scrap of the bag where the ingredients were listed. "This brand is made with fish and blood meal. If the bobcat was hungry enough, he might have torn into the bags and eaten some of it. I looked it up. It's not unheard of."

The sheriff gave up the pretext of paperwork and stared at her. Tess tried not to let those dark, impenetrable eyes disconcert her, but she felt like a kid at Catholic school all over again.

"Let's say I'll bite—*theoretically*, mind you—about the bobcat. That doesn't explain the jump to an exotic animal smuggling ring." When Tess opened her mouth, he added, "Illegal or otherwise."

She sat back with something like triumph. This was where things started to get good. Not even Detective Gonzales would have been able to resist a theory like hers. In fact, he wasn't going to resist it, despite the pressure coming from above. He'd already had a big fight with his boss and stormed out, determined to get to the bottom of things. Even Willow was having a hard time swallowing the whole story. It was too bizarre, too unusual, too—

"Well?" Ivy demanded.

"Sorry. I was wool-gathering." Tess took a deep breath and started again. "Did you know that bobcats are the most common exotic pet that people keep in the United States? After foxes and iguanas, I mean."

"Iguanas?" the sheriff echoed. "I don't see—"

"Toucans are also quite popular," she continued, determined not to let the sheriff take back any of the five minutes he'd promised her. "Not to mention king cobras. *And* monkeys."

"Ms. Harrow, if you're about to tell me there's a king cobra slithering around town…"

Tess shook her head. Thankfully, things hadn't progressed *that* far. At least, not that she knew of.

"No, but those books are missing from the library. Along with all the other ones on exotic animals. But get this. The books on domesticated animals—and on Bigfoot—haven't been touched."

He sighed. "I knew we'd get to Bigfoot eventually."

"You can't deny it—he's been a part of this from the start. Stalking the woods at all hours of night and day… Tranquilizing poor, unsuspecting bobcats…" She thought, but didn't dare add, *infuriating easily infuriated sheriffs of the law*… "We're located so close to the Canadian border here. There's no better place to set up a base of operations for moving illegal goods back and forth. Just think. If Bigfoot and his criminal counterparts have been keeping the animals in holding until they can be sold or moved across the border, they'd need information on how to care for them. But they wouldn't want to leave a trail of evidence behind, so they've been taking the books from the library without permission."

Library book theft wasn't much of crime—not unless you were talking about that first edition Shakespeare—but Tess was pretty sure you could still make an arrest over it.

"They'd also have to be very careful to keep all those animals caged up. If one of them escaped—say, a bobcat who takes up residence underneath an old lady's porch or a flock of toucans flapping through the forest—they'd have to hunt them down again. And *without* being detected. What's more ideal than to skulk through the forest disguised as Bigfoot?"

Since the question was a rhetorical one, she didn't wait for an answer. "Voilà!" She waved her hands with a magician's flourish. "*That* must be what's happening in the woods. There's a secret trove of animals located somewhere near my cabin. All your Bigfoot sightings and strange animals are connected that way."

She waited, her breath baited as she waited to hear the sheriff's response.

She needn't have bothered. That raspy, unexpected shout of laughter told her everything she needed to know.

"I know how it sounds," she said, rising to her feet and holding her hands out in supplication. "I get that you might need a few minutes to wrap your head around the idea. I'm even prepared to go over some of the more far-fetched aspects. But you know it fits. It's the only thing that does."

If he did, he wasn't prepared to admit it. Or, considering how hard he was laughing, *capable* of admitting it.

Ivy took her by the arm, her clamp firm, and began

dragging her toward the door. Tess tried to dig her heels in, but Ivy was a lot stronger than she looked—and she looked like the sort of woman who could climb a mountain with a dagger between her teeth.

"He's laughing now, but it won't last," Ivy hissed into her ear. "I promise you don't want to be here when he stops."

For once, Tess didn't argue. She allowed herself to be led out of the room, content—for now—that she'd planted the exotic animal smuggling seeds. Sheriff Boyd might not buy into her theory *now*, but she knew enough about his methods to feel sure that he'd follow through. He'd talk to Edna, look into case precedence, and mull over the possibilities. Then, and only then, would he start investigating.

As a woman who was used to her detective jumping feet-first into his leads, this cautious professionalism felt like a huge waste of time. As a woman who was learning that *real* detectives were a lot less exciting, she was willing to wait.

"I'm right, Ivy—you know I am."

Ivy wouldn't meet her eyes. "I don't know anything of the kind. The one thing I *will* say, however, is that the longer Carl remains missing, the closer the sheriff is to doing something drastic."

Tess found that difficult to believe. Sheriff Boyd didn't strike her as a man who'd done anything drastic a day in his life. "Like what?"

"I don't know," Ivy admitted. "But the last time he misplaced someone close to him, he ran away from town and didn't come back for twenty years. I don't like our odds."

"You mean…?" Tess gestured toward her head and

emulated a scrubbing motion, recalling the day Ivy had washed her hair for her, the day she'd hinted at the sheriff's dark past. There had been something about a sister, if she remembered correctly.

Ivy shook her head. "Forget I said anything."

"Yeah, right. You can't say something like that and expect me not to follow up on it." Since that was precisely something Ivy *could* and *would* do, Tess decided to change tack. "Did you guys know that Wilma Eyre was likely seeing Zach Peabody before she died? Romantically, I mean?"

Ivy snorted. "Zach Peabody sees every woman around here romantically at some point or another. You're going to have to try harder than that."

"I thought an illegal exotic animal smuggling ring *was* harder."

"And so it is, Ms. Harrow," Ivy said, chuckling as she showed her the door. "That's one story the sheriff will never be able to swallow."

Chapter Eighteen

"Microfiche is the last bastion of the glory days of library-hood." Nicki drew a deep, reverential breath and clicked a button on the enormous machine. It whirred and shook in protest, but the light behind the screen eventually came on. "We have a teenager working part-time to digitize all our records, but the most we can seem to get out of him is one or two pages a week."

Tess settled in the beige plastic chair Nicki had brought and rubbed her hands. "As soon as all this murder nonsense is done, I'll send you Gertie. She'll have it done in a few weeks—and you don't have to pay her, either."

"Mom, I'm sitting right here." Gertrude looked up from—what else?—the giant box containing Ivy's book. She was down to the last few chapters. Tess had started making her keep notes so she could send them along and pretend they were from her. "I'll do it, but I charge twenty dollars an hour."

"Gertie!"

Her daughter hunched an impatient shoulder. "I'm a child, not your servant. It's twenty bucks or nothing."

"Nicki could hire a fully trained adult for that much."

"Actually, Nicki couldn't hire anyone for any amount.

The guy doing it is an intern. You two realize this is a tiny rural library, right? We exist almost entirely on charitable donations."

Tess nodded. "I remember. Mr. Mason Generosity himself."

"Exactly." Nicki slid the film into the machine and showed Tess how to manipulate the dial. "I peeked at Sheriff Boyd's library account to get his year of birth. This puts us in the vicinity of his sixteenth year—that's when you said he ran off, right?"

"That's what Ivy told me, yes. But I don't know how much I trust her. They're in cahoots together."

Gertrude snorted. "No one has used the word cahoots since 1888."

"Be quiet and keep reading. I want detailed feedback on all of Ivy's character arcs."

"Impossible," Gertrude retorted. "There are like three hundred of them."

Of course there were. What was a thousand-page sci-fi epic without a wildly rotating and unnecessary cast?

"I'll be in the back going over accounts if you need me," Nicki said. She paused and fingered the bobbing corks that dangled from her earlobes. "Remind me why this is important to the case? I don't see what Sheriff Boyd's personal history has to do with anything."

Neither did Tess, but that wasn't going to stop her from searching through these perfectly legal public records to see what she could discover.

The events and happenings in Okanogan County in the early 1990s were nothing to write home about.

If Tess was being honest, they were nothing to write to the news about either, but that hadn't stopped the dedicated journalists of *Okanogan Times* from putting out their daily paper.

"Ma Penny's Secret Jam Recipe."

"Holiday Lights Cost Extra $0.20 in Daily Electric Bill."

"Two-Headed Calf Turns Out to Be a Sheep with a Tumor."

Tess propped her head on her hand and stifled a yawn as she continued examining the microfilm. Gertrude heard her and leaned close. "That one about the two-headed calf seems cool," she said encouragingly.

"Look at the picture." Tess stabbed her finger at the screen. "How anyone thought that was a second head—or a cow—is beyond me."

"You're the one who's always telling me that research is the most important part of writing a book. Shouldn't you be better at this?"

Tess stuck her tongue out at her daughter. Research *was* important, but she generally stuck to the kind that only required a quick google search or two. There was a reason she wasn't a *true* crime writer. Fake crimes were a lot more fun.

"Oh! Wait. I think I found something." She sat up as she caught sight of a promising headline about a landslide that took out several houses and a barn. Several people had gone missing, only…nope. They'd found them washed up with an entire herd of cows. Several limbs had been broken, but everyone came through intact. Everyone *human*, anyway. Based on the open-invitation, community-wide barbeque on the following page, she was guessing a few of the cows hadn't made it. "False alarm."

"You know, you could just ask the sheriff directly," Gertrude pointed out. "People do that all the time. It's called having a conversation."

Tess snorted. "You think that man opens up his heart to strangers? On purpose?"

"You could try being nice to him. Then you'd be friends. He probably opens his heart up to friends all the time."

"You want me to entrap a man into telling me his deepest, darkest thoughts?" Tess switched off the microfiche. "Shame on you. I raised you better than that."

"It's not a trap if you mean it."

Tess blinked. "Gertie!"

"What? You can be friends with a man, Mom. I won't freak out or anything." Gertrude got up and stretched. They'd both been sitting for so long that their limbs were starting to knit to the chairs. "You could even ask him out on a date, if you want."

"Gertie!" This time, Tess didn't blink. She couldn't. Her eyes had gone totally dry.

Nothing she'd said or done in the past two weeks should have led her daughter to suppose she was interested in Sheriff Boyd as anything other than an ally in solving this crime. Sure, he was attractive in a gruff, woodsy way—and there was no denying that uncommunicative grouches were basically her type—but he was too much like Detective Gonzales. It'd practically be incest.

"Don't be so dramatic," Gertrude said, rolling her eyes. "People do it all the time. Divorced people, I mean. I bet Dad has like twelve girlfriends already."

Any outrage Tess might have felt at her daughter's attempt at playing matchmaker disappeared at once. The bitter note in Gertrude's voice was undeniable—and justified. Every time they made it somewhere with internet access, Gertrude fanatically checked her voicemail and texts. She tried to hide what she was doing, but Tess saw the crestfallen expression that resulted.

Tess *always* saw it.

"I'm sure he only has five or six girlfriends," Tess said, trying to make light of things.

It didn't work.

"You know he was cheating on you, right?" Gertrude's eyes didn't meet hers. "Before you split up? I read one of his emails once. He left it open on the desktop."

Tess's heart sank. The one thing she'd done since the divorce proceedings had started—the one thing she was determined to do until the end of time—was avoid the trap of painting her ex-husband like the villain in all this. It was just like Gertrude to see right through her good intentions to the electronic trail Quentin had left behind.

"It doesn't matter," Tess said, forcing a smile. "We all do bad things sometimes. It doesn't automatically make us bad people."

Instead of making her daughter feel better, this response seemed to fill her with a rage as frightening as it was unprecedented. Gertrude's anger usually took the form of sullen retreat and a deepening blow to the chip on her shoulder. This active fury was new.

"Aren't you going to even pretend like you care?" Gertrude whipped to her feet, sending half of Ivy's book flying. "Can't you act like a human being for once in your stupid life?"

"I'm trying, Gertie-pie. I'm—"

Gertrude was in no mood to hear it. She turned on Tess, her whole face screwed up in a tight, angry ball. "Dad was *cheating* on you, Mom. He was sneaking around behind your back. He was smiling to your face and pretending like he cared, and the whole time, he was in love with someone else."

"It's not that simple."

Gertrude laughed without mirth. "Are you serious? It's *exactly* that simple."

Tess didn't have a good response for this. On the one hand, life—and especially the relationships that propped it up—were rarely as cut-and-dried as people wanted to believe. On the other, Tess had been fourteen once. She remembered well what it had been like; how black-and-white everything had seemed, how easy to tell right from wrong.

Before she could articulate this in a way that wouldn't send Gertrude into a further rage, her daughter's gaze turned suddenly sharp. "You really didn't know about the emails? Or who they were from? You never once peeked to see what Dad was up to?"

Tess shook her head, wishing with all her heart that

she could push rewind and start this conversation over. Of course she'd known that Quentin was cheating on her. She'd never seen the literal emails, but there'd been no escaping the furtive way he'd checked the computer late at night or how he always took his phone calls in another room. Given Tess's penchant for amateur investigation, she could have easily gotten proof of his activities. For crying out loud—she knew Quentin's computer password. Pulling up his private accounts would have taken her all of five minutes.

She'd also known what would happen the moment she did.

This. This was what would happen. He'd avoid the difficult conversations with his daughter, duck and hide instead of facing up to his mistakes. When Gertrude stood there and fumed over Quentin smiling and pretending he cared about Tess, what she really meant was that he'd smiled and pretended to care about *her.*

And there was nothing Tess could do about it. For years, she'd faked a smile and a marriage, done her best to eke out the remains of a relationship that had died a long time ago. It hadn't been pleasant, but it had been worth it for Gertrude's sake. She could be a writer and a mother, plowing through all the rest just to see her daughter smile. The one thing she couldn't do was make Quentin be anything other than what he was.

Gone.

"Oh, honey," Tess said, but it was wrong. It was all wrong. Gertrude took one look at the sympathy in her mother's face, and everything seemed to break at once.

"*Don't*," Gertrude warned, her voice dangerous.

But she didn't have a choice. She had to.

"He loves you more than you'll ever know," Tess said. "He's just not good at showing it."

Half of her expected Gertrude to fly out in anger; the other half thought she might finally burst the dam of tears that had been backing up all summer.

Neither of those things happened. Instead, Gertrude leveled her a look that was so uncannily penetrating that Tess felt sure her daughter could see how hollow she was on the inside.

And then Gertrude turned on her heel and stalked away without a single word.

Chapter Nineteen

"Is Gertie with you?"

Tess wrapped her arms around herself as she approached Sheriff Boyd. He was once again dressed in his black knit cap, though he'd opted for jeans and a sweatshirt instead of the wilderness heist gear. He didn't turn at the sound of Tess's voice, so she must have made more noise than she realized tiptoeing out to the pond.

"Yeah, she's sitting on that fallen log over there." He paused a beat. "You shouldn't let her wander around outside the cabin on her own."

"She's not on her own. You're here."

The sheriff's grimace told her exactly what he thought about that. She opened her mouth to defend herself, but then she caught sight of Gertrude's slouched posture and the way she kept stabbing a stick into the mud along the edge of the pond and changed her mind. There was no use pretending anymore.

"I told her not to leave, which was my first mistake." Tess sighed. "She's not speaking to me right now."

"What did you do?"

"What makes you think this is my fault?" she asked, but there was no use pretending about that, either. "I said the wrong thing. I also did the wrong thing, wore the wrong thing, blinked the wrong way, and coughed too loud. She hates me, and to be perfectly honest, I'm not sure I blame her. Coming up here for the summer might have been a mistake."

"It wasn't."

Tess started, surprise rearing her head back. "I'm sorry. Did you just say I was right about something?"

The sheriff's smile was slow but unmistakable. "You don't have to act so shocked. You're a pain in my backside, and you don't know anything about how law enforcement works, but you're a good mom. It doesn't take a genius to see that."

For reasons Tess couldn't even begin to understand, a flood of tears started to fill her eyes. Even though she dashed at them with the back of her hand, Sheriff Boyd still saw. He pretended not to, but that somehow made things worse.

"I remember the summer you visited here," he said suddenly. He fixed his gaze on where Gertrude sat repeatedly stabbing the mud. "I was eleven years old."

"Wait—what?" Tess turned to look at him, but he kept his face averted. "Did we meet?"

He hunched one of his shoulders. "Not really. I saw you a few times, but you always had your head buried in a book. Or a *Time* magazine, which I thought was a weird reading choice for a kid."

Tess laughed too softly for Gertrude to hear. "You should've introduced yourself. I was reading those magazines out of desperation. There was nothing else to do around here."

"That's the point, isn't it? The quiet?"

Tess found herself nodding along. That *was* the point, actually. Whenever she thought back on that youthful visit to her grandfather, she remembered a sense of deep, numbing boredom and very little else. Her grandfather had offered her no entertainment and even less conversation. He'd fed her and put a roof over hear head, and that was it.

It had been the worst summer of her life. And also, somehow, the best.

Sheriff Boyd indicated Gertrude with a tilt of his head. All that stick-poking had dredged up some kind of crawling insect or reptile out of the pond. Gertrude bent close and watched as it made its way along the edge.

"She feels it, too. Not everyone does, but you can always tell when it happens." He drew a deep breath of fresh forest air. "It's like someone turns the noise off so you can just *be*. Sometimes, you get a few minutes. Other times, you get years. Your grandfather got years."

Tess could feel those dratted tears welling up again. This time, she didn't make a motion to wipe them away.

"I don't know what you two are running from—or why— but bringing her to this place was the best thing you could do." He gave a slight cough. "Well, the murder isn't ideal, but you know what I mean."

Oddly enough, she did.

"My husband," she said. Catching herself, she amended this with, "Ex-husband, I mean. That's who we're running from. Rather, we're running from the *idea* of him."

The sheriff lifted a questioning brow, patience and

understanding in every line of his bearing. Tess realized with a start that Gertrude had been right when she'd suggested Tess stop fighting and just talk to him—as a human being, as a *friend*.

"Since the divorce, he hasn't made much of an effort to be part of Gertrude's life." She caught herself in the middle of the polite lie and sighed. "Actually, he hasn't made any effort at all. And the longer we stayed in Seattle, the louder the silence got."

"I'm sorry."

Tess believed him. There was such a note of sincerity in his voice that she had no other choice. "When I got word that my grandfather died and left me this place, I thought... why not? Maybe the quiet of the forest will drown out the quiet of all the rest."

"And has it?"

Tess didn't have an easy answer. For a few days there, it had seemed like Gertrude was doing better. Her daughter was making friends and showing an interest in the world around her. She was enthusiastically assisting with the investigation and whipping up new culinary delights for the team of cops outside her door. She was even laughing again.

Unfortunately, Tess was starting to realize that there was an expiration date on their time here, a thing Gertrude had known from the start. Eventually, Wilma's murderer would be found. Eventually, they'd have to return to Seattle. Eventually, they'd have to face the reality that had chased them all the way into the depths of the forest: Quentin didn't care enough to call, and there was a good chance he never would.

"He sounds like a jerk," Sheriff Boyd said as if reading her mind. "Gertie is one heck of a great kid. He has no idea what he's missing."

"No." Despite herself, Tess smiled. "He really doesn't."

She glanced over to where Gertrude was seated, surprised to be greeted by nothing but an empty log. After casting a quick, anxious glance around the forest's edge, she realized Quentin wasn't the only one missing out on his daughter right now. Tess had been so involved in her conversation with Sheriff Boyd that she'd forgotten everything else.

Her heart, which had already been feeling heavy, turned to stone.

"Victor!" In the sudden clench of Tess's chest, his first name just popped out. "Gertie's not on the log anymore. He took her. Bigfoot got her!"

It was ridiculous to assume that a fully grown teenager could be Bigfoot-napped a few feet away from them without making a sound, but Tess couldn't help herself. Panic drove all other considerations from her mind.

And when those considerations *did* return, well, Tess didn't feel much better. Bigfoot wasn't the only danger an angry, heartsick teenager might run into out here. Not while Carl's disappearance remained unexplained and Wilma's murder unsolved.

The sheriff's eyes widened as he raked his eyes over the tree line and found it empty, save for a light fluttering of branches settling back into place. With the same speed he'd used when chasing down Bigfoot that first day, he took off in that direction.

And Tess, despite being no physical match for him, followed right behind.

Chapter Twenty

"WHAT DO YOU MEAN, HER FOOTPRINTS STOP? THEY can't stop. Find them!"

Sheriff Boyd slapped a hand over Tess's mouth. She didn't appreciate this particular approach to silencing a woman, but there was no denying that she'd been growing shrill. She couldn't help it. She *felt* shrill. They'd been following Gertrude's size seven Doc Marten prints for the past hour only to find themselves facing a dead end.

"Shh," he whispered with a cock of his head.

"What do you hear?" she asked. Considering his fingers were still holding her mouth shut, it came out more like, "Mmhhwhoohrr," but Sheriff Boyd didn't need an interpreter.

"If I tell you to wait here, will you do as I ask?"

He lifted his fingers so Tess could answer. "My daughter is somewhere out in those woods—lost, scared, or worse. Do you think I'm going to wait here?"

The sheriff's only answer was a huff of air. Tess tucked a finger through his belt loop and held firm. He glanced a sharp question at her, but she had an answer ready. "This way we won't get separated. I used to make Gertie do it when she was little and we went anywhere with crowds."

She must have been growing shrill again because the sheriff nodded and said, in a gruff voice, "These tracks must stop for a reason. She's around here somewhere."

This reassurance went a long way in making her feel better, but not for long. As far as she could tell, they were several miles from the cabin by now, their path a haphazard one that followed no logical direction or destination. The only thing that was keeping her from flying into a full panic was the sheriff's promise that the footsteps didn't look hurried.

Nor were they accompanied by another set. Wherever Gertrude was going, she was going there on her own. She hadn't been kidnapped by a murderer, and she wasn't being dragged along by a man in a Bigfoot suit. That had to mean something.

Tess heard it then, the unmistakable sound of branches breaking. She jumped, sucked in a breath, and hooked her finger even tighter on the sheriff's belt loop. She'd have died rather than admit it, but she was mostly holding on because she needed to feel the heat coming off his body, the latent strength of the muscles in his back.

She needed to know she wasn't alone.

"There," the sheriff whispered, pointing some distance through the woods. "I see something."

Tess saw what he was indicating. She made a motion to bound joyfully forward—it was Gertrude! she was safe!—when she realized they were looking at not one, not two, but three small, dog-like animals snuffling and sniffling at something on the ground.

"Don't you dare say baby cougars," the sheriff said. "Those are coyotes, clear as the nose on my face."

"What are they doing?" Tess asked, but there was no need to voice the question aloud. One of the coyotes looked up at the sound of voices, a hunk of something fleshy and red dangling from its mouth. "Oh, no. No, no, no. Not—"

The sound of a gunshot caused Tess to scream. If she'd been paying attention, she'd have noticed that the sheriff had extracted his gun and pointed it toward the sky, but she'd been so fixed on the feasting animals that she hadn't been paying attention.

"I thought shooting your gun came with mountains of paperwork," she said, but not without a grateful underscore to her voice.

"Sometimes, the paperwork is worth it," he said grimly and started jogging toward the area where the coyotes had been eating. The sound of the gunshot had scattered them in every direction, leaving Tess with a clear view and an even clearer field.

Not that she needed to draw all the way up to know what she was looking at. The scattered remains of the scavenged meal were clear for anyone to see.

That was a dead body. A human one. And this time, Tess easily recognized who it was—or rather, she *would* have, had the world not suddenly opened up underneath her before going black.

Tess woke up to a slap on the face.

Okay, so it was more of a gentle tap, followed by a gruff, "Get *up*, woman," but the idea was the same. She came to awareness—and immediately wished herself somewhere else.

Anywhere else.

"I can't move my leg. I think you broke it." The sheriff groaned as Tess rolled off his body. His quick intake of breath indicated that she hadn't moved as gently as she'd thought, but that was hardly her fault. From the look of things, they were in a deep dirt hole that didn't provide much in the way of space. The sheriff's solid mass had cushioned her fall, but the way his foot twisted at a sickening angle indicated that his own descent hadn't been nearly as pleasant.

"Oh, no." Tess winced as the sheriff took hold of his knee and attempted to shift his leg to a more comfortable position. "How bad is it?"

"Bad." He grunted. "You fell like a bag of rocks."

"As opposed to what? A bag of feathers?" Panic made Tess's voice louder than she intended.

"I don't suppose you count emergency first aid in your long list of accolades?" the sheriff asked. He clicked his tongue as soon as he saw how white her face was. She could repair a cut with the best of them, and she made the whole family get their CPR certification every year, but broken bones had always made her nauseous. There was something so uncanny about them, so *wrong*. "Never mind. I'll live."

"Are you sure about that?" Tess couldn't help asking. She pointed upward, toward the circle of leaves and sky and the mangled body that they hadn't quite reached before falling in the hole. "Was that—"

The sheriff nodded. "Carl," he said, his mouth a flat line.

He scooted back toward the dirt wall of their hole, his broken leg extended. He was so tall that he had to crook his knee to fit, and even then, Tess was practically on top of him. There was no way he could be comfortable right now, but he didn't murmur a word of complaint. Only the quiet way he held himself, his breathing careful and labored, indicated just how badly he must be hurt.

"I guess we finally found him," the sheriff said. "Or, rather, Gertrude did. That explains why her footsteps stopped."

Tess didn't cry out, even though every part of her soul wanted to scream. She bit down on her lip instead, so hard the metallic tang of blood rose to her tongue. Seeing that carnage with her own two eyes was bad enough...to know that her daughter had also witnessed it, and with no one to shield her, was almost too much to bear.

"She's a smart kid," the sheriff said, still in that gruff way. "She probably saw the same thing as us and immediately turned back. She'll go for help as soon as she reaches the cabin."

"She's a smart kid, but she's still a *kid*," Tess countered. "How do you know she can find her way back?"

The sheriff hunched one of his powerful shoulders. "She has to. I don't know how else we're getting out of this hole. Do you think you can climb?"

For the first time, Tess registered where they were—*really* registered it, taking in the vertical dirt walls and impossibly far-off sky. To avoid unnecessarily jostling Sheriff Boyd, she got to her feet as gently as she could, but it wasn't easy. The hole was much deeper than it was wide, the walls so fragile that the moment she reached for a handhold, a cascade of loose soil came down over the heads.

"I'm not sure I should be poking at this," Tess said, spitting the taste of dirt from her mouth. "It's really unstable. Too much movement, and the whole thing could collapse in on us."

"Then please don't. We'll have to cross our fingers and hope for an airlift."

Tess had heard of sinkholes in places like Florida and Texas, where high levels of precipitation ate away at the ground from inside, but never here. Besides, this hole was so deep—so oddly placed next to Carl's body—that she knew there was nothing natural about the way it had been built. Even more to the point, several large fern fronds littered the dirt around them. Unless she was very much mistaken, those had been used to cover up the hole and had fluttered down when they had.

"Have we been booby trapped?" Tess asked.

To her surprise, the sheriff laughed. There was a smattering of dirt in his hair that she longed to brush away, but she didn't think he'd appreciate her maternal solicitude. He looked as though he was barely holding on as it was.

"I was going to suggest deliberate and malicious injury, but yeah, booby trap works." He closed his eyes and carefully rested his head against the wall of their hole.

"Does it hurt *very* badly?" Tess asked.

His eyes flew open. "What? Oh—my leg. It's not my

favorite thing, but I've suffered worse. I was just trying to remember what I saw before we fell."

"*Worse?*" Tess echoed. She couldn't imagine much worse than having a hundred-and-sixty pound woman falling several feet to land on your leg and crack it in half. Then again, there was whatever happened to Carl's body up there to account for...

"Gunshot. Two of them." He waved off her next question and ordered her to close her eyes instead. "I don't know how long Carl's been out here, but there's no way coyotes were responsible for that mess. *Think*, Tess. Use that annoyingly photographic memory. What did you see?"

Tess felt her stomach heave, but she did as the sheriff asked—partly because his leg was broken and he needed the distraction and partly because he'd used her first name. There was something powerful about the way it rolled off his tongue, as though it were a plea and a command rolled up in one.

Closing her eyes, she did her best to conjure up the scene above them.

"The area in front of him was flat—too flat. No natural shrubs or ferns. Someone dug this hole and then covered it up with leaves and branches, but it wasn't done well. They assumed we'd be distracted by the body and fall without noticing."

"No conjectures," he grunted. "Just facts."

She opened one eye. "I'm not wrong."

"I didn't say you were. But the longer you sit there arguing with me, the less you're going to remember. The first five minutes after an incident occurs are the most important for recall."

"I know that," she muttered, but she took a deep breath and tried again. "There were three coyotes, all of them eating. They must have just gotten here, because they were hungry. Ravenous, almost. They didn't kill him. Something else did. They were only scavenging after the fact."

"No conjectures."

"I can't help it!" She did her best to put her writer brain away, but it was never far from the surface. Besides, the more she brought that scene up above to mind, the more she couldn't shake a certain, terrible feeling...

"They weren't the first animals here. No—it's not conjecture. Hear me out. Carl's body had been...mauled. And by something large. I did a lot of research for *Fury on the Mountain*, including looking at pictures of large cat kills. There's a distinct pattern to the way each kind of predator leaves its prey. So, unless we're dealing with a crazed psychotic killer with a machete—which, given how Wilma was killed, isn't likely—I think we're looking at an animal attack."

The sheriff was eerily silent, so Tess risked opening her eyes. She was half afraid that he'd passed out or—worse— fallen victim to an undiagnosed concussion, but he was staring at her with knit brows.

"You saw it, too," she said. "You believe me."

She suddenly looked around the walls of their hole, at how rudimentary it was, how easy it would be to escape if the sheriff wasn't currently nursing a broken leg. Under any other circumstances, he could have easily hoisted Tess onto his shoulders and lifted her out the top. In fact, the sheriff was so tall that he might have even had a chance to get out on his own.

"This isn't a booby trap for us, is it?" Tess asked, her mouth suddenly dry.

"No, Ms. Harrow. I don't think it is."

"It's a booby trap for a—"

The sheriff interrupted before she could say the word aloud. "Tiger."

Chapter Twenty-One

Darkness had been descending for several hours now—and, with it, the growing suspicion that the two of them would die inside this hole. Not of dehydration or even exposure, but of a tiger falling on their heads.

It was pure conjecture, of course. There had been no signs of a tiger roaming the forest that Tess could call to mind, and she liked to think that anyone running an animal smuggling ring would take extra precautions with such a large and dangerous species, but all the pieces were there.

Random animals running through the forest, most likely fleeing from a predator.

A large and messy kill that looked unlike anything she had seen before.

A huge, baited trap from which there was no escape.

No sooner had Sheriff Boyd said the word aloud than he immediately tried to take it back, but some things were impossible to undo. A tiger unleashed into the wilderness of Tess's imagination was one of them.

She shuddered and forced herself to focus on the man she was practically sitting on top of. The sheriff's increasing annoyance at their situation—and at her—was preferable to thoughts about their inevitable deaths. Of that she was sure.

"Where did you get shot?" she asked, since it was the only topic she could think of that didn't involve enormous teeth and even more enormous claws.

Or Gertrude, all alone out there and wondering where she was.

"Physically or geographically?" he asked.

"Both," she said, pleased to find him playing along. "And if you say it's in the right thigh..."

His body shook with a slight laugh. "I was shot well before your silly detective, and no. I've got one hole in the shoulder and another in my flank. Surprisingly enough, the shoulder hurt more."

"Can I ask—?"

"No." He paused and sighed. "Okay, fine. Who shot me? How did it happen? What were my exact thoughts on the nature of death, and what did the blood spatter look like?"

"I was going to ask how long ago it happened, but the rest of those are good questions, too."

It was too dark to see much beyond the outline of the sheriff's face, but something in him tensed. "I was shot by my sister's boyfriend. She disappeared one night when we were both teenagers, and he held me accountable for it. I didn't think about death so much as how I was going to find her with a couple of holes in me, and I don't recall the blood spatter. I'm sure there are photos of it on record somewhere if you really want to know."

"Oh."

"Though the blood probably looked much like you imagined it did. Murder scenes are the one thing you always get right."

Tess could only blink in wonder at how honest the sheriff was being. Never, in her wildest dreams, did she imagine he could be so forthcoming. Perhaps it was the sense of impending doom, or maybe he was just bored—

"I know you've been looking into it, but I'd prefer if you didn't dredge everything up and set the town talking. Whatever you want to know, just save us both the trouble and ask."

This was an awful lot of information for Tess to suddenly wade through. She wasn't sure where to start, so she latched onto the most important part.

"Did they find her?" she asked quietly. "Your sister?"

The sheriff gave a small start of surprise. "No, they didn't, and they stopped looking after a few weeks. They found a bus ticket for Seattle and assumed she'd split town. She was written off as a runaway."

Tess found herself nodding along. That fit with the story she knew so far—of everything she knew about this man. A young Victor Boyd had left Winthrop at sixteen and moved to Seattle. He'd taken up law enforcement and was rigidly good at it. He'd finally found the nerve to return to his hometown, but he wasn't the same man, and people resented him for it. He was too reserved and too gruff, too determined to see every case solved the way his sister's never had been.

It would have made for an amazing backstory if it wasn't so painfully tragic.

"I'm sorry," she said. "That must have been terrible. You were so young."

Tess had no way of explaining what happened next. Either

her hand found his, or his hand came seeking hers, because their fingers were suddenly entwined. She'd always known that intense emergencies bonded people, and that those who suffered trauma together became linked in ways that defied reason, but she'd assumed a man like Sheriff Boyd would be exempt.

She also felt how small this hole was. The warmth of their bodies, the press of the sheriff's leg against hers...it was impossible not to feel it. To feel *him*.

"How did you know I was looking into your past?" she asked.

His hand slipped out of hers as easily as it had slipped in. "You're not exactly the most subtle woman in the world," he said. "I heard about your trip to the library. You should be more careful about what you're doing...and who you trust to help you do it."

That got Tess's attention. She sat up straighter. "You don't mean Nicki, do you?"

His silence was all the answer she needed. Bursting into a peal of laughter, she said, "She's a librarian who loves Cervantes and drives a bookmobile. She's not running an animal smuggling ring and digging elaborate traps to catch a tiger in the woods."

"How do you know that?"

Tess paused. She knew Nicki was innocent the same way she knew that Mason Peabody wasn't to be trusted. She knew Nicki was her friend the same way she knew that she liked Sheriff Boyd a lot more than was good for her.

"It's what I do for a living," she said, knowing her words

were inadequate but unsure how else to say it. "Finding what motivates people, what drives them. Digging deep until I know their character arc."

The sheriff chuffed a short, disbelieving breath. "And hers is that she's just an innocent, well-educated librarian who decided to move to the middle of nowhere to ramble around in a refurbished truck? And who happily throws herself into the first murder mystery that falls her way? That's the whole story that you, in your vast wisdom, have given her?"

Tess swallowed heavily. When he put it that way, it did seem lackluster. *Poor character development*, her editor would call it. *A real Mary Sue*, the critics would say. *I paid thirty bucks for this?* would come the collective screech from the Amazon reviews.

"There's more to her than that," Tess protested. "Nicki takes genuine interest in everyone around here. She's practically an encyclopedia when it comes to what people are reading—and what's happening in their lives."

"Exactly."

Tess didn't pretend to misunderstand him. "She's also the one who discovered all the missing library books about exotic animals."

"Ah, yes. The mysterious library thefts. I was wondering when we'd get to those. Tell me, if you please, who, in this day and age, uses *books* to research anything?"

Tess swallowed and stared at the dark shape of Sheriff Boyd's slumped body. It was a fair point, but there was no way she was going to admit it. She also wasn't going to mention how Nicki had helped her break into Wilma Eyre's mobile home. Or how Nicki's mobility—her job was literally to wander the woods without question—gave her the perfect alibi for just about everything.

She didn't need to. The sheriff already knew. He knew, and he wasn't going to stop until Tess admitted it.

"That's preposterous," she said. It was the closest thing to a concession as she was willing to get. "What could her motivation possibly be?"

"The same thing that anyone smuggling tigers and toucans through the woods of central Washington across the Canadian border would conceivably want. Money. I did my research, Tess, just like you knew I would. Wildlife trafficking can be a highly lucrative career for a criminal with the right connections. There are private collectors and research facilities that will pay a pretty penny for an animal in good condition."

Tess shook her head. She refused to believe that Nicki had any part of this. Granted, now that the sheriff had pointed it out, it *was* odd than an erudite and well-dressed woman with a vast store of knowledge and a great sense of humor would choose to live in a place like this, but Tess liked to think that she was all those things, too.

Well, with the exception of the well-dressed part.

"It wasn't Nicki. It was Mason. You and Ivy said so."

"The devil we did."

Tess had to take a deep breath and cast her memory back. Remembering, she amended her statement. "Well, maybe not you, but Ivy. That day of the parade—she told me your primary suspect would be there. Lo and behold, Mason

Peabody came driving through the center of town like he owned it."

"Mason Peabody owns a million-dollar logging company and half the town's retail properties. He's also a highly visible member of the community and has political aspirations. You really think he'd risk all that for a king cobra side hustle?"

Tess opened her mouth and closed it again, unable to believe what she was hearing. Actually, she *was* able to believe it, which was the whole problem. Especially since Nicki had been present that day at the parade, too.

"No," she insists. "It fits—I know it does. Mason's a smarmy, greedy entrepreneur who's trying to run you out of town. Maybe his business is in trouble. Maybe he's only smuggling animals to humiliate you."

"He killed a woman with direct ties to his own company and threw her body in a nearby pond because he wants to be a small-town sheriff *that* badly?" Sheriff Boyd made a rough tsking sound. "Please. If you tried to pull off that kind of garbage in one of your books, your career would be over, and you know it. No one would believe it."

The fact that his words carried nothing but the truth didn't make them sting any less.

"Then what's your grand theory?" she countered. "That Nicki moved here undercover as a mobile librarian to run exotic animals over the border? And she recruited the help of a female logger friend she may or may not have been having an affair with, who accidentally died when…what? The tiger they were smuggling bit off her head?"

The sheriff didn't say a word, but he didn't need to. Tess

was on a roll. By Nicki's own admission, it wasn't unusual for a woman to have a social life around here, even with the slim pickings. What were the chances that Nicki wasn't as celibate as she'd pretended to be?

"Of course, then she'd have to dispose of Wilma's body so no one could trace it back to her…or to the tiger. A local uninhabited cabin would be the perfect spot for it—and she could make it suspicious by removing Wilma's hands so it looked like a professional hit." Tess sucked in a sudden, sharp breath. This wasn't half bad, actually. "Only she didn't know I was moving to town so soon—or that Zach Peabody would use the cabin's pond for blast fishing—so the body turned up before she expected it to.

"And now that she's down her partner, she's having a hard time keeping the animals under control, so they're escaping left and right. The only way she can collect them is to dress up as Bigfoot and stalk the forest trying to tranquilize them. Except, when push comes to shove, you can't tranquilize a tiger. Not easily. If Carl happened to see Nicki stalking through the forest hunting for the animal, he'd have chased her down. Which—oh, jeez—would explain why Nicki was the one to rescue Gertie and me from the roof of the cabin, because she was there and knew we were trapped."

Tess was starting to feel dizzy with possibility, but she didn't stop. She couldn't. This was good stuff.

She closed her eyes and leaned back, ticking each thought off on a finger as she continued working through the plot.

"So, that puts Carl out in the forest with the tiger while Nicki is coming to my rescue. She plays the hero while poor

Carl is left to the animal's mercy. The tiger attacked him and dragged the kill here so he could return and feast another time. Tigers do that, you know. If they can find a safe space to hide their food, they'll come back to finish their meal—a thing Nicki would know because she has all those books on exotic animals that she took from the library without checking them out. Nicki realized that the only way she'd be able to catch the tiger is to dig a trap next to Carl's body and hope the tiger fell in. Only he didn't. We did."

By the time Tess was done, her heart was thumping. She knew, in that moment, that she'd just written her best book yet. Her solution was so ridiculously outlandish—but with enough plausibility—that no one would see the ending coming.

"Well?" she demanded. "Is that it?"

To her dismay, the sheriff didn't answer. She scowled and nudged him with her elbow.

"Come on—you can say it. I'm right, aren't I? You didn't want to believe me about the animal smuggling ring, but since we're literally sitting inside a tiger trap, you can't pretend anymore."

Despite the growing irritation in her voice, the sheriff didn't respond. Alarmed now, Tess struggled to her knees, but she'd been sitting still for so long that both her legs had fallen asleep. They wavered underneath her, but she braced herself on the dirt wall and leaned close.

"Sheriff Boyd?" she called, panic rising in her throat. "Victor? Are you all right?"

Nothing. She was close enough now to detect how pale

his face was, how tightly drawn the lines around his mouth. Lifting a hand to his forehead, she felt the clammy chill of his skin and cursed softly.

"Oh, for crying out loud," she muttered. "It's just like a man to pretend he's fine when he's in shock and knocking on death's door."

Then she did the only thing she could think of in a situation like this one.

She screamed bloody murder.

Chapter Twenty-Two

TESS WASN'T SURE HOW TO FEEL WHEN NICKI NICKERSON came to her rescue.

Her first thought at seeing that familiar face hanging upside-down over the top of the hole was one of unadulterated relief—especially since Sheriff Boyd had yet to do more than flutter his long eyelashes. But then she remembered the theory rattling around in her head and immediately tensed.

This marked the second time Nicki had come to her timely rescue. While she appreciated the opportunity to get out of this hole, she didn't appreciate the implication.

One rescue could be written off as a lucky chance. Two was downright suspicious.

"Oh, thank everything that's good and holy," Nicki said. The sun had started to rise by now, a soft glow surrounding the librarian like a halo. "We found you."

"We?" Tess echoed, but there was no need to ask. A sea of other familiar faces popped into her line of vision. Ivy and the two additional deputies from that first night in her cabin, and a man who looked like a paramedic—Tess had never been so happy to see so many uniforms in her life. "Please hurry. The sheriff is in shock. His leg is broken, and he's passed out. The break is bad enough as it is, but I'm scared he also hurt something internal."

She didn't dare move from her position. After her first bout of screaming had failed, she'd decided she was much better off doing her best to keep the sheriff comfortable. He now lay with his head in her lap as she murmured the same kind of soft nothings that had soothed Gertrude as a young child.

Although she'd done her best to quell all thoughts of Gertrude—and what might have happened to her—they came roaring back now with a vengeance.

"Gertie?" she asked as the squawk of several radios came on all at once. Calls for an airlift, a halt to the search party, and a coroner's van warred with one another. "Did you find her? Is she—?"

"Safe and sound back at the cabin, don't you worry," Nicki said. There was so much kindness in her voice that Tess had a hard time believing she was anything but a friend. "A little shaken up, but she'll be better now that you and the sheriff have been found."

Relief flooded through Tess in such a powerful wave that she burst into tears. She'd sat in this hole for hours, cold and scared and clutching an unconscious man, without tearing up even once. Knowing that her daughter was okay, that she'd *be* okay, was the thing that broke her.

Especially once she glanced up to find even more people starting to make plans to evacuate her and the sheriff.

"If she's at the cabin, and you're all here, who's staying with her?" she demanded, dashing angrily at her tears with the back of her hand. They better not have left a fourteen-year-old child on her own in that place. Not when there was a freaking *tiger* roaming around at large. "Please tell me you didn't leave her there alone."

Ivy was the first to answer. "Oh, she's not alone," she said, and something about the grim line of her mouth set Tess on her guard.

And a good thing, too, because Ivy's next words almost caused the world to open up and swallow her all over again.

"Your ex-husband is with her—and if you ask me, he's none too happy about it."

Chapter Twenty-Three

"HAVE YOU LOST YOUR EVER-LOVING MIND?"

Quentin looked the picture of paternal outrage in a wrinkled suit, his tie hanging loose around his neck and his hair yanked up to stand on end. He attacked Tess the moment she limped, weary and wary, across the threshold to the cabin.

Tess ignored him. "Where is she?"

The *she* in question came running through the back door, her eyes rimmed red from tears and a lack of sleep. The moment she saw Tess, she cried out and ran forward with her arms outstretched.

"Don't be mad at me, Mom. I'm sorry I ran away. I'll never do it again."

Any desire Tess might have had to recriminate her daughter for causing so much trouble dissolved in that moment. She crushed the warm, sobbing body to her chest and held her. Gertrude sagged into the embrace in ways that Tess remembered from her infancy, as though her daughter wouldn't be happy until she was once again a part of her body—sharing her blood and her oxygen, taking up the same physical space.

"It's okay, Gertie-pie. I'm not mad. I'm just glad you're okay. I'm glad everything is okay."

The words were meant as comfort—and if the way

Gertrude sniffled and calmed down was any indication, they worked—but Tess couldn't help but acknowledge the lie. Everything *wasn't* okay, and Quentin's grim expression proved it.

"How could you let a child—*my* child—wander off into the woods alone like that?" he demanded. "Not to mention living in this hell-hole in the first place. Murder, Tess? People being slaughtered in the backyard? What are you thinking?"

Even though Tess knew it was the wrong thing to say, she felt the tart words spring to her tongue. "I don't know what you've heard, but the woman wasn't slaughtered here. Her body was just dumped in the pond."

Quentin's eyes bulged. He'd always had a googly-eyed stare, more like a dehydrated carp than a man, but Tess had never realized how prominent it was before.

"I'm just saying." Tess shifted uncomfortably. "No actual crimes have been committed on these premises. And we've had police protection the whole time."

Quentin snorted. "Some protection."

Tess could feel Gertrude stiffening in her arms. The memory of their argument was still fresh in her mind—the way Gertrude had howled at her father's abandonment, how she blamed Tess for it—so she forced herself to breathe deep. No matter what it might cost her, she wouldn't fight with her ex-husband. Not in front of their daughter.

"You're right," she said. "This is no place for a child. I'm sorry to have put Gertie in harm's way."

"Mom!" Gertrude shook off Tess's embrace. Anger started to peek through her red-rimmed eyes. "I was never *in* harm's way. I needed to cool off, so I took a walk. People do it all the time. I didn't know I was going to run into...*that*."

"Of course you didn't," Tess soothed, but Quentin interrupted her before she could say more.

"I'm having Gertie pack her bags. There's no way I'm letting you keep her here another night."

Tess closed her eyes and counted to ten, but it did little to quell the rising tide of her anger. Let her? Since when did Quentin *let* her do anything? When he'd been MIA for six months? When the only way she even knew he was still alive was the regularity with which he cashed his palimony checks?

"Of course," she murmured. To the outside, it sounded like she was meekly agreeing, but anyone who knew her better would understand that she couldn't raise her voice any louder than that. If she did, there was a good chance it would crack—that *she* would crack. "You two should check into the hotel for a bit. You'll be much more comfortable there."

"I'm not taking her to some blasted hotel. We're going back to Seattle. We're going *home*."

Tess glanced at Gertrude to see how she was taking Quentin's sudden lapse into concerned paternity. She should have been ashamed of how happy she was to see that sullen, ironclad look of rebellion, but she wasn't. Gertrude wouldn't go down without a fight.

"No."

Quentin gave a start of surprise. "I beg your pardon?"

"You don't get to tell me what to do, *Quentin*," Gertrude said coldly, emphasizing the use of her father's given name.

"I'm not going to Seattle, and I'm not going to the hotel. I'm staying here to take care of Mom." Without pausing for breath, she turned to Tess and added, "It was Carl, wasn't it? Out there in the woods? All eaten up?"

Tess made a frantic motion for Gertrude to change the subject, but it was too late.

"Eaten up?" Quentin roared. Followed almost immediately by, "Who's Carl?"

Tess's legs finally gave way underneath her. The paramedics at the scene had wanted to take her to the hospital the next town over for observation, but she'd signed a release waiver so she could get to the cabin as quickly as possible. Unfortunately, the fall into the hole and the hours of holding an unconscious Sheriff Boyd and her *stupid ex-husband* were conspiring against her.

"Whoa, there." Quentin's arms were around her almost at once. His arms were so familiar, the low hush of his voice so much a part of her, that she could only sag against him. "Are you okay?"

"It's fine," she said. "I'm fine. They gave me some IV fluids before they let me go, but I'm still feeling a little weak. It was a long night."

Gertrude dashed to the kitchen and poured out a tall glass of lemonade. Quentin walked Tess to the couch and coaxed her down onto it. It hadn't been Tess's intention to play the victim card, but he looked genuinely alarmed for her, his movements gentle in a way she remembered all too well from the early days of their marriage.

She sighed and allowed herself to bask in the sensation

of being cherished, however temporarily. All evidence to the contrary, she and Quentin had been in love once upon a time. Young and full of plans for the future, her imagination and his ambition combining to create a formidable pair. They used to spend hours wrapped in one another's arms, talking and not talking as the mood struck, never needing to say what they both knew loud and clear in their hearts.

More than anything else, that was what she missed. Not having someone to empty the dishwasher or a warm body to reach for late in the night, but someone who knew her. Someone who saw her for who she really was...and who didn't balk at what he found.

Something like a sob must have escaped her because Quentin's voice turned soft with concern. "What *happened* out there, Tess?" he asked.

She shook her head, unwilling to give voice to all the things she was thinking and feeling. Chief among them was the overpowering desire to sleep, but she refused to do that until she and Quentin figured out what to do with Gertrude. He'd come at a terrible time, it was true, but maybe he was right. Maybe Seattle was the best place—

"Wait a minute." Tess sat up with a jolt and shook off Quentin's comforting arm. "What are you doing here? How did you know we were staying at my grandfather's cabin?"

Quentin looked so startled by this sudden line of questioning that he could only blink. Not that it mattered; Gertrude was ready with both the answer and Tess's glass of lemonade.

"I told him where we were," she said. "The last time I

stayed with Tommy and Timmy, I used their internet to send him an email. I thought he might get worried if he tried to text me and didn't get a response."

It was such a sweet and simple answer that Tess felt what remained of her strength give way. Quentin's ready flush brought it back again.

Tess could read that look as easily as other people read a book title. He might have come here because of the email, but he hadn't worried and he *definitely* hadn't texted.

"My phone's been really glitchy lately," he lied, not quite able to meet Tess's eyes. "I thought it would be best if I came down right away and rescued Gertie from...this."

This statement was accompanied by a disdainful sweep of his gaze around the cabin. Tess wasn't surprised to find that it didn't meet his fastidious standards, but she *was* surprised that he didn't offer a snide comment to go along with it.

Maybe the divorce had taught him a thing or two about taking things for granted.

"I'm glad you came, but there's no way I'm leaving," Gertrude said in a tone that brooked no argument. "Tommy and Timmy are cool, and I like the weird, old-timey downtown. What if I promised to go the hotel with you? Like Mom suggested? You'll like it here, I promise. We can go mountain biking together."

Tess didn't have the heart to suggest what she was really thinking: that both Quentin and the bikes she and Gertrude had rented could go into the pond, for all she cared. Not when her ex-husband had come all this way. Not when

Gertrude so obviously wanted him to stay. Only extreme desperation would get that child to willingly agree to bicycle up a mountain.

"You want to go out riding with me?" Quentin asked. He pushed his tortoiseshell glasses up his nose. "Really? This is supposed to be one of the best places in the state for it. I've been trying to get your mother to come here for years."

It was true. If there was one thing Quentin loved in this world, it was mountain biking. He liked the speed and the danger, the way it took several hours to go up a mountain only to whiz down in a matter of minutes. He'd mentioned the possibility of staying in her grandfather's cabin a few times over the years, but the timing had never worked out.

"You could get a bike from Tommy and Timmy's shop," Gertrude said. "They have maps of this whole area—even a few towns over, where there haven't been any dead bodies."

Mentioning the dead bodies was a mistake, but Tess could see Quentin struggling with himself. He *wanted* to stay, as much as he might hate to admit it. And Gertrude, never one to miss an opportunity, knew it.

"Please, Daddy?" she begged, reverting to a childlike plea. "It would make this the best vacation ever. Way better than the time Mom dragged us on that whale-watching tour in the pouring rain. Remember? We were out there for *hours*, and all we saw was one stupid porpoise."

That clinched it. Quentin, with gleeful memories of Tess's failure in his head and Gertrude's pleading eyes in front of him, gave in.

"Your father is more than welcome to take you to stay in town, but the biking is going to have to wait," Tess said. Gertrude opened her mouth to argue, but Tess held up a hand. "I'm serious. There's a good chance that whatever animal attacked and killed Carl is still wandering around out there. No one's going anywhere near the forest until its caught."

"But I—" Gertrude began, but it was no use. If mentioning the dead body put Quentin on his guard, introducing animal attacks into the conversation downright floored him.

"You mean Gertie wasn't exaggerating about that?" His throat worked anxiously up and down. "A man was actually eaten out there? By what? A bear?"

Tess took a deep breath and did her best *not* to conjure up the image of Carl's final moments, but it was impossible. She doubted a thing like that would ever fully leave her.

"Something like that," she said, unwilling to introduce a tiger into the conversation when Quentin was already up in arms. "It's the strangest thing. According to Sheriff Boyd, the man who died—one of his deputies—grew up in these woods. If anyone should have been able to avoid being attacked by a wild animal, it was him."

As soon as she spoke the words aloud, she realized how true they were. Granted, she'd never gone head-to-head with an escaped tiger before, but Carl must surely have noticed the tracks of such a large animal—or, if not Carl, then literally anyone else who lived around here. A bobcat was a small, wily thing, and toucans could be mistaken for crows by someone who wasn't an avid outdoorsman. But tigers were as visible and unusual as, say, Bigfoot. Someone must surely have reported a sighting by now.

"Why are you looking at me like that?" Quentin asked.

Tess shook her head to clear it. "I'm not looking at you. I'm lost in my thoughts, that's all. Let's just say I don't think either of you should start exploring the wilderness until they figure out what happened to that poor man and leave it at that."

Gertrude was more than willing to co-sign on this plan as she began tossing items into her overnight bag. Tess noted that her daughter didn't pack *all* her things, nor did she grab Ivy's giant stack of a book, which she was pages away from finishing. Tess's heart constricted to see it. Gertrude knew, even if Quentin didn't, that this father-daughter moment wasn't likely to last long. She'd get a few days, a few laughs, and then he'd be back to forgetting about them.

This thought made her reach for her daughter and hold her much more tightly than she'd planned. Instead of shrugging the embrace off, Gertrude glanced up, her sweet little face puckered with more worry than any child should have to wear.

"Are you sure you'll be okay if I leave you here alone?" Gertrude asked. "The police are busy with Carl, and you don't look so good…"

"You go have fun with your father," Tess said, fighting tears. "I'm going to take a long nap, and then head to the hospital to check on Sheriff Boyd."

"He's okay, too, isn't he?" Gertrude scanned her face. "He

didn't get hurt too bad looking for me? And he's not mad or anything?"

"Not in the slightest," Tess promised as she dropped a kiss on her daughter's forehead. She grinned and added, "And if he does decide to be mad at someone, I think we both know which one of us will get the honor."

Chapter Twenty-Four

"You brought the sheriff flowers? Bold choice."

Nicki stood in front of the hospital, one leg bent and her foot propped against the cement brick wall. She pushed herself off as soon as she noticed Tess approaching. Tess was about to comment that she hadn't noticed the blue bookmobile in the parking lot, but Nicki forestalled her with a grin.

"I don't drive it *all* the time. I have a real car." She pointed at a nondescript black SUV so covered with mud that it looked as though it had run through an off-road course on the way over. "Contrary to popular belief, I'm not always a librarian."

Nicki's appearance bore out this statement. For the first time since Tess had met her, she'd lost the retro glasses and had switched out her dangling earrings for a more sedate pair of silver studs. Even her clothes seemed more subdued than usual, a pair of black slacks paired with a pink silk blouse.

"I know." She frowned and tugged at her top. Sweat stains were starting to pool down the delicate neckline. "I had to drive all the way to Seattle this morning for a meeting. I feel like an imposter."

Tess didn't point out the obvious—that she looked and acted like one, too. Not only did her car appear as though it had gone the opposite direction of the metropolis, but there was no way Nicki should be this alert after her long night. She *said* she'd spent the whole time searching the forest for Tess and Sheriff Boyd, and Ivy's version of the story bore out that tale, but there wasn't a single bag under her eyes.

Tess, by comparison, was carrying around an entire grocery store under hers.

"Were you waiting for me?" Tess asked politely. *Too* politely, if the questioning lift of Nicki's brow was any indication. Tess forced herself to smile and add, "Or is he in a bad mood, and you're too scared to go in alone?"

Nicki relaxed. "A little of both. I was just mustering up the courage to go in but wanted to wait and see if you showed up first. I had a feeling you might. Where's Gertie?"

Tess couldn't think of any reason not to tell her. "Staying at the hotel with my ex-husband."

"Uh oh. You don't seem very happy about it."

She wasn't, but Tess didn't have the energy—or the desire—to go into details. "It's for the best. The cabin is too dangerous, and Gertie needs more attention than I can give her right now."

Nicki's look of disbelief added fuel onto the already-burning sense of guilt in the pit of Tess's stomach.

"You don't have to say it." Tess sighed. "I should have moved her away from this place the moment they pulled Wilma out of our pond."

"That's not what I was going to say."

Maybe not, but it was definitely what she thought. Along with Quentin and Ivy and pretty much every other person

Tess had talked to in the past twenty-four hours. Sheriff Boyd was the only one who'd even hinted that the cabin might be good for Gertrude. Good for them both.

Then again, he'd said that before they'd stumbled on Carl's mangled remains. A man was allowed to change his mind after an experience like that.

"What do you know about Carl?" Tess suddenly asked. Nicki might be the closest thing she had to a suspect, but she was still the best source of information on the people who lived and worked in this town.

"Carl?" Nicki echoed. "About how he died, you mean? The latest rumor is that he was killed by a tiger, but that can't possibly be true. I bet Zach and Adam Peabody made it up to mess with people."

Tess felt a blush start to rise. "Actually, Victor and I were the ones to come up with it. We had a lot of time to think while we were in that hole."

Nicki stared at her. "*Victor?* My, my. What happened down there?"

The blush spread like wildfire. *Not* because of the suggestion of romance underscoring Nicki's voice but because of the other theory she and Sheriff Boyd had floated. The one that put Nicki in the driver's seat to theft, smuggling, murder, and more. "Nothing. We had a lot of time to think, that's all. But I wasn't talking about Carl's death. I mean his life. He was super outdoorsy, right?"

"Most people of a certain age around here are. Biking in the summer, skiing in the winter, hiking all year round. I think Carl hunted, too. Why?"

Tess didn't respond. She didn't have to.

"You think there's more to his death than an animal attack, don't you?" Nicki asked.

Tess thought a lot of things, up to and including how unlikely it was that Carl would have fallen prey to a tiger without putting up one heck of a fight first. She also thought back on the location of his body, of how untouched and serene the surrounding forest had seemed. A mortal battle of man versus nature should have looked a lot more violent than that.

"But what about your exotic animal smuggling ring?"

"First of all, it's not *my* exotic animal smuggling ring," Tess protested. She may have come up with the theory, but she was hardly an expert on the practice. She'd never even had a dog; taking care of a bobcat and a flock of toucans would require a defter touch than hers. "Secondly, it's still the best answer to all this. I just wonder if maybe Carl was more involved than we think. If *I* was going to start smuggling animals into and out of Canada, I'd want a man who knew the forest like the back of his hand to help out, wouldn't you?"

Nicki stared at her with an expression that was difficult to read. Since Tess was starting to wade into murky waters—and with a woman she was no longer sure she could trust—she heaved a sigh.

"But his feet are the wrong size to be our Bigfoot, and there's no denying that *something* out there attacked him. Plus there's the whole tiger pit the sheriff and I fell into."

"A tiger pit?" Nicki's expression still held that strange, impenetrable gleam. "Is that what we're calling it?"

"What's that supposed to mean?" Tess demanded. "What else could it have been?"

Nicki turned on her heel and slipped through the automated hospital doors. Tess hurried to catch up, unwilling to let the subject drop there. By the time she reached Nicki's side, she was surprised to see a smile crinkling the edges of the librarian's eyes.

"What's so funny?" she asked.

"Oh, nothing," Nicki said and gave lie to this statement by falling into a deep, rich chuckle. "Just that no one except the illustrious Tess Harrow would fall into a deep, man-made hole next to a dead body and assume it's an elaborate trap for a five-hundred-pound jungle animal."

"As opposed to...?" Tess began, but the answer hit her the same time as the blast of air-conditioned, antiseptic-scented air.

There was only one other thing a hole like that could have been.

A grave.

———————————

If Tess could have come up with a way to get Nicki out of the hospital room so she could talk to Sheriff Boyd alone, she'd have done it in a flash. There were dozens of things she wanted to say to—and ask—the sheriff, but Nicki was watching her like a hawk.

Or a toucan, at the very least.

"I brought these to cheer you up." Tess held out the

bundle of colorful summer flowers, trying not to look as silly as she felt. "Don't bother telling me that you hate them and you don't need me to waste my money or my sentiment on you. I already know. But the nurses always appreciate the leftovers. When I was in for an appendectomy last year, I loaded them down with so many bouquets they could have opened a florist. They loved it."

"Thank you," the sheriff said and took the flowers. No argument. No fuss. As if that wasn't enough cause for alarm, he also carefully arranged the stems in a hospital-issued pitcher of water before returning his attention to his guests. "That was thoughtful, Tess. I appreciate it."

At the mention of her given name, Tess blushed. She was careful not to look over her shoulder at Nicki, but she could feel the librarian's silent laughter all the same.

"How long are you in for?" she asked, trying not to feel as discomposed as she did.

"Too long," the sheriff said with a sudden frown. "The break's not a bad one, but they want to keep me under observation for the shock."

Tess didn't like the sound of that. The longer this case dragged on, the more complicated—and deadly—it got. "That seems overly cautious, doesn't it?"

"It's protocol." The sheriff's mouth was grim. "And before you tell me that Detective Gonzales would rip out his IV and climb out that window, let me point out that I'm on the second floor. There's no way I'm jumping that far with my leg. I'd like to walk on it again someday."

"I wasn't going to say that."

Behind her, Nicki laughed—and so good-naturedly that Tess couldn't help grinning.

"I mean, I was thinking it, but I have *some* tact."

The sheriff grunted, but there was a smile lurking at the edge of his mouth. "Believe me. I don't like being trapped here any more than Detective Gonzales would. How can I be expected to solve a double murder while I'm stuck in this bed?"

"Double murder?" Tess echoed. She was surprised the sheriff was willing to discuss the case so openly in front of Nicki, but maybe that was part of his plan. To trap her into confessing or giving something away. "Is that what we're officially calling Carl's death? A murder? Not...an accident?"

"*We* aren't officially calling it anything, but yes. Carl's death was deliberate."

"But what about our tiger?"

This time, his grunt carried something darker— something *sad*. "If a tiger can tear a man apart using the same serrated knife that was used to remove Wilma's missing parts, then I'll eat this hospital gown."

Tess fell into the nearest chair. It was made of pink vinyl that crackled as she sat, but she barely registered the noise. Her senses were in too much of a whirl, all this new information flooding through her like adrenaline.

Whoever killed Wilma killed Carl, too. There is no tiger. Nicki's not under arrest. Everything I believe about this case is wrong.

"But I don't understand," Tess said aloud. "What about the animal smuggling ring?"

The only answer she got was a sympathetic cluck from Nicki. "Don't be too upset, Tess. It'll make one heck of a good Detective Gonzales story line."

The sheriff snorted. "I can't wait to see how he handles *that*. If I know anything about your detective, he'll single-handedly wrangle every last one of them even though he'd be much better off collaborating with Animal Control."

Tess looked back and forth between the sheriff and Nicki, unable to discard her theory so quickly...or to avoid the sudden, overwhelming feeling that she was being ganged up on. Okay, so the lack of a tiger or a tiger pit stretched her theory a bit thinner than she liked, but all those things the sheriff had said about Nicki last night—about how odd it was for a woman like her to live here, about how she had access to people and places that no else did—were still true. Even more to the point, Nicki was standing at the door like someone guarding it.

Though whether she was keeping Tess from leaving or another person from coming in she couldn't say.

Matters weren't cleared up any when the sheriff cleared his throat in a meaningful—and rehearsed—way. "Nicki, do you think you could give us a second?"

"Of course," she said cheerfully. "Want me to grab you anything from the vending machine while I'm out there?"

"I'm good, thanks."

Nicki waggled her eyebrows suggestively at Tess as she left the room. She was also careful to shut the door behind her and make sure it latched. Tess felt a perverse desire to beg Nicki to stay, but that was ridiculous. She'd wanted this opportunity to talk to the sheriff alone, to demand answers, to share theories, to—

"So," he said in what was his longest and slowest drawl yet. "I hear your ex-husband has arrived in town."

"Quentin?" Tess shook her head to clear it. Of everything they needed to discuss, *that* was the thing he wanted to focus on? "Yeah. He came to see Gertrude, but that's not important. Did you know that Nicki was the one to rescue us from that hole?"

The sheriff stiffened slightly. "Yes. I've been fully briefed by Ivy."

"Don't you think it's odd?" Tess scooted her chair closer and lowered her voice, careful lest Nicki be listening at the door. "That *she* should be the one to discover us? And did you notice what she's wearing today? Said she drove straight here from Seattle, but you should see her car. It's dirty and splotched and—"

The sheriff didn't let her finish. Taking her hand in a firm grip, he said, "Tess, I need you to be frank with me. Is your ex here to try and win you back?"

Tess blinked down at Sheriff Boyd—at Victor—her heart suddenly listing left and right. "Don't you want to hear what Nicki has been up to?"

"I'm fully aware of Nicki's actions as of late. *Yours*, however…" His eyes, always so dark, suddenly seemed to extract all the light from the room. "I need you to tell me whether or not he's here to repair your marriage before I say or do something I'll regret."

She tried to yank her hand back only to find that Sheriff

Boyd was a much stronger man than she gave him credit for. The way he clutched her—the way he *looked* at her—was almost desperate.

"How many pain medications are you on?" she demanded.

"Enough. Too many. That's not the point." From the way Victor tried to shake his head to clear it, Tess knew he'd been hitting the pain meds harder than he wanted her to think. "This isn't easy for me, you know. I'm not like other men. I can't…"

He trailed off and took a deep breath, determined to try again.

"Be honest with me," he said. "You and your…Quentin. Is it possible he still has romantic feelings for you?"

"I doubt it. He's the one who walked out, not the other way around. He left me for a younger woman."

Victor didn't appear to put much stock in this. "But he's back now."

"To see *Gertie*."

His look of disbelief said it all—if Quentin had wanted to see Gertrude, he could have done it any time these past six months, and with Tess's full blessing. It was only now that she was showing signs of moving on with her life that Quentin had resurfaced. She wished she could disabuse Victor of his fears, but she couldn't. Not when Quentin had been so good with Gertrude back at the cabin.

And, she was forced to admit, with *her*.

"It's not what you think," she protested, but it sounded feeble to her own ears. "My relationship with Quentin is… complicated."

"Complicated how?"

Tess wasn't sure what to say. Part of her—the part currently being squeezed by Victor's hot, hard grasp—wanted to reassure him that her heart was one hundred percent unattached. Unfortunately, the rest of her was too sensible for that. After everything she and Quentin had been through together—the cheating and the fighting, the divorce and the ensuing six months of silence—her heart would never be a hundred percent anything.

"He's Gertrude's father," she managed. It wasn't even remotely close to what she wanted to say, but she didn't know how else to explain the situation.

Just like that, Victor let go of her hand. His fingers slid from her grasp and he lay back against his pillow. With his eyes closed and all the blood drained from his features, he looked, for the first time, as exhausted as Tess felt.

All of Tess's motherly instincts—and, if she was being honest, some decidedly *non*-motherly ones—came rushing to the surface. She reached for him, but Nicki returned to the room before she could make contact.

Nicki saw the way Tess snatched her hand back and raised a knowing brow. This, almost as much as the flustered way all the heat rushed to the surface of Tess's skin, helped her focus on the maternal side of her emotions.

"You stupid man." Tess fluffed his pillow and yanked his blanket up to his chin. "Did you get any rest at all since they hauled you in here?"

He didn't open his eyes. "I thought about it, but, between snapping my bones back into place and then throwing me into every MRI and CT scan they could find, there hasn't been time."

"Did they decide you have a concussion on top of everything?" Nicki asked sympathetically from the foot of the bed.

The sheriff grunted in confirmation. Tess was just wiping a lock of hair from his forehead—more of those strictly motherly instincts—when his hand came up and gripped around her wrist. His hold was so tight and so deliberate that she thought, at first, that he was going to fling her hand away. But then he tugged, forcing Tess's head down.

With his lips just inches from her ear, he whispered, "The ship is closer to harbor than you think."

Tess blinked down, startled by the vehemence of his words, but the power of the painkillers finally took over. She was barely back to a standing position before his gentle snores pushed both her and Nicki out the door.

Chapter Twenty-Five

"WELL, THAT WAS INTERESTING." AS SOON AS NICKI AND Tess stepped outside the hospital, Nicki attacked with the full force of an inquisitive librarian who lived inside other people's business. "What did Sheriff Boyd say to make you turn that shade of pink?"

"I don't know what you're talking about."

Nicki laughed. "It's a shame you don't write romance novels. I've always thought Sheriff Boyd would make the perfect smoldering hero."

This was going too far, even for someone with Tess's imagination. "He's a middle-aged curmudgeon who upholds rigid and outdated ideals regarding just about everything."

"Yeah, he is. Bow chicka wow wow."

"Nicki! He thinks of me as a meddling nuisance who doesn't know the first thing about law enforcement or life."

Nicki put a hand over her heart and gave a mock swoon. "Enemies to lovers. My favorite trope."

"Enemies to slightly-less-antagonistic enemies, you mean." Even though Tess knew the librarian wasn't to be trusted, she couldn't help giving in. *This* was what she'd meant when she wished for more female friendships. Someone to bounce ideas off of. Someone to make light of everyday troubles. "If you must know, he didn't actually make a move on me. He just hinted that he might want to at some point in the future."

"Oh, wow. What did you say?"

Tess shrugged. "Nothing, really. The pain meds were starting to take over by that point. He probably didn't mean any of it."

"Or maybe he meant every word, but it took a highly drugged state for him to admit it."

Tess felt a thrill move through her—both of delight and of the realization that Nicki had hit on another great plot point. Maybe Willow and Detective Gonzales could fall down a ravine together. A broken arm and a few doses of morphine later, and he'd be putty in her hands...

Tess was recalled to her surroundings by Nicki's sudden cough.

"What about the other thing you two talked about?" she asked as she started to move toward their cars.

Tess did her best not to look as alarmed as she felt. "What other thing?"

"What he said when I came back into the room—I didn't hear everything, but it sounded like he was talking about a ship. What ship? Do you think they're smuggling the animals by sea as well as over the border?"

Nicki must have been listening *very* hard to pick up that much of what Victor had said.

"I think he might have been half unconscious by that point," Tess demurred. "He wasn't making any sense."

"But what did he say?"

Tess struggled to come up with a believable lie. After opening and closing her mouth two times, she gave in. As far as she could tell, there was nothing incriminating in it. "He said, 'The ship is closer to harbor than you think.' Really, Nicki, he hasn't had any sleep for like thirty-six hours, and they wouldn't have put him through all those MRIs unless he'd hit his head pretty bad. It was the ravings of delirium."

Nicki stopped dead in her tracks and began digging for her phone. "Say that again?"

"'The ship is closer to harbor than you think.'" Despite herself, Tess's interest was caught. "Why? Is it a famous quote or something? It sounds familiar."

Nicki's peal of laughter rang out through the parking lot. "You could call it that. Here. Look." Within seconds, she'd opened a reading app on her phone and was scrolling through a heavily highlighted book. The words *Detective* and *Gonzales* showed up enough times for Tess to have a good idea what she was looking at.

"Wait a minute…*I* wrote that? When?" Tess snatched greedily for the phone. Sure enough, it was a digital copy of *Fury on the Waves.*

Nicki tapped the screen to show her the line. "It's what Gonzales says right before he's taken captive by that band of merchant pirates. That U.S. Coast Guard guy never figured it out, because the ship was like five hundred miles out to sea, but the pirate captain did."

"You remember every line from the book?"

Nicki laughed. "The important ones, yes. What Gonzales meant was that the terrorist organization wasn't a foreign one, but an American one. Because the ship—the bad guy—was closer to the harbor—American soil—than any of the authorities realized."

Tess sucked in a sharp breath. "So Victor was telling me the same thing. The ship—*our* bad guy—is closer to the harbor—*us*—than we realize."

As soon as she said the words aloud, she frowned and shook her head. It didn't make sense. If they stuck to the theory that *Nicki* was the one behind everything, the quote worked. Nicki was as close to Tess and the case as she could get without drawing extra attention to herself.

But she and Victor had already talked about that. He'd already pointed out Tess's lack of caution where the librarian was concerned. There was no need to remind her...especially while Nicki had been literally standing in the room.

"Do you think he knows who the killer is, and he's just not telling us?" Nicki asked.

"Probably. That seems like something he'd do."

Nicki took her phone back before Tess could scroll further along in the book. There were an awful lot of highlights in there—even for a librarian and someone who considered herself a Tess Harrow fan. One might almost call them an *obsessive* number of highlights.

"If it's someone close to us, who do you think he means?" Nicki asked as she tucked the phone away. "Mason Peabody? Otis and his wife? *You*?"

"Me?" Tess's laughed sounded forced even to her own ears. "What reason would I have for killing a woman I've never met?"

"Who's to say you've never met her? Remember, she was found in your pond. It makes sense that you'd bury her in your own backyard, especially if you didn't know Zach was going to dredge everything up with dynamite."

Tess didn't much care for this line of thinking, so she turned the topic the best way she knew how.

By directing it at herself.

"I can't believe you recalled a specific line from my book faster than I did," she said. "I should be ashamed of myself."

To her relief, Nicki took the bait. "I think what you mean is that *I* should be ashamed of myself." She said this was such an air of good-humored self-deprecation that Tess relaxed. "I told you I was a fan. I have been for years. You moving into your grandfather's cabin was a stroke of luck I never expected. Even though I knew you had family here, I never thought you'd actually visit."

All of Tess's relaxation went up in a burst of flame. She'd been warned by her literary agent, early on, to be wary of the line between author and fan. Online interactions were fine, and book signings were a great way to meet the people who supported her career, but anything that went beyond the line was just that: beyond the line. Requests for personal meetings, demands made under the guise of friendship, people showing up outside your remote grandfather's cabin…those flags weren't just red. They were crimson.

Tess was guessing that, if she picked up the phone and called her agent Nancy right now, she would tell her that an over-qualified librarian who'd memorized every line from her books and happened to be living in the same place her grandfather had called home for forty years was the biggest, crimson-est flag of all.

"You know, we've spent so much time working on this case together that I've never asked you anything about yourself." Tess stopped next to Nicki's car, taking note of how tinted the windows were. They were so dark, you could murder a person in the full light of day.

"About me?"

"Yeah. I mean, I know that you're a librarian and you find the dating pool around here limited—and also that you're a master at microfiche—but almost nothing else. Where do you live when you're not rambling around in the bookmobile? Where are you from originally? What led you to a career in a rural county library system miles from anything even approaching a nightlife?"

Nicki laughed and put her hands up in a gesture of surrender. "Whoa there. Slow down. Are you asking as my friend or because you're trying to characterize me and put me in your book?"

"I don't do that!"

"Please. You're telling me there's not a rogue tiger stalking the woods in your next book?"

Tess had to smile. "I made him a lion. I'm not a complete plagiarist." She grew instantly serious. "I mean it, though. I feel like a jerk. I've been so caught up in my own affairs that it never occurred to me to ask about you. This is me making amends."

Nicki stared at her a long moment before finally nodding and giving in. She also held up three fingers, ticking them off as she spoke. "I rent an apartment above the honky-tonk bar. It's noisy, but it's cheap, and I'm almost never there anyway. I'm originally from Seattle, like you, although I went to college on the East Coast. And I work here because they had a job opening, and I thought it might be a fun change of pace. I didn't plan on staying for long, but then Mason donated the bookmobile and they let me be in charge of it. I like driving it around a lot more than I thought I would."

Tess had no reason not to believe her, but suspicion took firm root in her mind. Fortunately for her, most of the things Nicki had just divulged could be easily fact-checked online...or with a little poking around in town.

"Well?" Nicki asked, but with a brittle quality that put Tess on her guard. "Any more questions, or will that cover it for now?"

"Oh, I'll let you go for today," Tess said, forcing a smile. "But don't get too comfortable. You never know what else I might want to know. There's a reason they say a writer is always writing."

It was just Tess's luck to be caught skulking behind trash cans by her ex-husband.

"For God's sake, Tess. Please tell me you haven't been reduced to recycling old cans to make ends meet."

Tess jumped and whirled, her hands reaching for the closest weapon she could find. As this was an old broom handle that had snapped in half, she felt good about her chances.

The spiky bits at the end looked like they'd leave several unpleasant splinters behind.

"What's the matter with you?" she demanded. "What kind of monster sneaks up on a woman in a dark alleyway?"

Quentin smirked. "The kind who murders them and throws their bodies in a pond."

She pointed the stick at him in warning. "Too soon, Quentin. Too soon."

He rolled one shoulder in a half-shrug and drove a hand deep into his pocket. That move had once worked wonders on Tess—that casual, devil-may-care attitude was her sexual catnip—but now it just made her want to snap at him to stand up straight. Quentin had the worst posture of any man she knew.

"I'm just saying. Maybe now's not the best time to wander around alone after dark. No wonder you lost Gertie."

"I didn't *lose* her. She wandered off. Teenagers do that—a thing you'd know if you spent any time with one." She narrowed her eyes and examined her ex-husband closely. "Where is she, by the way? I swear on everything you love, if you said something to drive her off again—"

"Relax. I'm walking back from dropping her off at her friends' house… What are their names, again? Randy and Rudy? Peter and Paul?"

"Tommy and Timmy." A sound from inside the building had Tess giving a start of surprise. She inadvertently reached for Quentin's arm. "Quick. We have to hide."

"Why? What are you doing back here? I saw a dark figure and assumed it was a raccoon."

"Shh." She yanked Quentin behind the dumpster and fell

into a crouch. When he didn't fall with her, she grabbed his pants leg and tugged. Hard. "I swear, it's like you've never been on a stakeout before."

The door Tess had been standing next to swung open. At the heavy, crunching sounds of footsteps, she relaxed.

"Phew. That must have been the bartender. Nicki has a much lighter step than that."

"Are you going to tell me what we're doing on a stakeout outside a bar?"

Tess glared at him. "Are you going to tell me what you're doing rolling into our lives after six months of absolute silence?" She didn't wait for an answer. Any excuses he had to make were just that—excuses. "*Six months*, Quentin. Do you have any idea what that poor child has gone through? How much she's missed you?"

Quentin had the decency to look ashamed of himself. At least, that was what Tess assumed from the dim lights cast into the alleyway from the street. She had no idea what Nicki was doing, living in a place as shady as this. She'd been informed by the bartender that the back door served as the entrance to both the kitchen and the upstairs apartment, but it was sketchy as all get-out. Poorly lit, littered with broken bottles, smelling of stale beer and even staler french fries—it was a criminal's dream come true.

"I know," Quentin said. "I'm sorry. Things have been a little...messy since the divorce, that's all. I'm only just now starting to catch my breath."

"Your hot young girlfriend decide she could do better and leave you?"

Quentin's whole body tensed.

"I'll take that as a yes." Tess sighed before Quentin could launch into full battle. At least that explained why her ex-husband was suddenly here, suddenly interested, suddenly *nice*. Not—as Sheriff Boyd seemed to think—because he was rekindling the flames of their love, but because he was bored. Quentin had never been any good at being on his own. "I'm not going to start an argument, so you can relax. I'm just glad you're here."

"You are?"

"Contrary to all evidence, yes. I wish you'd reached out sooner, but I'll take whatever I can get." Her voice grew suddenly hard. "She needs you, Quentin. You and I might be over, but she's still your daughter, and she loves you. You can't just disappear off the face of the earth for months at a time. It *hurts* her."

"I know. I'm sorry."

"Don't apologize to me. She's the one who needs to hear it."

Tess would have preferred to continue her stakeout of Nicki's apartment without the presence of her self-absorbed and recently dumped ex-husband, but she didn't have much of a choice. This time, when the door opened, she heard light steps and the tinkling of long, dangling earrings that could only come from one person.

"You'll have to be my lookout," Tess said in a voice so low it barely counted as a whisper. "Stay here and hoot like an owl if she comes back. I'm going to peek inside her apartment."

"Tess, have you lost your mind?"

"I'm not going to touch anything. I just want a look around."

Tess darted around the dumpster, prepared to dash up the stairs and snap as many pictures of Nicki's apartment as she could get within a safe amount of time, but she stopped before she made it more than a few feet.

There, standing in the shadows along the back of the building, stood one tall librarian and one man of medium build—about a hundred and eighty pounds and with size eleven shoes.

Tess made a frantic movement with her hand to keep Quentin quiet and leaned in. She was too far to make out the details of everything Nicki and Adam—Zach? Mason?— were saying, but she heard enough to confirm her worst fears.

"I know it's getting dangerous, but you have to stick with it," Nicki said. "We're too close to quit now."

Low male murmurs were all Tess could hear in reply. *Panicked*, low male murmurs.

"Strike while no one is looking. Everyone's so distracted by Carl's death that it's your best chance to get inside." She paused and flung a hand up. "Shh. Wait. Did you hear something?"

Fast—so fast her reflexes were almost like that of a tiger—Nicki whipped around and stared straight at Tess. Like a child, Tess held her breath and wished herself invisible…and was astounded when it actually worked.

Later, she'd realize that she'd been standing in a direct shadow, and that there was no way for Nicki to make her out against the dark exterior of the bar's weathered stone, but there was only one thing she could think right now: Nicki was the one behind it all. Nicki had been playing Tess from the start.

Tess wasn't sure why, but she suddenly felt like crying. Even though all signs had been pointing to this, she'd so desperately wanted Nicki to be one of the good guys.

She'd so desperately wanted Nicki to be her friend.

"We can't talk here," Nicki hissed. "Not with everyone on edge and Tess Harrow watching my every move. She's starting to ask questions. Next time you need me, use the burner phone. And Zach—" Tess's whole body went rigid. *Zach and Nicki. Nicki and Zach.* "No mistakes this time around, got it?"

Tess and Quentin remained in place long after the two criminals walked around the edge of the building and parted ways: Tess because she was still reeling with everything she'd heard; Quentin because his leg had fallen asleep and he was busy massaging it back to life.

"What was that all about?" he grumbled as he rotated his knee back and forth. "Why did that woman say you were watching her every move?"

Because she *was*—and because, in her foolish desire to get to the bottom of things, she'd pushed too hard. Nicki had seen right through her.

Quentin glanced up at her face and immediately softened. Fifteen years of marriage had been good for one thing, at least—he knew on instinct when Tess was about to cry.

"Come here, you," he said as he pulled her into a hug. Tess fought it at first, her whole body rigid, but something about that familiar warmth broke down the last of her barriers. She'd come here with the expectation of finding clues inside Nicki's apartment—a black, lacy thong or an excessive amount of cat food under the sink. Not to solve the whole dratted case. "Whatever it is, I'm sure it's not as bad as you think."

"That woman is a murderer. The conversation we just overheard was her confessing to the whole thing."

"Well, then." To Tess's surprise, Quentin didn't let go. "Maybe it's *exactly* as bad as you think."

Chapter Twenty-Six

TESS WOULD NEVER ADMIT IT TO QUENTIN, BUT HIS arrival in Winthrop couldn't have come at a better time.

She loved Gertrude more than anything on this planet, and the time they'd been spending together had been wonderful, but it was much easier to investigate a murder without a teenager in tow. Gertrude was too impressionable, too young—and she would have enjoyed Ivy laughing her out of the sheriff's office *way* too much.

"Are you going to accuse the old woman who runs the charity shop next?" Ivy demanded, wiping at her tears. "Or maybe the little toddler who's always running away from daycare? It's never too soon to start a life of crime."

"It's not funny." Tess crossed her arms and tried planting her feet on the floor, but it was no use. Ivy's laughter was starting to draw a crowd. "Talk to Sheriff Boyd. Or better yet—I'll go talk to him. I *saw* Nicki with Zach Peabody, Ivy. I heard her confess."

"You heard her say 'I murdered Wilma Eyre'?"

Tess hesitated. "Not those *exact* words, but it amounts to the same thing."

"So she said the word murder?"

"Well, no."

"Body?"

"Not quite, but—"

"Kill? Behead? Maim?"

"Ivy, you're not listening!"

Ivy took a step forward. Even though Tess commanded her limbs to stay in place, she found herself backing toward the door. "Okay, then," Ivy persisted. "How about Bigfoot? Smuggling? Carl?"

"Yes!" Tess pointed at her. "That one. She said Carl. I distinctly remember her mentioning Carl."

Ivy snorted. "Every single person in this county is talking about him. I'd have found it harder to believe if she *hadn't* slipped it into conversation." She continued, no less ruthless now that she'd made her point. "Go home, Ms. Harrow. Relax. Recover. You've had a rough couple of days—it's no wonder you're starting to point fingers at everyone. Believe me. You play this game long enough, and everyone starts looking like a suspect."

It was true. The longer Tess stayed in this town, the more it seemed that everyone was sitting on something huge. Edna's pet cat was actually a wild animal. Zach Peabody was working with Nicki to run a smuggling ring with a bit of murder on the side. Quentin was being a good dad. Sheriff Boyd was basically in love with her.

Just once, it would have been nice to wake up and find that the world *hadn't* been tilted on its axis.

"At least look into it," Tess begged. "Nicki's not who she appears to be."

"Are any of us?" Ivy asked and shook her head. "In all my

years as a police deputy, I've never met anyone who's completely innocent. Not even you."

Tess wished she could argue, but there was no denying it. She'd been the first to jump on the Nicki bandwagon, using the librarian as a sounding board for all her theories and ideas, feeding her top-secret information about the case. For all she knew, she was the reason Nicki had lured Carl out into the woods in the first place.

"At least put a tail on her," Tess begged. "Assign someone to keep an eye on her movements."

"Who?" Ivy demanded. She was starting to look less conciliatory the longer this conversation went on. "Every spare man we have is out combing the forest for signs of Carl's killer. In case you've forgotten, we recently lost one of our own."

"I keep telling you—Carl's killer is living in an apartment above the bar. She goes by the name Nicki Nickerson, which should have been our first clue. No one has a name like that in real life." A thought occurred to Tess. "Take the man watching my cabin if you have to. I don't mind fending for myself if it means someone's watching her."

"An excellent idea," Ivy agreed, "if we hadn't already reassigned that officer. Our resources no longer stretch that far. You'll be fending for yourself from here on out whether you want to or not."

A rising sense of panic clutched Tess by the throat—and not only because of the lack of a private security detail. That expression on Ivy's face was hard, cold, *done.* It was the same look Quentin had given her the day he'd moved out.

I can't take this anymore, he'd said. *You're too much, Tess. Everything with you is always too much.*

Hearing that from a man who'd fallen out of love with you was bad enough. Hearing it from the only person who stood between you and a murderer was worse.

"Oh, and Ms. Harrow?" Ivy said as she ruthlessly showed Tess the door. "If I hear that you bothered the sheriff with this while he's still in recovery, you'll wish that I'd left you buried inside that hole."

———

"Tess, I know you're in there. Open up!"

Tess stood at the far end of her cabin, surveying potential hiding spots. All those promising places to stash a body— the chimney, the lean-to, the rickety old porch—were too small to hold a living, breathing person. And the only other option she could think of, to run, occurred only to be immediately discarded.

For one thing, it was nine o'clock at night. For another, she was fully exposed in her pink flannel pajamas, her feet bare, and wearing one of those weird facial masks with cutouts for the eyes. If Nicki had come to murder her, there was little Tess could do short of balling up the mask and throwing it at her. It was infused with seaweed and cucumber, so the smell might buy her a little time, but she doubted so determined a murderer would be put off for long.

"Hello? Answer me, Tess, or I'm going to break down the door. You're scaring me."

That made two of them.

"Just a sec," Tess called, stalling as best she could. For a fleeting moment, she wished Quentin were here with her. He wasn't great in a crisis, but at least he was a witness. The last thing she wanted was to die in this cabin without anyone to see. "I'm on my way."

"Thank goodness." The relief in Nicki's voice sounded so real that Tess relaxed enough to pull open the door—but not before first securing the security chain. She relaxed even more when Nicki took one look at the wet mask clinging to Tess's face and laughed. "Oh! Are you having a spa night? I wish you'd have told me. I could really use a manicure."

As if to prove it, Nicki shoved her fingernails through the gap in the door. Tess noted that her nails were short and bare of polish. A murderer's nails—utilitarian and sparse.

"Are you going to invite me in?" Nicki asked.

Tess saw nothing for it but to comply. If Ivy didn't think tailing Nicki was worth the effort—and if she felt Tess was safe enough to live out here without a uniformed companion—then Tess had no choice but to trust her.

Since she wasn't a complete idiot, however, she was careful to position herself between Nicki and the rusty shotgun above the door.

"Here. I brought you a present." Nicki reached into the leather cross bag she wore and pulled out a library book. Since there wasn't much chance of murder by literature, Tess took it.

"Oh. It's another Bigfoot one."

"Someone returned it earlier today. I know we're no

longer searching for a *real* Bigfoot, but I thought it might contain something useful. Besides, you seemed so worried about Sheriff Boyd, I figured you could use the distraction."

"Yeah. Maybe. Thanks."

"That's it? *Maybe?*"

Since the only other things Tess could think to say had to do with betrayal, backstabbing, and murder, she did the best she could. "Um…do you want a drink? I'd offer you a snack, but without Gertie here to feed me, my supplies are running low. I might be able to conjure up a cracker or two if you're desperate."

Nicki's gaze turned sharp. "What's wrong? You're acting weird."

Tess dropped the book. "No, I'm not."

"Yes, you are. You have been ever since you got lost in the forest with Sheriff Boyd. I know I joked about the two of you getting it on, but did something really happen out there? Did you discover something you're not telling me about?"

"What?!" Unable to prevent herself, Tess cast an anxious—and, yes, *weird*—glance up at the gun. Honestly, if she wanted to get out of this conversation alive, she needed to rein things in. She'd have made a rock suspicious by this point. "Of course not. What could have happened?"

"I don't know. That's why I'm asking."

"You mean, other than almost losing my daughter, stumbling onto a dead body, and falling into a grave and/or tiger pit?"

"It wasn't a tiger pit," Nicki said, and with so much certainty that Tess was instantly on her guard. She must not have done a very good job of hiding her feelings because a pucker of annoyance drew Nicki's brows together. "Why are you looking at me like that? And backing away? I swear, it's almost like you're afraid of me."

Since Tess was, in fact, afraid of Nicki, she did the only thing she could think of in that moment: She reached for the gun.

Unfortunately, it was much higher up than it looked. Tess stretched and even managed a quick jump, but her fingers only grazed the metal. The gun dislodged a few inches but remained steadfast on the wall.

It was the worst thing that could have happened. Nicki saw every flicker of fear on Tess's face—noticed the jerky way she moved for the door—and attacked.

Okay, so she didn't attack so much as reach one of her long arms up and pull the gun down, but it amounted to the same thing. Tess's hands flew up in surrender. It was a sobering thing, to know that her lack of physical prowess would be her undoing, but there was always a chance the gun wasn't loaded or was too rusted over.

Or that Nicki would expertly spin the gun around her finger and extend it, stock-first, at Tess.

"Here," Nicki said, her voice dangerous. "Is this what you wanted?"

Tess reached for the gun as though it were about to strike. "Yes, but—"

Nicki waggled it until Tess had no choice but to close her hand around the smooth wood. She felt awkward holding it in her hands—all the more so when Nicki nudged the barrel down until the cold metal pointed straight into her own face.

"Hold it firm but not tight. Keep the butt away from your face. Honestly, Tess, a third of your books are devoted to the description and use of firearms. Don't tell me you don't know how to handle one."

Tess's palms grew so sweaty that she was finding it difficult to keep her hold. "I don't like guns," she confessed.

Nicki laughed, but there was little humor to it. There wasn't much humor in her face, either. Gone were her easygoing laugh and gentle smile. No more could Tess see a gleam of anything friendly in her eyes.

"Isn't that rich?" Nicki said, her voice low. "Well? Now what? Are you going to shoot me? Kidnap me? What's the plan? I can't help you unless I know what the end goal is."

In all honesty, the plan only went as far as Tess getting her hands on the shotgun. As a woman who wrote about violence with ease, she'd always felt that when push came to shove, she'd have no problems taking down the bad guy. Detective Gonzales did it without batting an eye. She felt sure that Sheriff Boyd would do the same.

Tess Harrow, it seemed, was made of less stern stuff.

She started to lower the gun only for Nicki to tsk and point it back up again. "Oh no, you don't. Now that you've threatened me, it's too dangerous to take it back again."

"Why?" Tess's voice wavered almost as much as the rifle. "What are you going to do to me?"

Nicki flinched as though Tess had struck her with the gun rather than words. "I can't believe we've come to this. I thought we were allies, Tess. I thought we were friends."

That word—*friends*—acted much more powerfully on

Tess than she wanted it to. Not too long ago, she'd thought that, too. She'd been so happy to meet someone new, someone she felt an immediate kinship with, that she'd overlooked everything else.

And the worst part was, she'd do it again in a heartbeat. Even now, with a gun in her hands and all the facts on her side, she wanted to believe so badly in Nicki's innocence that her next words caused physical pain.

"I know it's you," she said, swallowing past the lump in her throat. "I know you're the one who murdered Wilma and hid her body in my pond. I know you're working with Zach Peabody to cover it up—and maybe kill again."

Nicki didn't move, not even to bat an eyelash. "Interesting. Anything else you'd like to accuse me of?"

Emboldened, Tess took a deep breath and kept going. She'd written enough crime fiction to know that this was backwards—and that the villain was supposed to be the one confessing to her, not the other way around—but that was just another thing that made fiction so different from real life.

"Your bookmobile is the perfect cover," she said. "No one thinks twice about a sweet, friendly librarian who bumbles her way around and always has a book recommendation ready. You love reading and gossip. You enjoy the classics and genre fiction equally. You know everyone's secrets and have access to literally every road and location in this county— and all without anyone questioning what you're doing here or why." Tess drew a deep breath. There was a look in Nicki's eye that she didn't trust, but she needed to get this out. "But it doesn't make sense. It never has, only I refused to see it. You don't belong here, Nicki. You're too smart. Too pretty. Too—"

"Black?" Nicki suggested.

Tess flushed. That hadn't been the next word on her lips, but there was no denying it. This wasn't the most diverse part of the state. There was a fairly large Native population hereabouts, but melanin was sadly lacking in the rest of the populace. She hadn't witnessed any overt racism, but that didn't mean it didn't exist.

Instead of taking offense, however, Nicki only sighed. "Who else have you talked to about this?"

"No one," Tess lied. "I only just figured it out."

She didn't know what chivalrous urge had her protecting all the people she'd told about Nicki, but she held onto it like it was a lifeline. Ivy would probably be able to stand up for herself, but she didn't put it past Nicki to hightail it to the hospital and put a bullet in the sheriff's head. And as for Quentin, well…Gertrude would need at least *one* parent intact when all this was over. Tess would have preferred it to be her, but she wasn't about to quibble over details.

Nicki studied her for a long, careful moment, as if deciding whether or not to believe her. In the end, she must have accepted Tess's words as truth because she nodded once.

"Let's hope you're the only one who sees it," she said. With a swiftness of action that Tess would never be able to work out, she shot her hand out and plucked the gun from Tess.

The author in Tess was disappointed to find that her life

didn't flash before her eyes. She didn't feel particularly hot or cold, she didn't see a bright light beckoning for her from afar, and she didn't even dwell with regret on the mistakes of her youth. As Nicki raised the butt of the gun and brought it down over her head, all she could think was "Now I'll never figure out how the book ends."

Chapter Twenty-Seven

TESS AWOKE TO A SPLITTING HEADACHE, A MOUTH AS DRY as dust, and silence.

She had no idea how much time had passed since Nicki had clocked her over the head, but it was dark outside. Either it was still the same night, or she'd been unconscious for over twenty-four hours. Considering that her clothes weren't soaked with anything but sweat, and her stomach felt more nauseous than hungry, she assumed it was the former.

Oddly enough, she was in her own bed. A pillow lay under her head, and her grandfather's colorful quit was tucked up to her chin. She tested her arms and legs to find that she hadn't been bound in any way, and there was even a fresh glass of water next to her nightstand. A bottle of sealed ibuprofen sat next to it along with a note that read, "Take two of these and *don't* call me in the morning."

Tess promptly tossed the bottle in the trash.

She did, however, gratefully gulp the water. A tender bump on the top of her head and a persistent throbbing at the back of her skull showed her where she'd been struck, but not why she'd been allowed to remain in her cabin.

Tess had no intention of sticking around long enough to find out. Even if Nicki didn't come back to finish the job she'd started, she might release a panther or crocodile from her exotic animal hoard to do it for her.

"I am *not* getting trapped inside this cabin by a crocodile Cujo," Tess said as she reached for her bag and began rummaging for her keys.

At first, she was afraid she'd misplaced them or that Gertrude had taken it upon herself to hang them on the hook by the door. After five minutes of fruitless searching, she worried she'd been hit harder on the head than she realized. After ten, there was no denying the truth: Nicki had taken them.

"Because of course she did," Tess said, not totally unimpressed by this new twist. If she was in the mood to write her book—a thing she decidedly was not—she'd make sure to throw this into the next chapter. To strand a helpless woman out in the dark woods with no cell service and no way into town, to remove everything except her fear, was dastardly enough to round out any villain worth the page she was printed on.

"Only...Wait." Tess stopped underneath the front door and glanced up. The shotgun had been replaced in its usual spot, but not before it had been carefully cleaned and oiled. There was even another sticky note offering a step-by-step guide to using it. She had no doubt that if she had the nerve to fiddle around with the bolt, she'd find that the gun contained its requisite bullets.

In other words, Nicki had been granted every opportunity to hurt, maim, or otherwise impair Tess...and hadn't taken a single one.

"*Yet*," Tess said with a wary glance at that gun. "For all I know, she'll be back any minute."

The thought should have been enough for Tess to slip on her tennis shoes and jog into town, but she couldn't help feeling that all Nicki had wanted was enough time to escape. The pounding of her head and the woozy way she staggered about the cabin reinforced this belief. The last thing she was capable of right now was tracking down a rogue murderer.

"Until someone decides to come check on me, there's nothing I can do," Tess said as she slumped at the kitchen table. She groaned as she realized how much her editor and agent would love this particular scenario. "Unless, of course, I sit down and write."

Tess didn't sit down and write.

She thought about it—she really did. She even made herself a pot of coffee, but the thought of weaving tales of intrigue while her own fate hung so precariously in the balance wasn't one she relished.

Without television, without electricity, and without her phone, the only option left to her was reading...and unless she was willing to tackle Nicki's Bigfoot book, there was just one thing in the cabin to read.

"Well, Ivy. You win this time." Tess hefted the box onto her lap and opened the flap. Gertrude, raised to be reverential to books of all kinds, had been careful to keep all the pages in order and neatly stacked. Tess lifted the first and set to deciphering Ivy's scrawls.

The flickering light of the oil lamp wasn't ideal for reading such closely-knit words while suffering from a head injury, but that didn't seem to matter as Tess was sucked into a planetary system far, far away. Every aspect of the plot was improbable and over-the-top, the cast of characters so large and varied that it was impossible to keep track of them all.

Until, about fifty pages in, Tess realized she *could*. Not only did she know exactly how Corstice Devuto was connected to the Nebula Amalgamation, but she was rooting for Taab Tevran to overthrow Pelle Newvan for the Zaltan Cup—and she was rooting hard.

"Ivy Bell, you sneaky little minx." Tess turned the next page with a thrill she hadn't felt in a long time—the thrill of losing herself in a book, of leaving this world behind and entering one that had been fabricated out of thin air. It wasn't often that she stumbled across a book so enthralling that the writer part of her brain turned off and let her enjoy. "This is good. Like, really, *really* good."

She had no idea how long she might have continued like that, hunched over the box, deciphering Ivy's atrocious handwriting and battling starborgs alongside Corstice, but she was pulled out of the book and almost out of herself by mention of the word Bigfoot.

To be fair, the word ended up being Borgfleet, and it made absolute sense in context, but that wasn't the part that caused Tess's heart to leap to her throat. The sun had started to come up by now, full of dewy pink rays that promised a beautiful day ahead, but she paid no more attention to that then she did the dull ache at the back of her skull. Tossing Ivy's book aside, she scrambled to the table. She held her breath and mentally crossed all her fingers before flipping through the pages of the Bigfoot book Nicki had brought over.

Sure enough, this one was just as chockful of useless information and scribbles in the margins as the first. She'd assumed, when she'd read that first book, that Timmy Lincoln and his love of damaging library property were to blame, but the sketches of Bigfoot footprints, rhetorical questions like "always bipedal?", and a heavily underscored "for maximum cover, dusk and dawn only" could have been written by one hand and one hand only.

"Ivy's been reading up on Bigfoot," Tess said in a whoosh of air and adrenaline. "*And* she's been taking notes."

Since Nicki's bookmobile rarely traveled to Wi-Fi hot spots, she still relied on the old-fashioned process of stamping books when they were checked out. Sure enough, when Tess pulled out the return card, Ivy Bell was scrawled above Tess's own name. While that in and of itself wasn't particularly shocking—a police officer who researched Bigfoot while an impersonator was on the loose deserved nothing but respect—the date was.

January fifth. A good six months before now. Back when the Bigfoot sightings were nothing more than a plague in Sheriff Boyd's life and not tied to a murder investigation.

Tess dropped to the chair, her hands suddenly shaking.

Corralling her thoughts with a head injury and this sudden influx of information was tough, so she did what she always did when confronted with a tricky plot problem: she pulled out her sticky notes.

Her normal approach was a carefully color-coordinated timeline of all the plot points, character arcs, foreshadows, locations, and clues contained within her work in progress, so she didn't alter her method now. The names of everyone who'd played a part in Tess's life since she arrived here, their possible motives, their alibis, the fact that they hit her over the head with a shotgun and/or researched Bigfoot long before he made an official appearance on the scene... it was all here, and it all pointed to one very incriminating conclusion.

"No way," Tess breathed as she stood back and appraised her handiwork. The entire south wall of the cabin was covered in sticky notes, several of which were already coming loose and fluttering to the floor. "Ivy and Nicki are working together."

The more she thought about the it, the more the pieces fit. Ivy and Nicki, and most likely Wilma, were in on the animal smuggling ring together. Ivy was the right height and size to play the role of Bigfoot, and naturally, she'd have always known where to find and taunt Sheriff Boyd. Tess wasn't sure about the size of her feet, but she could easily verify that.

Besides, there was no denying that she'd sent Tess home alone to the cabin without a police escort...and then likely told Nicki exactly where she could find her. She'd refused to let Tess go to Sheriff Boyd with information against Nicki, thereby freeing her up to tie any loose ends that remained.

In other words, the three of them were a lady gang of criminals, throwing dust in the eyes of the local law enforcement. A lady gang of criminals who ran exotic animals over the border in an operation that literally no one saw coming.

Tess was so excited by this—at the prospect of three women running a heist-like operation undetected for months, at her chance to make Detective Gonzales fall in love with Willow only to break his heart when she turned out to be a criminal mastermind—that she almost forgot that murder wasn't something she was supposed to applaud.

"Ivy and Nicki killed a woman and dumped her body in a pond. They were responsible for Carl's death. They might be coming for me next." Tess chanted the words in hopes that they'd make some impression on her befuddled brain. Those two were dangerous. They were her enemies. She couldn't trust them.

It was no use. She began snatching the sticky notes from the wall, unable to look at them any longer.

"I don't believe it," she said, crumpling up pastel-colored ball after pastel-colored ball. "I *can't* believe it."

And the truth was, she didn't. Not really. Nicki had gone out of her way to *not* kill Tess, and Ivy had written in the margins of a public library book in what was an undeniable trail of evidence. More to the point, Nicki had brought Tess that book on purpose, knowing full well that Tess had a sample of Ivy's handwriting in her possession to compare it to.

As if she wanted to be caught? Because she didn't know that Tess would make the connection?

Or, worse, to toy with Tess before swooping in and killing her for good?

Chapter Twenty-Eight

TESS DIDN'T REALIZE SHE'D FALLEN ASLEEP AT THE TABLE until she woke to the hammering sound of fists on her front door.

"Ms. Harrow, open this door right now."

"Tess! Tess! Are you in there?"

"Just let me go in through the window. I know I can fit."

This last remark caused Tess to sit up with a start. The other angry voices might blend into the background, but Gertrude's soft lilt had the ability to draw her out of a coma.

"I'm here. I'm awake. Stop yelling."

"Mom!" Despite Tess's promises that all was well, Gertrude popped in through the kitchen window. For reasons she couldn't understand, Gertrude was dressed in a yellow sundress—the type of thing she hadn't worn since she was six years old—but that didn't stop Tess from pulling her daughter into her arms.

"It's okay, Gertie-pie," she said. "I'm right here. I haven't gone anywhere."

"Let us in, Gertrude," Quentin said from the door. "We can't stand out here all day."

"Oops. Sorry. Coming, Daddy."

Tess blinked as she watched her daughter click open the

door and beam up at her father. In addition to the yellow sundress, she had low-heeled sandals on her feet and a daisy hair clip holding the pink strands out of her eyes. If Tess couldn't make out a faint outline of her own drool on the last of the sticky notes spread across the table, she'd think she was asleep and still dreaming.

"That's it," Quentin said as he swept inside. He took one look at Tess and firmed his lips in a tight line. "We're getting you out of here. It's not safe for you to be living in this town, let alone this cabin. You look like you were hit over the head with a club."

The third member of the party, Ivy, stepped inside holding a first aid kit. "That's because she *was* hit over the head with a club. At least, that's what Nicki said when she called in. What happened? Who hit you? Why didn't you run for help?"

"I… Uh…" Tess glanced down as Gertrude's hand slipped into her own. What she saw there startled her even more than Ivy showing up on her doorstep with a first aid kit in hand.

On each of her daughter's fingernails, a delicate daisy had been painted in blobs of yellow and white fingernail polish. She could still see the outline of Gertrude's favored hues—midnight blue and deep purple sparkles—around her cuticles, but it was obvious some effort had been made to remove them.

"It was Nicki—" she began, but Gertrude finished for her.

"Who called it in," she said. "We know that already. She said she came out here to check on you, but you were knocked unconscious. Does it hurt?"

Tess's mind was starting to clear—and, with it, a realization that her daughter had been replaced by some kind of Stepford version. Gertrude had never shown concern for Tess's physical well-being a day in her life. Not even after last year's appendectomy. The only interest Gertrude had shown in that was the possibility of keeping the appendix in a jar to put on the mantelpiece.

"I don't know what happened," Tess said, placing a hand to her temple. She was still so rattled that the gesture wasn't wholly feigned. To tell the truth—that Nicki had done this to her, and that Ivy was in on it—wasn't likely to result in a happy ending. Not while Ivy had a gun on her hip and the authority of the law behind her.

Since everyone was waiting for an answer, however, she had to say *something*. "Someone snuck up behind me while I was working," she lied.

"Working?" Ivy echoed with a glance at Tess's typewriter. It sat at its usual table, protected by its plastic cover and a fine layer of dust. She hadn't made any attempt to sit down and get her words in for days, and it showed.

"I was plotting," she said as she gestured at the garbage overflowing with crumpled sticky notes. With any luck, Ivy wouldn't look too closely at how many times her own name appeared on them. "I'm sorry. I wish I knew more, but everything is so fuzzy…"

Thankfully, her state was so weakened that everyone was willing to take her at her word. Ivy came forward with her first aid kit to examine the back of her head with the same rough tenderness she'd shown the day she washed Tess's hair.

She showed the same lack of concern, too, pronouncing the injury no worse than a light bruise. After that, she took a full description of the attack, which Tess shrouded in obscurity.

Her attacker had moved silently and stealthily.

She had no idea what he wanted.

Nothing was missing as far as she could tell.

Yes, maybe she *had* fallen and bumped her head, and, in the semi-consciousness that followed, she'd fabricated an elaborate and unrealistic tale to cover for her own clumsiness.

Quentin snorted over this last one, but Ivy's questions relaxed, so Tess knew she'd done the right thing. At least, she thought so until she caught Ivy examining the gun above the door. She'd forgotten that the deputy had spent several hours inside this cabin. Her keen eye would have picked up how rusty the weapon was before…and how sparkling it was now.

"I had it cleaned," Tess said to stave off any unpleasant questions. "In case I needed it."

Ivy cleared her throat in a way that was open to a hundred interpretations. She also scrawled some notes in her notebook, all those scrolls and loops filling the page. Neither of those filled Tess with much in the way of confidence.

"Where did Nicki go, if you don't mind my asking?" Tess asked in as casual a voice as she could muster. "After she reported my accident, I mean?"

Ivy shook her head. "I don't know. She called in the report, but the connection was bad. I didn't get all the details. Just that you were hurt and in need of assistance."

"And what time was it?" Tess asked sharply. From the way

the sun was slanting through the curtains, it was well into the day by now. "How long ago did she call?"

"An hour, maybe? She said she was in a hurry and couldn't stick around with you, but that she'd put you in bed with a cold compress." Ivy glanced around, as if just now realizing that Tess was nowhere near her bed. "Why did you get up?"

Tess didn't say anything right away. She was too busy working out the timeline of events. If Nicki put the call in an hour ago, that meant she'd waited all night before she placed the request for help. That gave her plenty of time to make a getaway...or to plan her next steps with Ivy.

Since it was obvious some sort of response was expected, Tess once again looked to the contents of the table. She picked up the half-empty mug and waved it. "I wanted coffee."

"Since when do you drink it black?" Quentin asked.

Ivy dipped her finger into it and narrowed her eyes. "Since when do you drink it cold?"

Tess avoided Gertrude's gaze, which was watching her much more closely than she cared for. Her daughter looked so concerned, and so sweetly innocent, that she couldn't help thinking she was missing something.

"Since you took Gertrude to go stay at a hotel," Tess said. "I can't work the coffeepot on my own, so I had to drink the dregs."

"Well, she's not coming back here, so don't blame me," Quentin said. "What if she'd been here when you were attacked? What if the killer was coming here to kidnap her? What's it going to take before you realize that dragging a child into a murder investigation is a bad idea?"

Guilt, made all the sharper for being deserved, assailed Tess from all sides. Everything Quentin was saying was true, and there was no use pretending otherwise. If she'd been a halfway decent parent, she'd have closed this cabin up at the first sight of an arm falling from the sky. But Gertrude was doing better—Tess was sure of that. She was happy and engaged in life again. She had friends. She smiled. She *laughed*.

The yellow sundress and daisy-painted fingernails were odd, yes, but Gertrude *was* a teenager. Drastic overnight transformations were part of the deal.

Ivy must have seen some of the conflicting feelings flitting across Tess's face because she sighed long and hard.

"I'll see if the sheriff is willing to post someone out here, but until then, it's best to stay in town with your daughter and ex-husband." She paused and stared at Tess in a way that sent a shiver down her spine. "Or, better yet, back home in Seattle."

The worst part of Tess's day came after Ivy left the cabin.

In the past twenty-four hours, she'd discovered a murderer, confronted said murderer, been hit over the head, plotted an intricate web of lies, and faced down a corrupt officer of the law.

She'd have gladly done it all again to avoid the next part.

"I've decided I want to go live with Daddy."

"What?" Tess blinked first at Gertrude and then at

Quentin, who was doing a poor job of hiding his smug expression. Clearly, he'd been prepped about this conversation ahead of time. "Gertie, what are you talking about? You can't live with your father."

"Why not? He's my parent as much as you are." Gertrude crossed her arms and adopted a look of fierce determination. That particular look was one Tess had fought for years to instill in her daughter—one she'd have normally defended to her dying breath—but right now, all she wanted to do was cry.

She *didn't* but only because she distracted herself by digging her fingernails into her opposite palm. "I know he's your father, but it's not that easy. You can't change parents like hair color."

The reference to Gertrude's hair only caused her to scowl. "I'm not *changing* parents, Mom; I'm *choosing* one."

Tess felt as though she'd been slapped. "You're choosing your father? I don't understand. Is this about the fight we had back at the library? About me…ignoring emails?"

Gertrude shrugged one shoulder and carefully avoided Tess's eye. "It's not that big of a deal. It's just something I want to try out for a bit."

"But what about your school?" Tess demanded.

"I'll be a freshman next year anyway, so it doesn't matter if I have to change to a new one. It's the perfect time to transition."

"Your old room…all your things…"

"It's just a room," Gertrude said, clearly disgusted. "And they're just things."

Tess couldn't argue with that—especially not with a teenager who'd already made up her mind.

"Fair's fair. You got your turn." Gertrude uncrossed her arms and reached for Quentin's hand. "I did six months with you and decided I didn't like it, so now I want to try something new. I bet a judge would let me live wherever I wanted. They do, you know, for teenagers. They want us to have agency. You're always saying that, too."

It was true. Tess *did* want Gertrude to have agency when it came to things like interpersonal relationships and advocating for herself at school. What she didn't want—what was causing a knot of tight, painful panic to form in the pit of her stomach—was for Gertrude to leave her for a man who'd never once proven himself worthy of her love.

And in a *sundress*, of all things.

"I'm sorry about all this cabin stuff, Gertie," Tess said, almost desperate. "I know living without Wi-Fi is hard, and there's been a lot of weird stuff going on, but—"

She cut herself off when Gertrude's lower lip started wobbling. Quentin saw it the same time she did and pulled their daughter into his arms.

"Now look what you did," he said over the top of Gertrude's head. "You made her cry."

"But I didn't say anything!"

"Exactly. Not once did you take our daughter's fragile emotional state into mind. Not once did you ask her what *she* wants."

Something wild and frantic was trying to escape Tess's ribcage, but she forced it to lie still. She stared at her daughter long and hard, her eyes examining the shaking body and bright-pink head. "What do you want, Gertie?" she asked, her voice so gentle it was barely a whisper. "What do you really, truly want?"

Gertrude whirled to face her, her gaze strangely intense. "I want to finish my stay in the hotel and then go home," she said. "To your home, Daddy. To *ours*. We can pick all my stuff up from Mom's house while she finishes writing her book."

That wild, frantic thing started flapping in earnest.

"I can't—" she began, but the words got stuck in her throat. Tess Harrow, a master at language and alliteration, whose prose transported millions of readers to a universe that only existed inside their heads, had nothing to say. Nothing that mattered, anyway. Not when her whole world was getting ready to walk out that door.

Quentin saw it and softened. "Why don't you grab anything you might have left and head out to the car," he suggested, squeezing Gertrude gently on the shoulder. "I'm sure your mom could use a minute to gather herself."

As Gertrude ducked her head in agreement, Tess let out a reckless cry. "Wait!" When Gertrude did nothing but look back at her with that same odd intensity, she added, "At least give me a hug before you go."

To her relief, Gertrude complied. The girl wrapped her arms and gave Tess the strongest, fiercest hug of her life. Her fingers clutched so tightly at Tess's waist that they were like talons, her face buried in Tess's shoulder as though it was the last time they'd ever touch.

It reminded her so much of the little girl Gertrude had

once been—the little girl she, in so many ways, still was—
that she forced a smile. She might have done everything
wrong where Gertrude was concerned, but at least Tess
could let her walk out that door knowing she was loved.

"Hey." Tess reached down and chucked her daughter
under the chin. "I'm agreeing to this, but only until this mess
at the cabin is settled. Then we're sitting down with a lawyer
to hammer out the details. I'm not giving you up entirely."

That burst of sentimentality proved Tess's undoing.
Gertrude scoffed and rolled her eyes before stomping away.
"Ugh, Mom. Whatever. You're so dramatic all the time."

As the door came to a close on her daughter's retreating
form, Quentin cleared his throat. "About that lawyer stuff…"

Tess lowered herself shakily to the chair. She despised
herself for appearing weak, especially while her ex was in the
room, but she wasn't sure how much longer her legs would
work. There didn't seem to be any way for this moment to
get worse, but she didn't put it past Quentin to try.

"It's not negotiable, Quentin," she said. "If Gertie wants
to live with you, I'm not going to stand in her way, but I want
the conditions in writing. For her protection."

He cleared his throat again, this time with so much
emphasis that Tess feared he was choking on his own phlegm.

"What now?" she asked, weary and wary.

"It's just that if I have custody of Gertrude now, there will
be added expenses. Dinners out, movie nights, faster Wi-Fi
at the condo…"

Tess wished she could pretend to misunderstand him.
Either that, or throw the Bigfoot book at his head. "What

you mean to say is dental visits, new clothes when she out-grows the old ones, and school fees, right?"

"Of course that's what I meant." He had the decency to color. "It's standard practice, Tess. If the situation were reversed, and a *woman* was the one asking for child support…"

Quentin was right, and Tess knew it, but that didn't make the situation any easier. She didn't mind the money—she minded losing her daughter. She minded having so mis-read this cabin situation that she no longer understood the person she'd given birth to. She and Gertrude had their problems, yes, but she'd genuinely thought they were getting somewhere.

"I'll call my lawyer next time I have cell service and see what we need to do to get things updated," she said, smiling tightly.

Quentin shifted nervously. "What about for the next few weeks? This hotel in town isn't cheap, and Gertrude only ever seems to want gourmet foods. I don't know what you were thinking, introducing her to truffles when she was only eight years old."

Tess closed her eyes and started to count to ten. The darkness and added oxygen only made her head swim, so she gave up about halfway.

"How much do you need?" she asked.

"Five or six thousand should do it."

"Five or six thousand *dollars*?" Tess echoed. "Did you rent out the entire hotel or something?"

"It's not like it makes a difference to you," Quentin said,

a mulish set to his jaw. "You probably have that sitting in a drawer around here. You're just upset because Gertie chose me over you."

"She didn't choose you, Quentin. She's acting out because we had an argument. It'll pass, and when it does, you won't find this parenting thing so easy." Even as Tess spoke, she rummaged around her desk for her checkbook. She had to shove past Ivy's giant manuscript, several of Gertrude's graphic novels, and for some inexplicable reason, a plastic-wrapped muffin before she finally found it. As soon as she finished writing it out, she handed both it and the books—finished and unfinished—over. "Here. She'll want to take these with her. The graphic novels belong to the library, so they'll need to be returned eventually. My grandfather's hardware store is on the hook for them."

"Your grandfather's hardware store?" Quentin echoed. "What does that have to do with anything?"

Tess sighed. To be honest, now that Nicki was a murderer and had clocked her over the head, she wasn't sure what the rules were regarding late fees. "I had to give the library an address with a mailbox in order to get a card. It's not a big deal."

"Yeah, but isn't it all closed up? When I walked by, it looked like no one had been in there for months."

Yes, but only if you didn't count the mystery guest who'd slept underneath the cash register. Or the bobcat that had ravaged the fertilizers. "It's just a formality, Quentin. What does it matter?"

"Nothing." He accepted the graphic novels but refused

Ivy's manuscript. "I'm not lugging that thing around. You can keep it."

"Fine. Whatever. But don't blame me when Gertrude refuses to go to bed until she finds out what happens in chapter fifteen million and sixty-seven."

Quentin stopped in the middle of heading out the door. "What kind of book has that many chapters?"

Tess sighed, her heart and head so heavy that it was a wonder she could breathe at all. "One that's finished... something I don't know anything about these days."

Chapter Twenty-Nine

"He's not accepting visitors right now."

Tess stood at the end of the hospital hallway with her arms crossed and her most belligerent expression on. She was facing two of the largest, meanest-looking deputies the sheriff had on staff, but she wasn't about to be intimidated.

"He'll see me."

"I'm sorry, ma'am, but we've been posted here to ensure the sheriff's privacy. Unless you're here on official business, we can't let you by."

"This *is* official business," Tess countered. "Just go into his room and tell him Tess Harrow is here. He'll throw open the doors and beg me to come in."

The two deputies shared a look that showed their disbelief, but Tess only tapped an impatient foot. She could literally stand here all day. She had nowhere else to be; her new best friend was a criminal, and her daughter had left her. And the only other thing she could feasibly do— write the ending to her book—was on hold until she figured out some kind of resolution. No matter how hard she tried to make Willow and her wily librarian friend, Lexi Lexington, out to be the bad guys, they fought her tooth and nail.

"Tell him it's about Zach Peabody. Tell him I have new information about the case."

Mentioning Zach got the two men to start moving, though they trudged rather than ran to the sheriff's hospital room. Tess didn't bother waiting at the end of the hall, so she was well within hearing range by the time they reached him.

"For the Lord's sake, get rid of her," Sheriff Boyd said. He sounded tired, irritable, and, to be perfectly frank, like he meant every word. "Tell her I'm sleeping. Or in surgery. Or dead. Whatever it takes."

The remaining shreds of Tess's dignity, already barely holding on by a thread, disintegrated. She'd always known that Sheriff Boyd's by-the-book approach to solving crime and her own somewhat unorthodox methods weren't compatible, but that was a large part of their charm. They were Fox Mulder and Dana Scully, Kate Beckett and Richard Castle, Scott Turner and Hooch.

Weren't they?

"She seems awfully determined, Sheriff," one of the deputies said. "Maybe you could just feed her a line to get her out of here."

"Like what? That woman has been a pain in my backside since the moment she rolled into town. Do you have any idea how much easier this would have been if she'd just left when I told her to? I don't have time for more of her crackpot theories right now."

Tess's whole body began shaking. She was tempted to push her way past the sheriff's two self-designated bodyguards and demand an audience, but she couldn't seem to make her legs work. They were cemented to the floor along with her heart, which was rapidly sinking lower still.

He doesn't believe me. He doesn't respect *me.*

Having spent the past fifteen years of her life married to a man for whom respect was a four-letter word, Tess recognized that feeling more than she cared to.

All of a sudden, the Bigfoot book in her bag seemed paltry. A few hasty scrawls in the margins were hardly enough to accuse Ivy of murder—and even the bump on her head was taking on less dramatic proportions. Beyond a slight bruising, Nicki hadn't technically hurt her, and she didn't have any hard evidence about Nicki's involvement in the animal smuggling ring—or that an animal smuggling ring existed in the first place. If she wanted to hand the sheriff a case he could actually prosecute, then that was what she needed to do: hand the sheriff a case he could actually prosecute.

As the men in the room began to guffaw over a joke that had probably been made at Tess's expense, her legs began moving again. Not *toward* that hospital room, where nothing but incredulity and heartbreak waited for her, but in the opposite direction. Back down the hall, toward the parking lot, and firmly seated behind the wheel of her Jeep.

She turned the key and floored it, determined to get to the bottom of things. And to do it, she knew exactly where she needed to start.

At the top.

"Mason Peabody. Just the man I wanted to see." Tess took the stairs to his seventies-style office two at a time. There was a spring in her step and a sparkle in her eye—the direct result of having churned out three thousand words of fiction.

They weren't three thousand words on *Fury in the Forest*, but that was beside the point. Tess had just finished writing what she considered her real masterpiece.

"I wanted to let you read the article before I sent it over to my friend at the *Seattle Times*." She thrust ten typewritten pages out. "I think you'll find it a very scintillating read."

Mason snatched so greedily at the pages that Tess almost screamed. The past few days hadn't been great for her nerves; at this point, a butterfly landing on her shoulder too fast would probably send her into hiding.

"You're really going through with it?" Mason asked as he started scanning the lines. The question was a rhetorical one—a point driven home when he finished the first paragraph, guffawed, and dropped into his cracked leather swivel chair. "You're right. He *is* like a corrupt king who's been on the throne too long."

The he in question was Sheriff Victor Boyd, a man Tess had painted in every color of villainy her vast imagination held. He was a corrupt king one sentence, an unrestrained dictator the next. He stepped on people to achieve his own ends and cared nothing for the little guy. It was all made up, of course, but Tess had been so infuriated by what she'd overheard in the hospital that she'd allowed her feelings to flow over onto the page. She may have gone slightly overboard.

As Mason continued reading and chuckling to himself,

Tess wandered around the vintage office, taking note of the faded details and slightly musty smells. She stopped when she reached a map showing a huge swathe of forest extending in every direction.

"Is this us?" she asked, tapping a gold star in the center. The topography around here was starting to become more familiar, and she thought she recognized the stream she'd crossed on her way in.

Mason glanced quickly up and grunted his assent. "That's a breakdown of all the areas that are getting ready for reforestation. Logging will continue well into the fall, but I like to plan ahead. The planting season will be on us in no time."

Tess nodded and continued studying the map. She was pretty sure she could see where her own cabin was located, not to mention the surrounding forest where the search parties had been out looking for Carl…and where she and the sheriff had ultimately found him. The logging map went much further north than she'd ever ventured, but Tess liked that she was coming to know the area. It made her feel more at home, almost—*almost*—like she belonged.

"Well?" She turned her back to the map and watched as Mason neatly stacked the papers. The grin on his face was all she needed to know she'd succeeded at her goal. "Would you like to add an official comment?"

His grin widened. When he smiled like that, so deeply that his eyes crinkled at the corners, he was an undeniably attractive man. "No, thank you. I'm not going anywhere near this thing."

She couldn't help laughing. "Scared of what Sheriff Boyd will do to you?"

"Of course not." He gave the appearance of being genuinely insulted. "My campaign is a clean one, that's all. I wouldn't want people to think I had anything to do with this piece."

Considering that Mason Peabody's entire platform was based on making himself out to be the opposite of Sheriff Boyd, a man of the people and champion of the downtrodden, Tess wasn't sure how true this was, but she was willing to play along. "And why would they?" she agreed blandly. "It's merely one investigative journalist's look at life and bureaucracy in small-town America."

"And a fine look at life and bureaucracy, it is. I like the part you added about my donations to the library—the blue bookmobile is just the start. We have a whole fleet planned for the next few years. Not many people know about that."

"Nicki is always singing your praises," Tess admitted.

Mason greedily rubbed his hands. "When will the article run?"

"Well, now." She hesitated. Things were progressing so nicely that she hated to upset the apple cart. "That depends."

"On what?"

"You." She positioned herself in front of Mason's desk and stared down at him. She made no move to take the article from him, no attempt to win her way through this with a smile. The apple cart was toppling over one way or another. "I'm happy to overnight this to my friend but not until you tell me about your brothers."

"My brothers?" He shot out of his chair like a bullet. There were several dozen people milling around outside this office, so Tess didn't fear for her life, but that didn't make getting stared down by a man over half a foot taller than her any more pleasant. "What do they have to do with anything?"

"I don't know," she said with perfect honesty. "That's why I'm asking. They're more tied up in this murder investigation than you've let on—that much I'm sure of. How they're involved, however, is still a blank. I'd like you to fill it in."

"With what?" he demanded.

Tess bit back a sigh. Clearly, this was a man who didn't do well with an empty page. "Let's start with whether either of them is homeless right now. Would they need to crash at, say, an abandoned store for a few nights?"

"No. They live in our parents' old house." Mason's brows knit tightly together. "What does this have to do with anything?"

"Telling you isn't part of the deal." Tess reached for the article. When Mason didn't try to stop her, she knew she was on the right track. He wanted this thing in print so badly he'd probably rattle off his social security number if she asked for it. "Does Zach really go blast fishing in people's ponds?"

"No. Yes. Probably." Mason threw up his hands. "They're always doing stupid things like that. The Lord only knows why. To give me a headache, most likely. As kids, they were always getting in trouble and then begging me to pull them out of it."

"Is that why you got the logging company and they didn't?" Tess asked. She thought but didn't add, *and why they might be willing to go to great lengths to make some extra cash?*

"What are you talking about? We all have an equal stake in the business. They don't care to take on the day-to-day running of things, but we all own it. Together."

Tess's heart gave an odd thump. "What do you mean? They aren't just your employees?"

Mason looked at her as though she'd grown an extra head. Possibly two. "Are you serious? Of course it's not all mine. What kind of parent would give a company to one triplet and leave the other two out?"

To be honest, Tess had no idea. While it was obvious that Mason was the more level-headed of the three—and that he did the lion's share of the work—cutting the other two out of the business altogether would have been the height of cruelty. It also would have been a perfect motive for helping Nicki and Ivy run their animal smuggling business right under their brother's nose, which was why Tess was having such a hard time tossing the theory out.

If the Peabodys weren't hurting for cash—if they were nothing more than your average, garden-variety delinquents—then what was Zach doing skulking around with Nicki? And what had Zach and Mason been arguing about the first day she visited?

"Adam drinks too much, and Zach is always coming up with some crackbrained and unnecessary get-rich-quick scheme, but they're not a bad pair." Mason spoke with something approaching affection. "You could put that in the article, if you want. Our family's been a part of this place for over a hundred years. You can't go five steps without hitting some kind of Peabody history—most of it positive."

Mason spoke with a different kind of pride than usual. When he was puffing himself up as a potential sheriff candidate, he was bombastic to the point of being unbearable. This sounded less like a politician and more like a man who loved his family.

Which, yes, *could* be a motive for murder, but not for an animal smuggling ring that likely pulled in a fraction of the income this place did, if the size of the map on that wall was any indication.

"What was Zach's connection with Wilma Eyre?" she asked, determined to get through her questions before Mason threw her out the door. "Was he sleeping with her?"

"Of course not."

"But someone was. You said so yourself."

Mason's eyes narrowed. "What's this about? What do you really want from me?"

"The truth, Mr. Peabody," Tess said. "Zach wanted to sleep with her, didn't he?"

"Probably. My brother isn't the most discerning man when it comes to women. He even fancied you for a bit." Mason smirked. "But it's like I said—Wilma was in a relationship. Some hot city buck, by all accounts. Why does it matter? I told Sheriff Boyd all this the day he toured the logging camp. If he doesn't think it's worth following up on, why should you?"

Tess struggled to keep herself from saying something she'd regret. *Of course* Sheriff Boyd had known about Wilma's love affair, and *of course* he'd never once thought to mention it to her. Every single person who was connected to this case was hiding something.

Edna's cat was a wild animal. Nicki wasn't just a librarian. Ivy knew more about Bigfoot than all the rest of them combined. Zach owned one-third of a logging corporation. Sheriff Boyd had spent this entire time pandering to her ego. The only person who *hadn't* lied was Mason, the man she'd pinpointed as the murderer from the start.

How was that for irony?

"Is that enough?" Mason asked with a nod at the article in her hand. "Will you print the article now, or did you want me to tell you something else?"

Tess wouldn't have minded a quick peek at his financial records, and Detective Gonzales would have been sure to demand an interrogation room with Zach Peabody and no witnesses, but the information Mason had supplied was more than enough for now.

"I'll send it to him tonight," Tess promised. She *would* send it to him, but she knew there wasn't even a remote chance he'd print it. The last thing anyone in Seattle cared about was the political landscape of a town almost no one had ever heard of. "Thank you, Mason. You've been more helpful than you realize."

Mason walked her politely to the door. "As have you." He didn't reach for the knob right away. Tess was alarmed until she glanced up and noticed his thoughtful expression. "That thing you said before, about whether or not my brothers would be staying at an abandoned store... You mean your grandfather's old hardware shop, don't you?"

Tess nodded. "I'm sure you've heard by now that the sheriff and I found signs of a makeshift camp in there."

Mason heaved a sigh. "Which goes to show you how far things have fallen under his watch. When I'm sheriff, I'll make sure to ship those homeless bums out of town on the first Greyhound that passes through. I saw him skulking around several times."

Tess had to bite down on her tongue to keep from sharing her thoughts on such a cruel—and unhelpful—approach to the homeless epidemic and focused instead on the second half of this statement. "What do you mean, you saw him? You literally saw the person who broke in? You know who it was?"

"Well, I can't say as I *know* him, but there was some pretty strange activity going on there right after you moved into your cabin."

Tess heart stopped dead in her chest. "What kind of strange activity? Who was he?"

Mason scratched his chin thoughtfully. "I never got a good look at the guy, but he seemed pretty average. Better dressed than most bums but that's not saying much. He probably stole the hunter's jacket I saw him in."

The mention of a hunter's jacket snagged lightly on Tess's memory, but that was no surprise. People around here seemed to own them by the dozen.

"Why didn't you think to let Sheriff Boyd know?" she demanded. "Or me, for that matter? It's my hardware store."

"I've been meaning to speak to you about that, actually. I've already bought up most of that block; we're planning on tearing everything down and building some luxury condos. What would you say to selling me the building? I'll take it as-is, no questions asked."

"Luxury condos?" Tess echoed. She couldn't think of anything more incongruous to the historical flair of the town. The people of Winthrop didn't need Sub-Zero fridges and cathedral ceilings. Not when they had the vast wilderness and the entire midnight sky to call their own. Sheriff Boyd would rather gnaw off his own arm than see his precious Main Street become a haven for tourists.

"You think on it," Mason said in lieu of an answer. "You might even consider getting in on the ground floor with a unit of your own. The return on investment is sure to be a selling touch point for years to come."

Since Mason was back on his buzzwords, Tess knew she wasn't likely to get anything approaching sense out of him now. Pulling open the door, she trotted out to her waiting Jeep, her head in a whirl.

There really was a person staying in the hardware store. A male person. A male person who skulked.

That might not fit in with her lady gang of criminals, and it might not be enough to bring the case home to Sheriff Boyd, but it was a heck of a good start.

———

The police tape around the hardware store had been removed by this time, but the building was in as much disarray as the last time Tess had been here. It also smelled just as bad as before, which was a point in favor of Mason's luxury condo offer. The task of cleaning this up wasn't one that appealed.

There was still no electricity running to the store, but

daylight held out long enough for Tess to make a beeline for the cash register area. The sleep-rumpled blankets were there along with the potato chip packages and a bottle of Gatorade that looked suspiciously as though it had served as a midnight urinal. If anything else was needed to convince Tess that Mason had been right about her trespasser being male, that was it. Anyone with female anatomy would have to do some serious maneuvering to make that work.

She poked the bottle out of the way with the end of a rake and crouched low, taking in the scene with what she hoped were fresh eyes. There was no sign of a hunter's jacket, but when she picked up one of the blankets, she noticed that the wool was heavy and of exceptional quality. Pendleton, probably—a theory that bore itself out when she found the tag.

"These things are two hundred bucks a pop." Tess snapped a picture of the tag before tucking the blanket carefully back into place. "Why didn't the sheriff and I notice this before?"

She knew the answer to that already—because they'd been so blinded by the footprints, both feline and human. Even though they'd solved the riddle of the bobcat, those stupid size nines kept coming back to haunt her.

"Our mystery man wears size nine shoes," Tess said. "He appeared in this store around the same time I moved into the cabin. He eats high-end blue cheese potato chips, pees in empty Gatorade bottles, and sleeps on nothing less than merino wool. He knew about the bobcat and most likely was the one who tranquilized it that day in the forest."

With a flash of insight so profound that it almost knocked

Tess flat, she realized what she was looking at—or, to be more exact, *who*. And unless she was very much mistaken, the answer wasn't Ivy Bell, Nicki Nickerson, or anyone with the surname of Peabody.

"Tess, thank God I found you."

Tess screamed and whirled, the rake now held in her hands like a weapon. She lowered it once she recognized the flushed, breathless face of her ex-husband. "Quentin! What's the matter with you? You scared me half to death."

Quentin took a staggering step toward her. His hair was matted to his forehead with perspiration, his eyes wild as he reached for her. "It's Gertie," he said, gasping. "I can't find her anywhere. Something's wrong."

Chapter Thirty

"Is this supposed to be a joke?"

Sheriff Boyd stood looming in the doorway to his office. A heavy cast covered his lower leg, and he leaned on a cane, but he didn't look any less in command because of it. If anything, he looked even more like a rigid man of the law. Not even cracked bones could slow him down.

They wouldn't have slowed Detective Gonzales down, either. Or, Tess realized with a firm set of her jaw, *her*.

"If you think I'd joke about my daughter going missing, then you have no idea who I am—or what I'm capable of." Tess pushed her way past the sheriff, though she was careful not to jostle his injury. "Quentin, give him your report, please."

"My report?" Quentin echoed blankly.

Tess waved an impatient hand. Her ex hadn't recovered either his breath or his composure on the run over to the police station. She, on the other hand, was in peak form. The moment she'd heard those ominous words—*something's wrong*—she'd practically sprinted over here. All her search partying and tramping around the forest lately had done wonders for her physique; she wasn't even winded.

"Tell him what you told me."

"Just that—she's gone." Quentin spoke with so much force—so much fear—that flecks of spittle flew from his lips. "I didn't think she needed constant watching. She asked me for change for the vending machine, so I gave it to her. Then she left the hotel room to get her cookies or whatever. That was the last I saw of her."

Tess held her trembling rage in check, but it was difficult. If Quentin knew anything at *all* about his child, he'd have realized that nothing short of the apocalypse would drive Gertrude to vending machine snacks. Not while gourmet trail mix and yucca root crisps existed.

She'd obviously used the vending machine as an excuse to sneak off again. Only this time, Tess had no idea why…or where she might have gone.

"And what time was this?" Sheriff Boyd asked.

"When she left the room? An hour ago, maybe two."

"Wait—what?" Tess swiveled her head to stare at her ex. "You said you came straight to the hardware store to find me. How can she have been gone for that long?"

"It's all my fault." Quentin dropped his head in his hands. "I didn't notice right away. There was a movie on cable that I wanted to watch, and she was so quiet when she was in the room—"

There was no holding back the rage after that. Every limb in Tess's body shook with adrenaline, and she was prepared to use that adrenaline to make her feelings known. Sheriff Boyd took one look at her, however, and intervened. In what was possibly his drawliest voice yet, he asked, "Did she leave a note behind?"

"No, not that I could find."

The sheriff chewed on this for a long moment. "And did she give you any indication that she was upset with you?"

"No! We've been getting along great. In fact, we'd just decided that she'd come live with me for a while. She and Tess have been fighting."

Unbeknownst to Tess, Ivy had entered the room. Just as she was ready to explode, the other woman placed herself next to Tess, her body a warm, pulsing presence at her side. In a low voice meant only for Tess's ears, she said, "Let him do his thing."

Tess couldn't pretend to misunderstand her. Her nerves were stretched to the limit with the urge to participate in this conversation. She wanted to rant and rave. She wanted to wail and gnash her teeth. She wanted to protest that she and Gertrude might not always have been on the same page, but they were united when it came to the important things.

But the sheriff had locked eyes with Quentin by this time—eyes *and* horns.

"So she walked out without saying a word to you?"

"Yes!"

"Leaving behind no note or any indication of her destination?"

"That's what I keep saying! I think she must have been kidnapped." Quentin took his lower lip between his teeth and groaned, his head dropping to his hands in anguish. "Oh, God. And I know who took her. How could I have been so stupid?"

Tess could have recited a long list of answers to that

question, but her heart was pounding too hard for her to pick up the metaphorical cudgel.

"I'm not following you, I'm afraid," Sheriff Boyd said. "Who took her, and why are you so sure?"

"It was that woman in the blue library van," Quentin said. "She's been skulking around the hotel for days. She's the one who stole my daughter—I'm sure of it."

"Nicki?" Sheriff Boyd and Ivy shared a look that contained more knowledge than a Biblical tree. They were shocked and worried and—most important—unsure of what it all meant. If anything more had been needed for Tess to feel certain that they'd solved this case weeks ago, it was that.

They knew about Nicki. They'd known about Nicki all along.

And if that was the case, then Tess was pretty sure she knew the rest.

Chapter Thirty-One

IT WAS AMAZING HOW FAST THE SHERIFF'S DEPARTMENT could move when faced with a missing child believed to be in the company of a suspected murderer.

Tess and Quentin were all but forgotten as the entire office jumped into action. Calls were put out to neighboring departments, alerts were put up on the airwaves, and Sheriff Boyd had eyes for no one and nothing but the task ahead of him. Tess would have given her right hand for a chance to speak to the sheriff alone, but there was no opportunity. Not only did he refuse to acknowledge her many speaking looks, but Quentin was stuck to her side like glue, peppering her with questions she didn't know the answers to.

"Why would she do this to us?"

"How could she get into a stranger's van without saying a word?"

"Why don't you make her turn her cell phone tracking on?"

As annoying as Tess found all this, it was the last question that sent her over the edge.

"What's wrong with her?"

Despite the fact that everyone standing inside the room could hear them, Tess was unable to refrain from answering.

"You mean, other than the fact that her father had an

affair with a woman half his age and left? That he disappeared without a word for six months, refusing to answer a single one of her texts or phone calls? That she's spent the better part of the last year feeling as though the one man in the world she loves most abandoned her? Gee, Quentin. I don't know. What *could* be wrong with her?"

This proved too much for Quentin—especially in such a public setting. He grabbed Tess by the upper arm and hauled her from the sheriff's office, his whole body shaking with rage and, Tess was forced to admit, fear. Whatever else Quentin might have done, his feelings over losing Gertrude were real.

"It's not what you think, Tess. I know I've messed up, but I never meant for this to happen." He sounded so genuine, the anguish on his face so real, that Tess's heart gave a sympathetic pang. "What could that woman want with her? Ransom? Extortion? Revenge?"

"Do you want to hear my honest opinion?" Tess didn't wait for an answer. Her honest opinion wasn't something she generally asked permission to give. "It's not Nicki who approached Gertie. I'd put everything I own on Gertie approaching her."

"What? Why?"

Tess's lips lifted in a slight smile. "Because that child is more like me than she'd like anyone to know. She figured this thing out long before I did. I'm guessing she grabbed the first able-bodied adult she could find and took her to where the animals are being kept."

Quentin's whole body jerked. He still had his hand

clamped on Tess's arm, his grip digging so deep that Tess cried out in pain.

"What do you mean, *the animals*?"

"Tigers, bobcats, toucans...I'm not sure what kind of exotic creatures are being held anymore. I bet Gertie does, though. It's funny. I never thought that all this murder and intrigue was something she'd enjoy. If I'd have known that, I'd have asked for her help plotting my novels years ago."

Quentin's hold on Tess's arm didn't soften in the slightest. "How can you stand there cracking jokes at a time like this? You have no idea who that woman is—or what she might want with our daughter."

"You're right," Tess said. "I don't. Which is why I think you should take me to her."

"Me? *Me?*"

For the first time since he'd arrived in Winthrop, Tess allowed herself to look at her ex-husband—*really* look at him. He wasn't wearing a hunter's jacket, it was true, but all the other signs were there. Unlike her, he'd lost quite a bit of weight lately, his clothes hanging off a body that had always been lean to begin with. His hair was a little too long, his skin more tanned than usual. Even more telling were his finger-nails, which used to always be fastidiously clipped and main-tained. Today, however, they were jagged and bitted down to nubs. Tess was sure, if she asked him to roll up the long sleeves of his button-down, that there would be tell-tale claw marks all over his arms.

"Wilma Eyre was the woman you were cheating on me with, wasn't she?" Tess asked, her voice surprisingly calm considering the roiling of emotion under the surface. She was *finally* starting to understand why Gertrude had been so upset about the email she'd read all those months ago—and why she'd been so furious at Tess for studiously avoiding it. "Was that before or after the two of you started smuggling exotic animals over the border using my grandfather's cabin as your headquarters?"

"I don't know what you're talking about." Quentin's voice grew shrill, his clamp on her arm now tighter than a vise.

"What happened? Did she decide she could do better and drop you? Find out you were skimming a little off the top? I already know how willing you are to cut out the people in your life as soon as they're no longer of use to you. I thought abandoning a teenager was as low as you could go. I guess murder is a close second."

In that moment, Tess realized that she'd underestimated her ex-husband—both in terms of his strength and his love for Gertrude. As he yanked her arm so hard that she felt it wrench out of its socket, he pulled a gun from out of his waistband and pointed it at her. Unlike the shotgun above her door, this one looked brand new and highly lethal.

"I wouldn't, if I were you," Quentin warned in a voice low with loathing. The gun didn't waver once. "You and I are going on a little trip to get our daughter back. And for once in your life, you aren't in a position to argue with me."

She opened her mouth and closed it again, feeling the weight of his words like the gun he had pointed at her head. She'd known it would be a gamble—to confront Quentin like this, to trust that the man she'd once loved still existed somewhere deep inside—but she hadn't known how far he'd take it.

She had her answer now, and she wasn't so sure she liked it.

He'll take it all the way.

Chapter Thirty-Two

A FEW MINUTES LATER, TESS FOUND HERSELF IN THE trunk of a car she didn't recognize. She knew down to the exact inch how much room was in the back of Quentin's Lexus sedan because she'd had him tie her up and stuff her inside a few years back. She'd been researching escape possibilities and needed to know—for authenticity's sake—how easy it was to get out.

It had been remarkably easy, much to her surprise, due in large part to a glow-in-the-dark emergency release lever.

The car she was in now was either a rental or a loaner, because she hadn't seen Quentin behind the wheel while in Winthrop. It was also much older than the Lexus, because no such escape hatch existed. There was nothing but scratchy carpet and the tang of old oil to keep her company as they bumped over the heavily rutted roads.

Quentin hadn't bothered to secure either her hands or her mouth before he'd commanded her to crawl inside, but she didn't use either of those things to her advantage. She merely tried to find a comfortable position and keep track of the twists and turns of a road that seemed to be taking them deep into the heart of nothing.

Her feeling of calm acceptance abated as first one hour

passed by, then another. She'd known, from her study of Mason's map, that the expanse of forest out here was a large one, but familiarity didn't make it any easier to be traveling with an angry, armed ex-husband who'd already murdered two people in an effort to cover his tracks.

Considering that he was still listed as the beneficiary on her life insurance policy—and that the bulk of her money would go to whoever cared for Gertrude until the girl reached adulthood—Tess's chances of making it out of this alive were slim. She could only cross her fingers and hope that she wasn't wrong about what they'd find once they arrived at their destination.

The car came to a lurching stop at around the same time Tess's bladder started making pulsing warnings that it wouldn't hold out for much longer. When the trunk popped open to reveal darkness broken only by Quentin's grim expression, Tess knew that all the crossed fingers in the world wouldn't save her.

"They're not here. I should have known better than to trust you."

He took a few steps back, clearing the way for Tess to unfold her creaky, tingling limbs and restore the blood flow to them. She took stock of their surroundings as she did, but she didn't need her eyes to tell her where they were. Her nose had that covered.

At some point in its history, it must have been a commune of some sort—a haphazard collection of rusted shipping containers and wooden sheds arranged around a fire pit. A laundry line between two of the trees and a cooking pot hinted that human life had existed in some fashion in this locale's past.

Now, however, it was the wasted remains of the world's worst zoo. The only livestock Tess could see was an enormous snake inside a dirty glass aquarium, but the piles of dung told their own tale. So did the skeletal cages holding nothing but scratchy, mildewing animal bedding. One looked large enough to house an actual tiger; a few smaller ones hinted at a home for the bobcats. And the piles of straw spilling out of the shipping containers hinted that they, too, had been used as temporary living quarters for animals of all shapes and sizes.

"For God's sake, Quentin." Tess pressed the back of her hand to her nose to quell the overwhelming stench. "Couldn't you at least have cleaned up after the animals? It's a wonder no one found your hideout by following the scent trail. A pack of well-trained dogs could have found this place in a matter of hours."

"I don't know what you're talking about," he said, but they both knew it was a lie.

"Was Wilma the one who did the caretaking?" Tess demanded. "Is that what happened? You killed her and took all the money before you realized that taking care of a living, breathing creature is actual work?"

"It was an accident," Quentin said, his voice rising. "I didn't mean to kill her."

"But you did. Something to do with her head, right? What was it? A tranquilizer dart gone astray? A rock to the temple in a fit of anger?"

Quentin's eyes widened, and he looked at her as if she'd just pulled a rabbit out of a hat. Either that or climbed aboard a broomstick and taken flight. "How can you possibly know that?"

"Because you took the time to remove her head afterward, obviously." Did he think she was an idiot? It was the oldest trick in the book—and she would know, because she'd once written that exact one. "You didn't want anyone to be able to identify either her or the murder weapon."

"You…you…" Quentin quavered.

"You got that from that time we went to the mobster museum in Vegas," Tess scoffed. She remembered the trip well. She'd learned all kinds of useful things about removing identifying parts. Quentin had acted bored the whole time, but it seemed he'd been storing that information for later use. "Where are her other body parts, by the way? I'm surprised you didn't feed her to the animals."

From the way Quentin's face contorted, she realized that was what he *had* done.

"Good God, Quentin. What's the matter with you?"

That was when the rest of it hit her.

"You were going to do the same to poor Carl, weren't you? He chased after you that day in the woods, but you killed him. And then you cut him up to feed to the animals, but you'd either sold or lost most of them by that point, so you decided to bury him instead."

"It's not what you think, Tess. I didn't have a choice. Wilma was the one who oversaw everything. She was the one who knew what to feed the animals and how much they needed and—" He groaned. "You know I've never been good at the details."

It was true. She did know it. She also knew that she was to blame for a lot of what had happened here. When she'd first arrived, she'd noticed how clean the cabin was, detected the scent of Quentin's cologne in the air. If she hadn't been so distracted by the body in the pond, she'd have realized it had been inhabited long before she got there.

Which meant that *her* grandfather's cabin had housed her husband before he'd been forced to take up residence in the hardware store. *She'd* been the one to introduce him into the ways and means of being a criminal. *She* was the one who'd taken care of him for fifteen years, leaving him ill-prepared for a life on his own two feet. She'd probably even been the reason he stole all those books from the library in a last-ditch effort to turn his operation around.

In the Harrow household, books were always the answer.

Quentin must have started thinking along the same lines, because his whole demeanor underwent a dramatic shift. Instead of taking responsibility for his own actions, he cast a frantic look around.

"They're not here," he said, both the gun and his voice wavering. "Gertie and the librarian. You said they'd be here."

"I said they *might* be here," Tess corrected him, though not without some wavering of her own. She didn't trust the way Quentin looked right now—like an animal who knew he was one step away from a lifetime in one of those cages. "Maybe I was wrong and Gertie wanted nothing to do with this place. Maybe Nicki really is just a librarian who needed to spend some quiet time alone in the woods."

"I'm no such thing, and you know it." Nicki stepped out from behind a tree. Her hands were up in a gesture of surrender, but Tess didn't fail to notice the holster that held a gun tight against her ribcage.

Neither did Quentin. In one quick movement, he hooked his free arm around Tess's neck and yanked her in front of him in a back choke hold, his gun pressed to her temple. Unless Nicki was a crack shot, there was no way she could touch Quentin without going through Tess first.

"I come in peace," Nicki said, still with her hands up. She didn't attempt to approach them, but her whole body was tense with potential energy. "There's no need to act drastically."

"Where's Gertie?" Quentin demanded. "What have you done with her?"

"Don't worry. Gertie is safe and sound."

Nicki's eyes flicked to Tess's for a brief moment before moving back to Quentin's face. Tess realized, in a wash of relief, that the message being relayed was a hundred percent true—and offered for her benefit. *She* might have been deeply and categorically wrong about Nicki's motives in all this, but Gertie wasn't. When faced with irrefutable proof of her father's crimes, she'd gone to the one place—and the one person—where she knew she'd be safe.

"I want her back." Quentin tightened his hold on Tess's neck. She could still breathe, but not well. The hard steel of his arm was making it difficult to swallow. "Give me my daughter and half a million dollars, and we can all walk out of here safely."

"Give you Gertrude?" Tess demanded. "Have you lost your mind? If you think I'm letting her get anywhere near you after this, you might as well put that bullet in my head and get it over with."

If there was one thing Quentin knew about Tess, it was when arguments would be futile. She didn't have too many absolute lines she refused to cross, but this was one of them. She'd swallowed Quentin's infidelity for years. She gave him way more money than he'd been granted by the divorce courts. She'd even said goodbye to her daughter—however temporarily—when she'd thought it was what Gertrude really wanted.

But there was no way, short of a bloodbath, that Quentin was getting anywhere near their daughter after this.

"Fine." Quentin bit the word off and spat it at her. "Just the money, then. But I want it in cash."

What remained of Tess's patience snapped. "You aren't going to fight for her? Not even a little bit?"

"For crying out loud, Tess!" Quentin's whole body started to vibrate with anger. "You just said I can't have her."

"Of course you can't. But that doesn't mean you shouldn't *try*."

With a growl, Quentin pressed the cold ring of steel against her temple. Tess had written this moment countless times before, but she'd never realized how powerful it could be—not because she was scared but because there was a limit to fear. Once death was literally jabbing you in the head, survival took over.

Survival and a determination that your lying, cheating, murdering ex-husband wouldn't get away with this.

Like being locked in a trunk, being held at gunpoint was something Tess had practiced before—and with Quentin, of all people. Detective Gonzales had once been taken hostage, and she'd wanted him to escape using nothing but his own wits.

She knew now that he never would have done that in real life. Sheriff Boyd had taught her that. In this kind of situation, a *real* officer of the law would call for backup or let a hostage negotiator take over or allow Nicki Nickerson to do her thing. Police training demanded patience and protocol above all else—even if it meant the bad guy got away.

Tess Harrow, thriller writer and woman scorned, had none of that training. And Quentin was going to get away over her dead body.

With a deep breath, she put all her research into action. Step one was to thrust one leg out to the side, stepping away from the gun and forcing Quentin to adjust his hold. Step two was to raise her arm like a pendulum. Step three was to bring it crashing down against Quentin's favorite and most vulnerable anatomy.

In the aftermath, both Nicki and Sheriff Boyd would rake her over the coals for her stupidity. Sheriff Boyd would tell her what a foolhardy, annoying pain-in-the-backside she was. Nicki would point out that, since Ivy was literally creeping up behind them at the time, there was no need for such theatrics. In the moment, however, with adrenaline coursing through her, Tess could only feel triumphant as

Quentin howled, bent over double, and sent the gun flying to the dirt.

Now that her part in all this was over, Tess stood back and watched as Nicki dove to retrieve the weapon, followed almost immediately by Ivy tackling Quentin to the ground. The two of them fell in a tangle of limbs that ended up with Quentin pinned to the ground underneath the sharp jab of Ivy's knee. Nicki trained the gun at Quentin's head to hold him back, but there was no need. He knew when he'd been beaten, and he'd been beaten hard.

"By a lady gang," Tess said aloud. She felt a smile tug at her lips, her relief mixed with so many other emotions that it was difficult to pinpoint them all. "A lady gang of law officials and an ex-wife who knows a thing or two about self-defense."

"I like to think I had a little something to do with it," Sheriff Boyd grumbled as he came limping out of the tree line. The radio attached to his chest squawked with activity as the events were called in and reinforcements called out. "And what in the devil's name were you doing with all that ducking and flailing about?"

"I didn't flail," Tess protested. "I was using my moves."

She might not have spoken for all the attention Sheriff Boyd paid her. "He could have easily shot you, and then where would we be? If you think the paperwork for firing a gun is bad, you should see what happens when a hostage is killed at the scene of a crime."

"Uh oh. Does that happen to you often?" Tess couldn't help asking.

"I swear on everything you love, Tess Harrow, if you knew what was good for you…"

It was a shame Tess hadn't brought a tape recorder with her, because the torrent of words that Victor released were worthy of a Pulitzer. She'd made his case difficult at every turn. She'd scared Bigfoot away just when he'd been close to catching him. She had no business introducing her greedy ex-husband to Winthrop so he could conceive the ill notion of running exotic animals over the border in the first place.

"Where's Gertie?" Tess asked the moment Sheriff Boyd paused for breath. Ivy had Quentin well in hand by this time and was assisting him into the back of the squad car she'd parked at the end of the drive. Quentin had been so busy trying to find his daughter that he hadn't noticed they'd been followed the entire way.

"I told you. She's perfectly safe." Nicki approached with a light, careful tread, her gun holster still in place. Although Tess hadn't had time to give her a full assessment while staring death in the eyes, she took a moment to do so now. Like the day she'd seen Nicki after her trip to Seattle, her friend was dressed simply and neatly in well-cut navy slacks and a white button-down. "And if I know anything about her, gleefully devouring the latest issue of Nightwave."

"You left her in the bookmobile, didn't you?" Tess asked.

"It seemed the safest place, under the circumstances. No one will be able to find where I parked it, if that's what you're worried about."

"And by no one, you mean Mason Peabody, right?"

Nicki's glance turned sharp. "Since when do you care about Mason Peabody?"

"To be perfectly honest, I don't. But since you're investigating him for money laundering and who-knows-what-other-kinds-of-fraud, I imagine you care a lot." Tess paused. "FBI, right? That means he must be laundering money across state borders. Or out of the country."

Behind her, Sheriff Boyd groaned.

"What?" Tess turned a pair of wide eyes on him. "I know all about it, remember? *Fury in the Big City*. Detective Gonzales's FBI friend never would have been able to help him out if that mobster from New Jersey hadn't tried opening a second floating casino off the coast of Virginia."

"I've read the book, thanks."

"In real life, that FBI agent would have been pulled from the case long before he got that far," Nicki put in. "If he hadn't been fired outright. He broke at least seven security protocols, by my count."

"Nicki, not you, too!"

Nicki shared a grin with Sheriff Boyd. "Sorry, but it's true. If it makes you feel any better, I'm impressed you caught on. What was it about me that tipped you off?"

"Other than you leaving me painkillers and cleaning my gun after you knocked me out?" Tess shook her head. "Nothing. Mason dug his own grave. There's a map on his office wall that outlines all his replanting efforts, but I've spent enough time out here to recognize that half those forests are old growth. There hasn't been any logging done there in decades."

Tess felt her chest puff up a little. Her grandfather would be proud to see how far she'd come. Living in—and loving—this forest was something he'd spent a lifetime doing.

"That's how he does it, right?" she persisted. "Putting on a big show of ecologically sustainable logging? Pretending to sell more expensive wood to a bunch of shell companies up north? You can clean a lot of money by making it look like it's coming from forward-thinking businesses, especially if he's running most of his timber over the border. Money coming in from Canada would be a lot harder for the IRS and feds to track."

"It's not *his* money he's cleaning, but yeah. That's the gist of it. He's got ties to several shady characters who don't mind having a friend who regularly treks back and forth from Canada." Nicki narrowed her eyes at Tess. "You got all that from a map?"

"Not all of it," Tess admitted. "I wrote an article about his political platform for the *Seattle Times*. To help him win the next election."

Sheriff Boyd gave a start of surprise. "You *what*?!"

"Relax. They won't actually print it. But it got him to open right up. He mentioned that the bookmobile he donated to the library was just the first of many he was working with Nicki to implement. But that got me thinking…how many bookmobiles could a place like this possibly need?" She paused for dramatic effect. "If you'll recall, inflated charity donations are what tipped Detective Gonzales off in—"

There was no chance for Tess to finish. Both Nicki and Sheriff Boyd loudly voiced their protest to the continued reminder of their least favorite officer of the law.

"The less we hear about that man, the better," the sheriff grumbled, but Tess could tell he was impressed, so she kept going.

"Did you know Mason's planning on building luxury condos where my grandfather's hardware store is?"

He didn't, and, if the martial look in his eye was any indication, he was going to rectify that deficiency at once. "Not if the planning board has anything to say about it," he said. "That must be why he's so keen on getting me out of office. Well, that and the fact that the net is closing in on him, and he knows it."

"Yeah, which is why you have to swear not to do anything to blow my cover," Nicki said. "I was forced to take Ivy and the sheriff into my confidence, since they were digging deep into everyone's background for this murder case, but my work is far from done. I'm close to flipping Zach. If I can get him to testify against his brother, that's the end of all this."

Tess felt a spike of excitement drive home. "So *that's* why you were sneaking around with him outside your—" Too late, she realized what she was admitting—and who she was admitting it to.

"Wait. You were following me? You heard us?"

"It was just a little stakeout," Tess protested. "It could have been worse. At least I didn't hit you with a ten-pound rifle."

"That was for your own protection."

"The bump on the back of my head would disagree." Tess paused, frowning a little. While she adored the idea of Nicki

Nickerson operating as an undercover FBI agent bringing down a logging money laundering scheme in the wilds of rural Washington, she didn't love what it meant for the long-term. As soon as the case ended, Nicki would likely be gone with it. "You could have just told me the truth, you know. I wouldn't have said anything."

"She could have, but I asked her not to." The sheriff spoke with his customary drawl. "We needed you to be on your guard. Until we could catch your husband at this actual location, there was no way to link him to the murder. Officially, I mean. We've suspected his involvement for a while now, and we have an eyewitness who can confirm that he and Wilma were romantically involved, but we needed more before we could bring him in."

"Wait a minute…" Tess whirled on the sheriff, her fears about losing Nicki temporarily set aside. This was too important to allow to pass. "Are you saying you broke the rules? To catch Quentin in the act?"

"Don't be ridiculous," the sheriff said stiffly. "Not a single rule has been broken for this case."

Tess wasn't buying it—not by a long shot. Especially since Sheriff Boyd seemed to be having a difficult time meeting her gaze. "But you didn't have enough evidence to arrest him without luring him to the scene of the crime, right?" she persisted. "So you used me. You used me and my daughter to catch him."

"I didn't do any such thing. Did I assume you'd eventually stick your nose in so far that Quentin would have no choice but to take you into his confidence or try to do away with you? Yes. Did I prevent that from happening in a timely manner?" He couldn't help the sides of his lips from twitching. "Maybe not as well as I should have. But ever since you fell on top of me and shattered my leg, I haven't been acting as fast as I normally would."

"How dare you. It's barely a snap."

"I'll probably never run again. Did I tell you that?"

She didn't buy that, either. It would take a lot more than a broken leg to slow Sheriff Boyd down. "You banished me from your hospital room and said all those terrible things to your deputies on purpose. You wanted me to have no one to turn to but Quentin. You wanted me to solve the case for you."

Sheriff Boyd rolled a laughing eye toward Nicki. "Agent Nickerson, is that how you saw things roll out?"

Nicki took a step back, her hands up and a look of unholy glee on her face. "I'm only part of this because of the crossover into my own case. I have no jurisdiction here."

"Chicken," the sheriff muttered.

Nicki heard him and laughed. "Don't worry. I'll swear on my oath of honor that Tess Harrow acted of her own volition every step of the way." She turned her grin on Tess. "I don't think she's capable of anything else."

Tess was no longer able to contain herself. In a burst of joy and sorrow and overwhelming relief, she sank to the ground, her head in her hands as her whole body shook. Both the sheriff and Nicki stepped forward to comfort her, but there was no need. She wasn't crying; she was laughing—and she wasn't sure she'd ever be able to stop.

"Well, really, Tess," Nicki said. "I don't see what's so funny."

"I do," the sheriff replied dryly. "She's thinking about how much Detective Gonzales would love every minute of this."

Epilogue

THE ONE THING TESS NEVER SAW COMING WAS HOW GOOD an ex-husband-murdering-people-in-the-woods story could be for the Winthrop economy.

"We want to extend your contract for six more books," her editor said the moment the first article went live. Much to Tess's chagrin—and, she was forced to admit, her delight—her headshot from Nicki's bookmobile was now slapped across every newspaper in the country. "No, seven. *Eight*. Heck—let's take 'em all."

"Don't sign a thing," her agent warned. "I've got no fewer than three Hollywood directors on the hook. I'm thinking we should hold out for a Netflix series."

"Business has never been so good," Otis said as people flocked out of his bicycle shop, determined to explore the woods where the murders had happened. "Tourists are heartless bastards, God bless them."

The only people who seemed to resent the outcome were Mason Peabody, who was livid over all the positive publicity Sheriff Boyd was getting, and the sheriff himself. It was probably the only time he and Mason had ever seen eye to eye on anything.

"If I'd have known we'd be saddled with a pack of nosy

busybodies for the next six months, I'd have kicked you out of this town the moment you sauntered in," he told Tess when she popped by the sheriff's office to ask if he had any requests for who should play him in the cinematic portrayal of events. She rather thought Adam Beach or Gil Birmingham was a nice fit, but if the look on the sheriff's face was anything to go by, he didn't find the comparisons flattering. "Can't you do something to get rid of them?"

Tess could do quite a few things to get rid of them, up to and including selling her grandfather's cabin and moving back to Seattle. But despite the terrible events that had happened here, Gertrude had begged her to let them stay.

"I know it's weird," Gertrude had said when Tess brought up the idea. "But even with what Dad did and all the things that happened in those woods...I dunno. I guess I just like it here. It feels like home."

After everything the poor girl had been through, it seemed cruel to deny her request. Especially considering that she'd put the clues together long before Tess had. Gertrude had harbored suspicions ever since she'd heard the name Wilma and remembered it from the email, but it had taken Quentin's arrival in town to really set things off. The yellow dress and the attitude shift, the way she'd played along with Quentin, had all been all to lower his guard and get him to divulge the details of where the animals had been kept.

Tess would have been furious with her if she wasn't so proud. She'd been so fixated on Nicki and Ivy, who, as it turned out, just really liked stories about Bigfoot, that she'd failed to see what Gertrude had noticed in a matter of minutes.

A man who could leave a kid like that behind was a man who was capable of anything.

"If I promise we can stay—" Tess had begun, cutting herself off at the first shrill note of Gertrude's delight. "And that's still an *if*, then we have to find a counselor who can help us work through all this. I know it doesn't feel like it now, but it's going to take a while to process everything. For both of us."

To Tess's surprise, Gertrude had thrown herself into her mother's arms. She'd gone back to the black clothes and black fingernails, and her mood returned to its customary pendulum swings, but Tess had never seen her so happy.

"I'd like that," Gertrude had said, sniffing loudly. Tess had no doubt that her inexpertly applied eyeliner was probably transferred all over her shirt, but she hadn't minded.

"And maybe," Tess had suggested gently, "you can help me plot the rest of *Fury in the Forest*."

Gertrude's sharp intake of breath could have been taken one of several ways, but the light in her big green eyes meant only one thing. "Are you serious? You'll let me help?"

"To be honest, I don't think I can finish without you," Tess said, not altogether truthfully. Since life and fiction couldn't be too closely aligned, she'd decided to make Willow the villain of her story. It never would have worked out between her and Detective Gonzales, anyway. He didn't need someone with a background in crime; what would do him good was an outside perspective, someone to shake him out of his broody, uptight logic.

"I also don't think I can finish without electricity and

running water," Tess had also admitted. "It's time we talk renovations."

That had been all that was needed to transport Gertrude to new heights of euphoria, especially since Nicki stopped by with regular deliveries of all the latest graphic novels to keep Gertrude entertained in the meantime. Librarians still had to be librarians, even if it was only a cover for an ongoing money laundering investigation.

In fact, everything was working out so well that Tess only had one order of business left.

"Well, Ivy." She nodded as the officer entered the police station, looking busy and satisfied, though what there was to do now that the murder had been solved, Tess had no idea. A place like this could hardly be a hotbed of criminal activity *all* the time, but what did she know?

"Oh, jeez. Whatever it is, I don't want any part of it." Ivy took a wide step backward—a thing that the caused the sheriff to snort in laughter as he returned his attention to the stack of paperwork on his desk.

"I think you might." Tess reached into her purse and pulled out a small white card. It contained very little except a name and a phone number, but those ten digits were about to open a door that had the potential to change Ivy's life forever. "This is my agent's home phone. She's expecting your call."

Ivy didn't make a move to take the card. "What? Why? *What?*"

"You can thank Gertrude for it. She's the one who scanned the first hundred pages of your book into her phone so I could send them. You should probably set one of your minions onto scanning the rest. Nancy's going to want them right away. She was practically salivating the last time I talked to her."

Tess wasn't sure what reaction she expected, but the sudden burst of tears that broke out on Ivy's face wasn't it.

"Are you serious? You sent it? She liked it?"

"She *loved* it," Tess assured her. "And since I told her it only gets better after the first hundred pages, you can understand why she wants to talk to you."

Before Tess realized what was happening, Ivy's arms were flung around her torso and she was being squeezed in a giant bear hug.

"I can't believe it. You really read it all? And you didn't hate it? I'm going to have an agent?"

Tess shared a glance with Sheriff Boyd over the top of Ivy's head. He didn't seem the least bit surprised to see Ivy's overflow of emotion. Instead, he nodded at Tess in a way that she didn't dare interpret. He was sympathetic yet rueful, mocking yet pleased.

More than anything, however, that nod carried a promise of more to come.

He also turned and walked away, leaving her to deal with Ivy. Tess wanted to call out to him, to ask what a look like that was supposed to mean, but she didn't. That conversation would have to wait for another day.

"I'm going to be the biggest and best author this town has ever seen," Ivy announced, her arms still locking Tess in an uncomfortable embrace. "People will come from all over the world to see me."

"I beg your pardon," she said stiffly.

"I'll put this town on the map," Ivy added, blithely disregarding the fact that Tess had, in fact, already done that. "You wait and see, Tess Harrow. The literary world won't be able to stay away after I'm done with them."

About the Author

Tamara Berry is the author of the Eleanor Wilde cozy mystery series and, under the pen name Lucy Gilmore, the Forever Home contemporary romance series. Also a freelance writer and editor, she has a bachelor's degree in English literature and a serious penchant for Nancy Drew novels. She lives in Bigfoot country (a.k.a. Eastern Washington) with her family and their menagerie of pets. Find her online at tamaraberry .com.